NUN TAKEN

BRADY PHOENIX

Nun Taken

Brady Phoenix

This book is a work of fiction. All names, places, characters, and events are all products of the author's imagination and are fictitious. Any similarities to actual events, places, people, living or dead, is coincidental.

Cover Design by miblart.

First Edition: February 2024

ISBNs: 978-1-7362394-2-1

978-1-7362394-3-8

To Loretta and Stafford,
Their unconditional love sparked my love of reading and writing.

Chapter 1

November 1986

THE SUN SET OVER THE pumpkin patch. Frost formed as the temperature declined, introducing the ever-darkening night sky. The vigorous gusts of wind made the decayed burnt-orange and brown leaves dance to the lullaby of the sinking sun as the moon stirred. Single strands of hay soared off the oscillating scarecrow. Specks of snowflakes fluttered from its flailing limbs with the powerful howl of Mother Nature's intense breaths.

Beyond the pumpkin farmland was a delicate, gothic-style structure, standing alone in the cold, open region. Clusters of weeping willows encircled the stone building like a fortress. Two gargoyle statues greeted incoming visitors at the bottom of a deep cement staircase; their eyes drooped in sadness with their mouths crying out in agony. A division of the garden was submerged in mud with a metal brick-red toolshed in the rear. Next to the flowerbed by the field and behind the adjoining willow trees, the clock tower's grim, monotone gong announced the nine o'clock hour, signaling from its withered foundation that it was time for the residents inside to adjourn for the evening.

Griffwood Manor was a home inhabited by nuns strengthening their faith. It housed troubled youth in need of behavioral correction, each with their own distinct backgrounds. It was a space for adolescents to find their inner strength and integrate back into society with their body, spirit, and mind pure.

Children saw this place as a refuge from their lives to develop under the guidance of the sisters. Several worked strenuously to transform their perspectives and be the finest versions of themselves. Most juveniles saw this experience as an opportunity to accept direction.

Others, however, refused to take the program seriously, and used it only to withdraw from their homes. A few turned a deaf ear to the nuns' wisdom and neglected to abide by the rules.

This was the case for Buck and Frank.

The chapel excused the group of minors as four nuns exited out to the great hall. The youngsters went in their respective directions, trudging up the wobbly spiral staircases to their respectable dormitories, each containing ten miniature, separate chambers. They dismissed half of the sisters from the groups to their secluded rooms and study spaces, which boasted piles of bookshelves and tall, plush vintage chairs.

Buck and Frank were the last two boys to depart the chapel. They poked each other in between the sisters' observation of obedience between every gawk; their stares felt like ravenous hawks.

"Tag, you're it!" whispered Buck as he moved his arms under his armpit, concealing them.

Frank's nostrils thrusted out deep laughing breaths, trying to not attract the eyes of the sisters in the group's front. A cackling cough jolted the sister's body, gathering her attention as she turned around. Her robes rippled like waves in a black puddle.

"Stop it!" Frank said, attempting to contain his laughter; his sinuses rocked as he huffed a gusty exhale. "We're going to get in trouble."

The nuns checked on the boys as they approached the tower door. Luckily, the two were able to conceal their fun before getting caught by straightening their faces to seriousness. Snapping in and out of their demeanors became a pleasurable game to them, continuing to bounce in and out of their silence until they reached their dormitories. The change in lighting halted the trajectory of their escort, halting their joy.

"All right, children," said the first nun, her oversized glasses magnifying her serene, aqua-blue eyes. "Into your pajamas, then off to bed. Sister Magdalena will be here to check on you before lights out. So please be ready by the time she arrives."

The vibrancy of the orange carpet deepened into a vermillion shade of red from the dim candlelight. The egg-white walls crept into shaded darkness.

"Yes, Sister June!" the boys confirmed.

Their monotone prepubescent voices groaned like uninterested zombies was pleasant in her ears.

"Bless you all, my children."

The kids entered their own rooms. A slow creak expelled from the rusty hinges of the dungeonous door after Sister June and Sister Alice left. Dusty whines screeched from the old boards on the winding staircase with each trudging step.

All of the boys' tempo increased into a playful rush the further the women were. They scattered into their prospective rooms, which were comparable to the size of a rich, socialite woman's walk-in closet. The emptiness of their lone, twin-sized bed was supported by chipped-metal frames. Their nostrils took in the musty stench of their dressers; the faint smell of mothballs and wood stain had become monotonous.

The sunset peeked through the stained-glass window, showcasing the drifting willow trees that danced in the night wind. Buck went into his room to pull out his baby-blue striped pajamas. He ignored the rush of his peers running down the hall towards their bathroom. His neck found freedom from constriction as his fingers unbuttoned the placket of his crisp-white dress shirt. His chest expanded further with each button unfastening closer to his abdomen.

"I heard her ghost comes out at midnight and walk the grounds," one uttered from outside his room.

"I hear she terrorizes naughty children!" said another.

Buck joined the other boys to inquire further about their claims, intrigued to know more about their conversation.

"Who are you all talking about?" he questioned, his fingers fiddling with the roots of his shaggy carrot-red hair; his generous spread of cardboard-colored freckles peeked through the strands.

"Didn't you hear?"

"No," Frank answered as he marched into the hall, his interest also piqued.

"About who?" Buck asked.

"The ghost of the late Mother Superior. Don't you know?"

"No."

"She died a long time ago. They say her spirit still haunts the old grounds, punishing any children who disobey the rules of the land."

Buck and Frank's eyebrows rose; their noses wrinkled. The stale dread of their days called for more; something special to add flavor to their drab daily lives.

"Do you know what happened to her?" Frank asked.

"No," the child voiced without confidence. "I heard she passed away from too much wickedness in her heart!"

"No way!" said Buck, unconvinced. "You can't die from that!"

"Yes, you can!"

"Who told you such crap?" Frank interjected, rolling his neck from his slumped stance. "She's a *nun*, for goodness' sake!"

"Sister Tate," one boy said. The drumming of his foot punctuated his firm tone. "She told me in the infirmary a couple of weeks ago."

"Sister Tate is a *joke*!" Buck spoke coldly.

"She also said that when twelve o'clock rolls around, the ghost of Mother Superior comes out to check on the children. She makes sure that all of them on her property abide by the rules."

"And what will this *so-called* Mother Superior do if we don't follow them?" Frank asked, his throat clear as he huffed out a gust of air from his nose.

"She punishes them!"

"You are so full of shit!" Buck hissed. Their passionate defense meant nothing to him.

"Well then, don't believe me!" the child said, sneering with his lips pinched together. "You'll see!"

"I'm sorry to break up a close and touching moment," one of the other boys jumped in, "but we should get ready for bed before Sister Magdalena returns. She can be a real grouch if we piss her off!"

"You're right!"

They grabbed their toothbrushes and scurried closer to the staircase to the nearby opening, where the rest of the group paced as they waited to empty their bladders and perform their evening's personal care routine.

One by one, they ran around the hallway into their rooms to prepare themselves for bed, their frantic movements exhausting them. Frank and Buck glanced at each other; their mutual interest evidenced by the slow glide of a raised, bushy eyebrow.

"Mother Superior, huh?" queried Frank, curious.

"You don't believe this crap, do you?" asked Buck, crossing his arms.

"Are you thinking what I'm thinking?"

"Oh, you know it!"

"Tonight?"

"Tonight!"

The door opened, and Sister Magdalena entered. The two young men still donned in their day clothes brought heat upon her cheeks.

Her foot echoed in the room as she stomped over to grab Buck and Frank by the tops of their ears. Her fingernails dug deep into their lobes; waves of pain pulsated into their heads. The cartilage crackled similarly to a piece of mylar.

"I believe Sister June and Sister Alice requested for you to prepare for bed! You two are always disobeying. Please get ready this instant! Don't make me ask again!"

Frank and Buck scurried into their rooms like cockroaches caught in a sudden burst of light to change into their sleepwear with rapid haste. They threw the rest of their half-undone outfits onto the floor, next to the chairs by their windows. They ignored the brief chill of their nude skin as they pulled their pajamas over their thin boxer shorts.

In under a minute, they were ready for their bedtime prayer. They joined the others, bowing to the small wooden cross above the head of their beds, preparing for their blessing without enthusiasm.

"*Now I lay me down to sleep.*

I pray to the Lord my soul to keep.

And if I die before I wake.

I pray the Lord, my soul, to take."

"All right, my children," said Sister Magdalena, her hands fell gently to her sides. "Off to bed!"

The visibility of the hallway disappeared as the youths turned off their lamps that brought the faint bit of light from the underpart of their closed doors. Their backs prepared for the semi-plushness of their mattresses as they crawled on top of them; the firmness comparable to a cheap futon.

"Sweet dreams, my children," said Sister Magdalena.

"Goodnight, Sister Magdalena," the children responded in unison.

"Bless you."

The keyhole echoed an eerie *click* after she locked it behind her. The children's heads drifted away deep into their pillows; the down feathers crept closer around their ears as they greeted their nighttime dreams. Their brains complied to their eyelids getting heavier with the transition into their overnight imagination.

Everybody...except for Buck and Frank.

FRANK'S GAZE REMAINED on the branches to occupy himself while they swung like a pendulum. The swaying limbs of the drifting willow trees kept him awake. He waited for the hands to move, counting to sixty before checking for change. The dull tapping of his foot echoed through the silence.

It was eleven thirty.

He put on his navy-blue flannel robe and slippers before heading out into the hallway. He tiptoed across the corridor towards Buck's room; his fingernails lightly scratched the door like a hungry cat to grab his attention.

"Buck," Frank whispered.

No response.

"Buck, are you awake?"

The door opened with a groan. Buck's jutting chin stood out from his slouchy demeanor. His baggy eyes brightened by the moonlight the further the door swung open.

"You aren't serious about doing this, are you?" Buck grunted, his knuckles turning white as he grasped the frame.

"Yes, I am," Frank said, trying to contain his volume to a dull roar to keep the other kids from waking.

"All right."

Buck let out a deep sigh as he slipped on his plush maroon robe and coordinating slippers before joining Frank on his expedition.

They delicately walked to the stairs like Indiana Jones, striving to avoid the creaky steps of loose wood. Upon reaching the door, Frank took out a petite tool from his pocket; a paperclip that he kept safe under his mattress. The clip emitted a faint tap. The grip continually escaped his grasp from the dampening sweat with each faint echo. Each attempt slowed time even further with the rapidity of his beating heart. The door wouldn't give in to manipulation, and their frustration grew.

Click!

Buck closed the door carefully to hush the slow creak before descending the winding staircase toward the deserted entrance hall. Their toes treated the worn wood with reverence, trying to not put pressure on them to avoid the loud friction against its hardware. Frank reached inside the other pocket, removing part of a mirror to find out if anyone was still awake in the entrance hall.

The place was empty.

The custodian left through the front. His navy-blue jumpsuit saturated bright against the glowing moon. The waved curve of his unibrow made their spines tingle. His silence always made them tentative, unable to trust him if he caught the kids in their rule-breaking. None of the adults can be trusted, even the ones employed by the sisters.

They turned further away from him to enter the tiny, confined hallway. Their arms were within mere inches of scraping against the stone walls. The plastic bottoms of their plush slippers magnified on the stony floor of the narrow corridor.

The boys walked around the three prep stations after swinging the kitchen door. Pots and pans dangled above the empty surface; the smell of baked chicken and broccoli still engulfed the space. The reflection of the sky bounced off the chrome surfaces.

They opened the rear door, and a brisk chill whipped through their robes, tingling their spines. The muscles on their torsos bunched closer together, flinching from the freeze. Their arms locked near their chests, trying desperately to find an ounce of heated reprieve.

"Are you sure you want to do this?" Buck asked Frank, his jaw chattering like a wound-up joke prop.

"Yes, I do," he answered without hesitation.

The two proceeded to their right. Loose metal slabs slapped the overflowing water trough's foundation that neighbored the tool shed. The mossy rot firmly grounded the lone stump. A reflection from an embedded ax winked in their eyes. Stubs of roots searched the air for their formerly nourishing sprouts which peeked out from the vegetable garden, their desperation for a reunion apparent.

The boys' faces were slapped by the recurrence of willow branches flailing with the increasing wind. The tips felt like small needles kissing their rosy cheeks. Their soles sank into the drenched, muddy soil. The bottoms of their feet began to marry with the ground, becoming harder to move forward. Rerouting their path, they used the aid of the foliage to thrust their weight to the entrance, taking the longer route towards the clock tower. They found refuge in the four walls that protected them from the rushing wind taunting them past the swinging door. Relieved, Frank slammed the door shut behind them, locking the rusted handle with a firm grip.

"Oh, thank goodness!" Frank said, letting his head fall back looking heavenward. "Away from this awful wind!"

"No kidding!" Buck agreed graciously, his face warming with comfort. "It's colder than a witch's tit out there!"

Frank's stringy arms clamped around his back as he huddled closer for warmth. Their heartbeats rapidly beat against their chests while their necks warmed up to the exhausted breaths exiting their chapped lips.

An interminable wooden staircase enfolded them, scaling the boundary of the square interior towards the attic. They waited for the arrival of the ghost, eager to prove themselves wrong, hoping they made this story up.

Whistling gusts crept through slivers of holes in the lumber siding, interrupting the bleak silence.

"Do you think we'll see anything?" Frank asked, rubbing his hands onto Buck's forearm to warm him up. His fingernails sank into his flannel sleeves.

"I highly doubt it!"

THUMP!

They huddled closer for security, jittering in fear. Their breaths kept cutting shorter as panic settled further. Knots in their stomachs became tighter, combating the lightness in their heads.

"What was that?" shrieked Frank.

"Probably just the wind!" said Buck, concealing himself behind Frank for coverage.

The thudding continued. Their bladders loosened with a trickle of urine dampening their bottoms. The hairs on the nape of their necks stood up, stiffening.

Giving in to his fear, Buck headed to the exit, no longer motivated by his curiosity. The dry straw crunched under his slow steps.

"Enough of this," Frank said as his trepidation reached capacity. "Let's go back!"

He opened the door. The visual of a figure blending with the night sky made the boys embrace in panic, wailing from the fright of the ghost's revenge. Their lives flashed before them, a brief reflection on all the times they broke the rules grew, allowing their regret to grow with each infraction. They were too young to die and didn't want their innocent errors to be the reason for the end of their life's journey. When their parents learn that a spirit killed their sons for being bad-mannered, what would they say?

This shouldn't be the end, it just shouldn't.

Their eyes fixated upon the dark shadow of a cloaked woman with a structured headdress confirming their fears. The stories were indeed true. Mother Superior had returned to take the naughty children away. Their goose was cooked.

But it was not Mother Superior.

It was Sister Magdalena.

Sister Magdalena was more perturbed than she ever presented. Her cheeks flushed with deep red hues, huffing out of her flared nostrils like an instigated bull. The whites of her eyes brightened as they widened. Her stance was stoic, leaving no room for them to run past her to escape her fury.

"What on *earth* are you doing here?!" she said, planting her hands on her waist; the silhouette of her hips became visible from her grasp.

They declared nothing, both paralyzed from astonishment mixed with the wind.

"I have had it with both of you! Ever since you arrived, you have been nothing but trouble! You are a disgrace to the principles of Griffwood Manor, and I will see that you shall be punished!"

"But Sister Magdalena, we—" Frank started quaveringly, attempting to defend their actions.

"BUT NOTHING!" she said. The stomp of her foot rustled the straw beneath her shoes. "NOW COME WITH ME THIS INSTANT!"

Buck's head sank as he led the group out of the clock tower. He stumbled towards the nearby tree. The cold, chilly wind overtook his body again. He cradled his arms for warmth. His sorrow broke his heart, his tears becoming frosty. It was too much for him to prepare for Sister Magdalena's punishments. The rage that powers her exercises is not something he was equipped to tolerate. He was not prepared to be separated from Frank.

The clock gonged its first ring of the midnight hour. The limbs whined and crackled as a gust of wind swelled. A heavy branch fell nearer to the ground, coming closer to him. The edges of his slippers piled on top of each other as he jumped back allowing the layers of thick branches to entangle his forearms and knees, reeling him back into the wooden arch of the tree.

Buck hollered for Frank to save him. The whistling gusts were too loud and too strong as they muffled the sounds of distress from his struggle. He ached for relief as the clock continued to chime. He yelled louder for help as he stumbled further into a deep, hollowed-out nook. The intense winds brought isolation, despairing as though he were being eaten alive by the tree itself. His limbs danced with the entanglements of the willow's multiple cold, dangling branches. Buck's hope began to fade as he hyperventilated, causing the spots in his sight to grow while his throat closed in. His tightening lungs squeezed out bits of air while he sank deeper into the earthly abyss. An icy hand seized Buck's, yanking him towards safety as the branches started to separate from his tense, fear-stricken body.

It was Frank.

They ran as fast as they could away from the trees. They evaded every branch that swung in their direction, narrowly avoiding any additional conflict with the malevolence emanating from howling winds. It was as though the vegetation was hungry for children. Branches whipped across their faces, cutting their cheeks and tearing the thin fibers of their pajamas. They raced past the tool shed and the garden before approaching the kitchen door, closer to safety with each step. They slammed it behind them, trying to catch their breath as they leaned against it to ensure it was secure against the powerful breeze.

"Thank you for saving me," Buck said to Frank, holding his chilled hand for a second to acknowledge his gratefulness.

"Don't mention it." Frank's panting started to slow into a shaky laugh.

They both paused to catch their breath, feeling safe despite the terror they had experienced. The adrenaline had weakened their muscles, and they were desperately trying to take deep breaths. The duo walked toward the hallway. Buck froze with abrupt concern, his neck stiffening. His gaze became watery as he looked out the window. The slight visibility through the tree branches revealed brief glints of the clock tower. Their hearts began pounding again, the warmth of their blood pushing through their veins as he clutched the cuff of his robe.

"Where is Sister Magdalena?"

Chapter 2

June 2006

ONE WEEK AFTER SCHOOL had closed for the summer, the local Winterset Mall opened for the upcoming day. Security guards began their shift by making their customary rounds with a walk through the nearby food court. Frustrated, they escorted a misbehaved child to their mother who had picked up a coffee to take the edge off her upcoming stressful shopping escape. Assistant supervisors left their storefronts, ambling through the swarm of carts planted in the center of the jade marble tiling to deposit the previous day's earnings at the neighboring bank across the street. The elderly ladies' clean, white sneakers squeaked on the glossy surfaces, passing by the entrances to each store in their distinct two-toned velvet tracksuits from their jaunting power walk. The lingering scent of deep-fried cuisines overwhelmed the primary entrance, where three teenage girls strolled through the main doors. Their all-black ensembles contrasted with their greasy, pale skin as they scuffled their feet with apathy.

"There's nothing to do in this stupid town, so what should we do today?" asked one girl, groaning with little interest, "We could go to the bookstore and find those smutty graphic novels. Or do we go to the toy store and play with their cheap shit until we get kicked out?"

"Or do we harass the overweight security guard?" added the other young woman, her lack of enthusiasm matched. "Sonya, what do you think?"

Sonya was more of a positive influence between the trio of adolescents. She had no desire to rebel against one of their mischievous plans, so they constantly thrust her into situations outside her comfort zone. She didn't want to be looked at as a different person than she already was. Scoping out the area, the busier stores brought interest for camouflaging their mischief.

"Hmmm..." Sonya pondered while she thought of a plan, tucking her choppy, pixie-cut bleach-blonde hair behind her protruding ears. "Why don't we get some coffee? I cannot do anything productive without my caffeine. What are your thoughts?"

Blade and Darris seemed like almost perfect twins, despite no blood relation between them. Both had powdery-pale skin contrasting against their plaid crimson and onyx schoolgirl skirts that barely covered the tops of their night-black lace-up boots and *My Chemical Romance* t-shirts. Their only physical difference was the shade of their hair, which changed with any opportunity they could. Darris' most recent choice was amethyst, while Blade had chosen vermillion, both pulled into drawn-out, tousled pigtails straight out of a manga. Sonya had a hard time distinguishing which girl was which without their contrasting hair colors.

The three walked by the sizzling dog stand, passing by a young couple squirting their ketchup and mustard across the foot-long sesame seed buns. After taking in the decadent smells of cooked French fries, deep-fried doughnuts, and sizzling fiery Angus burgers, they made it to the small coffee shop. Blade and Darris ordered their blended mocha Frappuccino with extra whipped cream. Sonya requested her usual hot chai latte with extra cinnamon. Drinking their beverages in silence, they approached a bistro table in the food court, glaring at the increasing number of pedestrians as they observed and criticized each passerby.

"Check out that loser over there," proclaimed Darris. Her elbows nudged the two girls to look at the average-looking couple, sneering at their conformity with their basic clothing and demeanor. "What dorks!"

Blade laughed in agreement before taking a sip from her tall straw; the liquid rose, changing the plastic in color like mercury in a thermometer's glass tube.

The couple sat at one table to enjoy their large hot fudge sundae with two red plastic spoons. They gazed into each other's eyes full of love, indulging in the ever-growing moat of melting vanilla ice cream.

"I don't know," said Sonya, the awe of their affection fluttering her heart as she watched their hands grasp tight. "I think they look adorable. They really like each other."

"Ew. Why do you always find the good in people?" Blade cut in, her upper lip curled with vexation.

"I don't know. It's just that they aren't doing any harm, so why pick on them?" she defended meekly, wiping the foam from her lid with her fingers.

"You take the fun out of everything!" Darris barked.

"Yeah, it just seems like whatever we do, you seem to find a way out!"

"That's not it at all!" said Sonya, trying to defend herself while maintaining her facade.

People had always viewed Sonya in a different light. As a younger child, she had tried to take part in as many activities as possible. She had found little success with feeling welcomed or valued as a member of any group, no matter how hard she tried to fit in while being her authentic self, whether that would be in extracurriculars or social groups. If it were not for Blade and Darris taking her under their wing, she would have been stuck going through her senior year alone. She didn't have what it took to handle the exile, so Sonya compromised her morals and values one last time to settle for some sort of acceptance with them. She was obligated to deflect their mean-spirited antics throughout the school year. As much as their decisions fractured her heart, she wanted to wait until after graduation when she would go away to college and break ties with them. They were leeches of their parents and would stay behind in the comfort of their stagnant lives, refusing to grow up.

"Oh, really?" asked Blade, the wrinkles on her forehead became more defined as she slurped another long sip from her straw.

"Yes, really."

"Then why did you bail on us when we went to trash Principal Miller's yard during homecoming?" asked Blade.

"And what happened to you when we agreed to flood the shower rooms after gym class?" Darris said.

Sonya was speechless; her track record of shying away from their mischief piled against her, cornering her from their interrogation.

"I wasn't feeling up to it."

"How come I feel like you aren't our *real* friend?" Blade said, her black penciled-in eyebrow growing to a ninety-degree angle to punctuate her accusation.

"I *am* your friend," said Sonya, her head tucked between her shoulders with innocence.

"Then why don't you prove it to us?" Darris interjected snarkily.

"How?"

Their pupils bounced as they gawked around the boundaries of the mall, trying to conjure the most provable act that Sonya could do to show her devotion to them. They detected two kids sitting at the fountain and contemplated if she should knock them over into the clear, cold water. Then she noticed the security guard; his oversized belly prevented him from reaching his feet to tie his shoes. Fantasies presented of kicking him in the rear, knocking him to the ground. They yearned to watch him struggle to get back up like a turtle on its back with asthmatic wheezes bawling for help.

An employee pulled out a cardboard sign. The advertisement of the debut of a makeup store's updated smoky-matte eyeshadow palette collection piqued their interest. Light reflected off the glistening of their smiles. Their mutual thoughts synced as if they were one like a well-oiled machine with the perfect plan.

"We want you to steal some eyeshadow palettes from that store," said Blade. Her chipped, black polished fingernail pointed toward the shop.

"You mean shoplifting?" asked Sonya, her fingers fiddling with the excess skin of her cuticles.

"Yes, *shoplifting,*" Darris confirmed, her soft pitch mocked Sonya like a younger, snotty sibling.

"Isn't that a bit much?" Sonya uttered with reluctance. "I mean, it's *shoplifting.*"

"Call it what you'd like," said Blade. "It's time to step up and prove to us how much of a friend you really are."

"Can't I just push those kids into the fountain? They need a good kick in the pants anyway."

The children across the way tossed their food to strangers as they passed by. Patrons cringed in disgust as a French fry bounced off their shoulder. Waterfalls of tears drained out of a seven-year-old girl's eyes as she processed the spit landing into her scalp.

"It's the eyeshadow or nothing," said Blade sternly.

"Take it or leave it!"

The pair crossed their arms over their chest in unison like small children. Sonya's nerves rattled from the seriousness radiating from her friends. She had no other tactics that came to mind to avoid their plan without losing their support. Her head nodded slowly in compliance, pledging her allegiance for a quick steal.

Standing up from their table, Sonya walked out of the food court to enter the long row of shops. She trudged by the security guard as he regained his unsteady stance from the chaotic snarl of his shoelaces before collecting a justified snack at the doughnut shop. Her quivering chest battled sporadic breaths while she tried to devise a plan to elude what was becoming an insurmountable task to her. Either that, or a way to appease Blade and Darris without having to break the law.

After taking in the odor of summer sausage and ripened brie cheese wheels from the nearby kiosk, Sonya approached the makeup store. She moved by the advertisement that attracted many women of all ages into initiating their adrenaline-inducing shopping expedition. Her strut was wobbly; her shoulders tensed next to her ears by the shelves of lipsticks. She passed two teenagers trying every color imaginable with swatches streaked upon the tops of their hands. Her lungs tightened from the overabundance of musty fragrances tested by a cluster of elderly women yearning for aromatic euphoria without making a purchase. A youthful woman in all black approached her, carrying mesh shopping bags, amiable in demeanor with a beaming smile that distracted from her hyper-toned physique.

"Hi there!" boasted the cheerful employee. "Is there something I can help you find?"

"Uh, no," mumbled Sonya, her tongue drying up. "I'm just looking around."

"Let me know if you need anything."

"Thank you."

She scrutinized the set of brushes, swiping her fingertips atop the hairy bristles while she traveled further to the back of the store. A pyramid of the new smokey matte eye shadow palettes began to call her name. Its ghoulish chant allured from a table standing alone across from the check-out registers.

"Sonya...Sonya!"

Panic crept through her bloodstream; her hand clenched onto her coffee cup, almost crushing it and creating a mess on the store's glistening, white-tiled floor. Saliva pooled at the back of her teeth, nearly suffocating her; her throat became constricted, unable to swallow.

"Sonya!"

She couldn't do it.

She turned around and started to walk away, cowering from her predicament. Blade and Darris were leaning on a neighboring kiosk. Their eyebrows crept closer to their colorful hairlines. Their pigtails swished behind their shaking heads with disappointment.

Sonya was trapped.

She lost all sense of reason. She was not prepared to be abandoned by her only two friends and spend the rest of her senior year alone. Her mind went blank as she took one generous, dry gulp.

Her fingers pinched two palettes before she scurried towards the entrance like a cockroach to light. Sonya's determination to leave the store grew with each rapid step. She ignored every single syllable coming from the employee's mouth as she attempted to get Sonya's attention.

"Excuse me!" the staff member said, her voice growing stronger in demand.

They nodded their heads to acknowledge her actions, perked with pleasure. The palettes kept whispering to her, louder and more defined, persuading her to finish the deed.

Sonya started to run, hoping to silence the voices in her head that pulsated her temples.

"HEY!" the employee roared, the shopping bags clapped onto the floor. "STOP HER!"

Sonya strode out the door, her heart tapping against her ribcage. The employee was within arm's reach, fingers close to grabbing her. Being caught would mean the future she hoped for would be ruined.

Sonya threw down her coffee with hesitance, causing her opponent to slip as if she had stepped on a rotting banana peel. Sonya glanced back, relieved as the employee's silhouette drifted away into the distance with each stride. The worker screamed in pain while she writhed in the puddle of lukewarm liquid. The rush of adrenaline flowing through her body allowed her to ignore the cramping of her calves as the elation set in that she had gotten away.

THUMP!

Her face squished without warning as she plowed into the security officer and tackled him into the fountain like a stout linebacker. The poking ends of her soaked hair stung her eyes, accepting defeat as the officer's doughnut floated in front of her nose. Multi-colored sprinkles sank in her lap as Blade and Darris pointed at her, their faces flushed with pink hues from fulfilled laughter. They each snatched a small meat stick before turning their backs on her, walking away without a second glance.

She had been set up. All they had wanted was one final payout from Sonya before cutting ties with her. Her body became heavy, depressed with defeat; she was too stunned to retreat anymore.

The employee limped to the fountain and seized the two palettes on the floor. Dusty hues speckled on the tiles from shattered pieces of vivid colors below the broken containers. Vast amounts of water flooded out of the officer's pants as he struggled to stabilize himself. He marched in front of her disconcerting disposition, splattering generous amounts of liquid on her face with each determined step.

"You're in big trouble."

SONYA SAT IN THE SECURITY office, full of shame. Her jaw chattered as she tried to dry off her soaked clothes with an equally damp towel. Goosebumps popped on her forearms when the next wave of cold air shot out the vents. Her sinuses clogged her nostrils as she fought back her tears.

She flipped open her phone, tentative to type. Her bright screen was blurry as she scrolled down her small list of contacts. Her fingers shook, typing the first thing that came to mind after pulling up Blade's contact information:

"Why did you leave me?"

She drummed her fingertips on the screen with impatience, knowing they were glued to their phones. As much as they liked to play the part of non-conformists, they sure enjoyed it when they got a text to fulfill their desires for attention. Her palm vibrated as the notification came through, her soul ached when she saw the three letters that shattered her spirit:

"LOL"

Another notification came up right away.

"U R Pathetic!"

She returned to her contacts list and scrolled to Darris's name, trying to suppress the ache growing in her chest, and typed the same message. Darris' response was almost immediate:

"I'm sorry, but this had to happen."

At least Darris showed an ounce of compassion. She wasn't as harsh as Blade, but she still had to play her game to avoid being alienated like Sonya.

"How long were you two planning this?" Sonya typed.

"A while."

"Why not just tell it to me straight? You know Blade is using you as much as she is me."

Sonya had to say it. She had to expose not only Blade as the source of the problem but Darris for enabling it. Sonya had nothing to lose; she had to get some closure to get past her angered sadness. She wanted to call out Blade for how toxic she was. About five minutes passed; the longest five minutes. Sonya became hopeful as she might've gotten through to her, eagerly waiting to welcome her satisfaction. The possibility that she wouldn't be neglected by both of her friends and would walk away with at least one motivated her. Her phone vibrated, and in came another message:

"She isn't using me! How could you say that? You are a piece of shit for thinking that!"

Not the way Sonya imagined. She gave it another try.

"I've been there for you, and I meant every word I said. Please don't leave me. You mean so much to me."

Not even a minute later, she got one last response.

"Pathetic!"

Sonya knew Darris didn't use the word "pathetic." It was then she realized Darris was with Blade and that her strings were being pulled by the puppet-master. She had tucked away the ounce of humility she rarely showed. It was then that Sonya fully comprehended they were finished with her.

Tears formed as she waited for her mother to finish meeting with mall management and find out her verdict. She yearned to be a compliant, law-abiding teenager. Still, she had to face the reality that she had become a delinquent. Staring at the ceiling tiles, she tried to distract herself from her near-hypothermic state by counting them. All she thought about was returning to the church she once devoted herself to and away from trouble and mischief.

Sonya was the only one in her immediate family who took part in church growing up. Her parents were too busy working to accompany her to service. If they weren't working, they still weren't willing to make the time to practice, using work burnout as their excuse. She had several relatives that she would accompany to a more traditional sanctuary for holidays and special occasions out of respect for them. As her circle of friends changed with the passing years, the places of worship she would go to changed, which progressed away from traditional services the more she grew into her adolescence.

Sonya had been devoted to the youth group in addition to the bell choir and Sunday school. Her heart felt full as she was welcomed with open arms despite her over-the-top personality. She was well-suited for the Christmas programs, and channeled her energy into the love for the faith she passionately believed in. As the years went by, the congregation aged. There were moments she felt out of place in the community that had once embraced her. She distanced herself from the church and kept her beliefs to herself after being let down time and time again by those she had previously sought acceptance and guidance from.

Another sharp chill surged through her body as she recalled the cold desertion from her past. A door opened, and three individuals approached Sonya as she nervously waited for her punishment. She raised her widened blue eyes up towards her parents and mall management. Her lips quivered, holding back tears like a five-year-old who felt guilty for breaking an expensive vase passed down by their ancestors. Her mother's eyebrow perched along the rhythm of her father's disbelieved, huffing breath expelling from his nostrils.

"Sonya, I want to tell you how disappointed your mother and I are," her father scolded her.

"I know."

Sonya wiped the tears of guilt that glistened her cold cheeks; her fingers intertwined each other.

"I could press charges and have you placed into a juvenile detention facility to have you think about what you've done," the mall manager spoke, his breath wheezing with anxiety, his circular spectacles fogging.

Sonya's body became numb as though her fate was being sealed for the rest of her teenage life. The vision of the Queen of Hearts, yelling "*off with your head!*" echoed in her mind.

"Please, don't," Sonya pleaded, kneeling at the feet of the manager, her face close to kissing his ankle. "I swear I will never do this again! You can even ban me from the mall. I guarantee you won't see me again!"

Her mom's hand was steady when it rose, preventing her daughter from begging any longer.

"We negotiated an alternative for you."

"Y-you did?"

A small breath of relief exhaled through her rapidly chattering teeth.

"Because this is your first offense, your father and I have agreed to enlist you into a program. One that will hopefully guide you to not make these mistakes again," she said.

"Help?" Sonya asked, confused. "Like therapy?"

"Something of the sort," a breath-filled female voice shot out from behind Sonya, startling her as the office door slammed shut.

Sonya peered in the door's direction. The slender outline of a woman moved toward her. An enigmatic, middle-aged dame appeared orderly and genteel as if she came directly from the 1940s. Her emerald-green chiffon blouse billowed over her gray calf-length pencil skirt. A long, purple feather danced atop her oversized houndstooth-printed wool hat, which accentuated her porcelain-white complexion.

"Sonya, I would like to introduce you to Lady Ophelia," said her mother.

"Lady Ophelia?" said Sonya, more confused as she took in her garishness.

"She runs a weeklong program for troubled teenagers that need guidance in the appropriate direction," her father added matter-of-factly with hope.

"Direction?"

"Sonya, darling," Ophelia declared, her vibrato-like alto voice resembling a ghoul. "What you've done today is unacceptable behavior. Your parents and mall management both know that this was an act of poor judgment driven by a lack of focus. I am here to help troubled teenagers, misguided in their decisions, and turn them into more responsible individuals as they transition into the real world as full-grown adults. I collaborate with small groups, establishing distinctive programs each week that highlight certain opportunities."

Ophelia's outrageous style not only made Sonya uneasy, but her mission to alter individuals did as well. She had just made one mistake, a harmless choice made to try to fit in with a pair of naughty girls.

"Do I have a choice in the matter?" Sonya said to her parents, whining with reluctance, belting out a groaning sigh.

"No, Sonya, you don't," her father responded with authority.

"You're heading out tomorrow morning."

"Really?" Sonya moaned, helpless and surrounded again for the second time in the same day.

"Really," said Ophelia, leaning in closer to Sonya.

Her thin, penciled-in black eyebrows rose in anticipation as she scoped out her fear like a quiet, ravenous dog about to attack.

"You will be one of my best subjects."

Chapter 3

June 2006

RAIN CLOUDS SWARMED city hall the following morning, fretfully greeting the sun blanketing the streets. Joggers encircled the heart of the town to prepare themselves for the long day ahead. Bikers dodged a pewter minivan arriving through the fog towards the bench on the corner of the street to drop off the teenager.

"Do I have to do this, Dad?" Sonya asked with disinclination, her seatbelt slowly freeing her from her seat as she gnawed on her fingernails like a hamster to a metal tube on a sipping bottle.

"This is not up for negotiation," he responded, his fingers tapping on the leather steering wheel.

"Can I just ground myself for the summer? I can do all the chores in the house. I'll even volunteer for the Sunshine Scouts! Please, Daddy, reconsider."

"You need this, honey. Your mother and I both feel that you need to make some adjustments in your life."

"Adjustments?" she asked. "If you're talking about my friends, there's no need to worry. Blade and Darris are no longer in my circle."

"Well, that's terrific! Those two little punks were bad news."

"Then why can't I stay home? You know I don't have any other friends. I've learned my lesson. I promise."

"This is final."

He slammed his hand onto the dashboard, asserting his parental authority. The motion shook Sonya to her core, knowing she has no say in the matter.

"We will not discuss this anymore. You need to change. Period!"

Headlights grew in size as a short, orange bus got closer, periodically halting for pedestrians crossing the streets.

"Your ride awaits," he continued. His dismissal was cold as a glacier. "Off you go. Your mother and I care for you a lot."

"Love you too, Dad," said Sonya, grumbling in defeat as she took her suitcase out of the vehicle and wheeled it towards the nearby park bench.

She collapsed into the seat; her breath huffed in accompaniment with her rolling eyes. The minivan disappeared from sight into the morning fog; the unbelievable sadness and abandonment weighed her down. She had been given no choice, no fighting chance to prove to her parents that this was just a one-time mistake. It didn't matter anymore.

This is what she had to do.

Sonya kept her frown hidden, suppressing her sadness like a sturdy suit of armor. She wanted to show a strong exterior, under-prepared to be judged by the passengers for showing any sign of vulnerability.

The bus pulled to the street's curb, parking a few feet away from Sonya before opening its door. A gentleman emerged. His reddish-orange hair was cut short, which gave his pale skin an open canvas to showcase a cascade of sun-kissed freckles, distracting her from his chiseled muscles silhouetting through his tight white shirt.

Sonya's sweaty palms grasped her suitcase's handle while her feet grazed the gritty sidewalk. The headlights looked like wide eyes staring at her with warning.

"You must be Sonya?" the man asked, his raspy voice grunted.

"Y-Yes, sir," she answered, her knees buckling.

"The name's Craig. I'm the nurse taking care of you this week."

"Nurse?" she asked, confused. "Is it an asylum or something?"

"Not necessarily. I am only a member of the staff to help you."

"Okay."

Her stomach churned, uneasy with no other choice but to play along. At least she had others to talk with to combat her nerves and save herself from pinching her skin.

"As part of the program, we ask you not to converse with the other members for the entire ride. You'll have plenty of time to do so later."

"Why not?"

"It's part of the process," he said. "Lady Ophelia believes that genuine recovery will begin as a collective when you all enter the four walls of the establishment."

"Recovery?"

"Look, Sonya," Craig chimed in impatiently, "just abide by the policies set in place, or else you may not have the best start once we get there. Understand?"

"Yes, sir," she confirmed with apprehension, wincing in pain as her nail pinched her cuticle.

"Very good," he said, his tone lowering closer to a welcoming soothe. "Now, if you take your belongings and have a seat away from everybody else, we will be arriving in approximately three hours."

Three hours? *Are we being dropped off in the middle of the desert*?

She grabbed her suitcase and hauled it up the stairs onto the bus, passing by the heavy driver as he devoured his cold-cut sandwich.

"G'morning, ma'am," he said. Crumbs flaked out of his mouth, trickling into the lap of his navy jumpsuit.

"Hi," she muttered.

Sonya continued to walk down the narrow aisle, passing two boys seated across from each other, their deep slumber uninterrupted by her entrance. Drool trickled out of their mouths like simmering cauldrons bellowing with their grizzly snores. Next, she passed a young teen, her skin shaded in olive with locks of thick, jet-black curls burying her white headphones. She glared at Sonya, examining her like a predator. Sonya's mousy trepidation was more enticing than her music.

In the back, she saw another girl, her straight hair cascading down her backside like the tail of a show pony. Her eyelashes fluttered cheerfully before the bulky hood of her heather-gray sweatshirt covered her head. A high-pitched sigh hummed out her vocal cords as she made herself comfortable for the lengthy wait.

Sonya became hypnotized by her startling beauty; her luscious, melanin skin reflected the highlight of the peeking sun from the dusty window. Sonya's stomach churned; her abdomen swished with a tickle. Warmth grew from her blushed cheeks; her lips tensed together. Forgetting to breathe, her shoulder fell back before the firm grasp of a hand pulled her out of her euphoria.

"Please take your seat," Craig interrupted. "And no talking."

Sonya nodded her head in compliance before venturing to her seat. The weight of her duffle bag sank her onto the uncomfortable pleather; tension faded from her bicep while the imprint of the strap disappeared from her palm's release.

The bus began to move, cruising by the nearby structures. She looked through the fog for a final goodbye before cruising past the athletes' exhaling vapors like a bunch of laid-back cigarette smokers. She gazed at the young woman as she started to doze, succumbing to the pulse of her music.

Sonya's hair lowered from the nudge of her lifted chin, concealing the faint dark circles cradling under her slightly bloodshot eyes. Her self-consciousness faded away as decrepit buildings transitioned into open, uninterrupted scenery. Ears of corn swayed on their stalks, hypnotizing her as her lungs absorbed the fresh stench of moistened, dewy grass. Her eyelids were heavy, anchoring closer to their resting place. Her head sank further as she escaped reality, entering her drifting, dreamy trance.

TEN-YEAR-OLD SONYA arrived at the church as the bells chimed to signal the congregation to enter the pristine brick establishment. She skipped down the sidewalk before crossing the street to join the jubilant group, taking in the colorful vibrance of stained-glass windows glistening in the beaming sunlight. Elderly couples greeted her after her fingertips clapped her palm as they caught up on their weekly updates.

"Hello, cutie pie!"

"Don't you look adorable today!"

She pranced into the dome-shaped chapel, taking her seat in the second closest pew. She savored the grand piano's peaceful, mellifluous, lullaby-like music, inhaling the musty, dry air. The rest of the assembly took their seats within time, stretching to adjust their spines in preparation to settle into the firm, unupholstered pews. The room became silent when the pastor walked up to the center of the stage, his white polyester robe gliding on the eggplant-purple carpet in a way similar to a ghost.

"John the Apostle reminds us, 'He has given us this command: Anyone who loves God must also love their brother and sister.' It is our responsibility to be the examples of love and unity in our homes and communities," said the elderly pastor, raising his arms high towards the cross that hung in the middle of the wall behind him. "Let us pray."

The entire congregation bowed their heads in unison, embracing silence.

"Dear God, we thank you for being a loving, gracious God. We thank you for all you've offered us, giving us forgiveness and the gift of new life through you. Thank you that your love is perfect, unconditional, and never fails. Nothing can separate us from your love. We pray that your love will fill and overflow our lives so we make a difference in this world and bring honor and glory to you. We ask for your help, reminding us that the most important things are not what we do outwardly. They're not based on any talent or gift, but the most significant things we can do in this life are simply to love you and to choose to love others. In Jesus' name, Amen."

"Amen," the assembly murmured in conclusion.

The pastor dismissed the crowd after ninety minutes, and they conversed casually about the rousing sermon as they approached the cafeteria. Sonya strolled to the kitchen to help get the coffee pots and treats ready for the adults to enjoy during fellowship. The musty smell of the inexpensive tea permeated the room while she collected a tray of brittle chocolate chip cookies. After peeling off the cling wrap from the assortment of desserts, she passed back through the swinging door to the tables. One table was composed of three pairs of people varying in age, exchanging an engaged conversation with a younger mother rocking two twin toddler boys fast asleep in their tattered stroller. Sonya's heart fluttered with enjoyment from the woman's glowing, pearly-white smile that resulted from the company of the welcoming group. Sonya carefully placed the snacks on the miniature Styrofoam plates at one of the adjoining tables, pinching the treats with little plastic tongs. The mother said her goodbyes to the group. As the last cookie left the pile of crumbs on her plate, she overheard the remaining pairs discussing their encounter.

"What does she think she is doing?" asked one female in the group, her dry lips curling in revulsion.

"I know," a man responded with equal repugnance. "She has no business being here."

"Did you hear she is on her *fourth* marriage?"

"Really? No way!"

"I'm glad she settled down after dating so many men in this neighborhood," a different woman added sarcastically.

"She better stay away from *my* husband."

Hearing the group's comments upset Sonya. She struggled to understand how the same members preaching about love and acceptance could be quick to judge without knowing someone. The quick change from their friendly façade to their harsh judgments gave her whiplash and made her stomach churn. Crumbs sprinkled onto the floor as her lack of focus unbalanced the teetering empty tray.

"Sonya, did you have any more cookies?"

She detected a feeble voice coming from the kitchen.

She froze up as her name was repeated, her memories fading away as her consciousness drifted back into the back seat of the bus.

"Sonya."

"SONYA."

A rumbling voice resounded in her ears as she opened her eyes.

She groaned, irritated.

"Sonya, wake up!"

Her eyelids ascended quickly, resembling a sheathing projector screen. The other passengers had vacated the ride. There was no driver or sleeping boys; even the girl across from her was no longer alluring in her slumber. Her lungs tightened with her staggering breath; an eerie chill overtook her as she took in the grim scenery. Bare branches of the neighboring willow trees resembled long, dry, untreated hair with wilted brown leaves holding on with desperation.

"Where are we?" she asked, her body locking with nerves.

"We're here," said Craig, gesturing his arm towards the door. "Welcome to Griffwood Manor."

Chapter 4

November 1986

"WHERE IS THE NUN?" Buck asked Frank, grabbing his arms feverishly. His spine tickled from the chill refusing to leave his body.

Frank's body quaked with panic. His quivering hands shook Frank's tight biceps, which tensed with terror with each frantic jolt.

"I don't know!"

"When did you see her last?"

"I don't know! What about you?"

"I'm not sure," Buck said, confused, shivering the cold from his shuddering slender body. "I was too busy being eaten alive by that tree!"

"Oh, yeah. That's right. I don't know how that could happen. Creepy stuff has been happening here!"

Frank struggled to catch his breath; the chill in his lungs was a lot for him to fight off. The darkness made his fingers tremble.

"What happened to you?" Buck asked, attempting to understand what happened while his flushed face faded back to pasty-white hues.

"When?"

"When the clock struck midnight," Buck said, clarifying with certainty as he recalled his trauma. "A branch shoved me into the tree, and I couldn't find you. I kept calling your name for help, but you never came!"

"The branch whacked me in the head and knocked me out."

Buck noted the cuts on Frank as little streams of blood flowed along his right temple.

Buck hurried to one of the nearby drawers to search for supplies to help his friend. Silverware jangled together with each fast, scavenging dig. Sharp pains pricked his fingers from the pointed edges of steak knives, as though he were looking for a tiny sliver of hay in a large stack of needles. A large soup ladle catapulted out of the drawer like a jack-in-the-box. His eyes shut tight from the nerve-wracking noise, jerking as if he was prepared to be punched. He clenched his teeth together, hoping to avoid drawing attention.

"Shh, quiet," Frank said, his dread mounting.

"Okay," Buck said, paralyzed from trepidation, culpable for initiating the unwelcome uproar.

A strain tugged on his lower spine as he picked up the sporadic spread of cutlery. Each handful of silverware made the muscles by his tailbone twitch.

"Didn't you notice me calling out your name?"

"Everything was a blur while the bells were chiming. I couldn't see or hear anything!"

"It must've hit you pretty bad," Buck said with concern as he returned the silverware into the drawers with care, sliding them into their compartments. "Should you go to the infirmary?"

"We can't tell anyone what happened."

"Are you sure?" Buck asked, fretful.

He took out a swatch of a worn-down cheesecloth before resuming the cleanup.

"Yes, I'm sure," he assured, walking closer to Buck as he inserted the last few knives back into the drawer. "We've done so well with keeping our secret. So why ruin it now?"

"Well, all of our other adventures didn't end up with us getting caught."

Frank laid his hand on Buck's to stop his racing anxiety. Buck looked into Frank's green eyes, ignoring the dried-up blood and dirt-covered scratches on his face, exchanging a slight reassuring grin with Frank. His two front teeth peeked out from the slow glide of his upper lip.

"Good. We have to keep everything we've done together here a secret. We'll be ruined if they find out."

Frank grabbed the nape of Buck's head and kissed him. Buck's lower back ache vanished as Frank's hand touched it. Their dry lips moistened from their shaky breath. With his knees buckling, Frank smashed his body closer. Their rapidly beating hearts warmed their once chilled exterior.

The institution rarely allowed them a period to spend together because of its spiritual nature and stringent guidelines. Frank never took their time together for granted. During the daytime sessions, they joked around in silence while trying to keep their distance, giving the façade that they were just best friends adhering to directions. As annoying as it made the sisters of Griffwood Manor, their bond had distracted them from the teenagers' *true* intentions.

The two would sneak off in the middle of the night or during their daily recess to enjoy their young, innocent, romantic relationship in many hiding spots throughout the establishment. They found a thrill in sneaking away to study rooms and confessional stalls to remain in each other's company. They knew if they were caught, someone would indeed punish them for their indiscretions.

"I promise," Buck said, his smile beaming bright.

"Thank you," Frank said, relieved as he leaned in for one last peck on Buck's forehead. "Let's get out of here."

Buck's smitten, hazel eyes sparkled in the peeking moonlight creeping through the window. He nodded in agreement as they walked to the other side of the kitchen. Frank scoped the room's parameters, noticing the darkened silence of the area, before tapping on Buck's shoulder, signaling they were okay to proceed. They cramped their toes from tiptoeing up to the threshold to the spiral staircase. Once at the top, Frank clutched his paperclip pick to seal the door back in place once they had arrived. The two meandered back towards their rooms, the adrenaline enshrouded their bodies like damp blankets. Buck clutched Frank's hand to hold him back another moment, barring the end of their adventure.

"Could you stay in my bed until I fall asleep?" Buck asked him, desperate for company. His nerves exuded from him as he bit his lower lid, rocking back and forth.

"I don't want to get caught," Frank said with a heavy yawn, declining the proposition. His unease grew with frustration.

"Please? I only need thirty minutes, and then I'll be out. You can leave if I'm asleep or not. I could use your comfort. You don't know how terrifying it was to feel like getting suffocated by a bunch of vines and branches. I thought I was going to die."

Frank couldn't turn away from Buck's innocent face. His fear was evident as tears moistened the base of his lower lid. Concerned, he yielded to Buck's proposal, nodding his head with an accompanying smile. His arm wrapped around Buck's shoulder, ushering him back to his cot for the night. They crawled into his twin-sized mattress, wrapping their legs with the thin bed sheet before burrowing into the warm comforter. Frank rested his arm around Buck's head as he wriggled to make himself comfortable. Buck turned to give Frank a tiny peck on the lips.

"Goodnight," said Buck, reclining onto his pillow.

His eyelids slammed shut like garage doors, hypnotized by the heated contact of his back snuggled against Frank's chest. Their cold, sore toes transitioned out of numbness as they held onto each other. Relaxation took over as his body became heavy, sinking into his mattress.

"Goodnight," Frank whispered, looking out the window toward the moonlight.

He reflected on the night's crazy adventure as he snoozed away into time from the silhouette of dancing willow branches flailed from mother nature's gusty breath, huffing its leaves into the night.

Chapter 5

June 2006

SONYA'S MUSCLES STRETCHED out, shaking her grogginess to grab her nearby duffel bag. She exited the bus and examined her surroundings, noticing an assemblage of decayed willow trees beginning to bloom. The rising sun welcomed a wave of the fresh afternoon heat with radiating warmth. Baby green leaves on healthy branches rippled from the tiny gusts of wind.

Behind the vegetation loomed a multitude of nuns, gloved up and wrapped in traditional garb, pulling weeds and piling bunches of roots and plants. Unfocused on their new guests, they gathered their assortment of tools rested by the broken-down water trough that stood next to an unsteady decrepit toolshed.

An aged clock tower peeked through tree branches like a rising sun, where its tarnished hands remained still at two o'clock. The rest of Sonya's peers walked up the staircase to the pair of tall wooden doors at the center of a U-shaped building surrounding them. She trudged to the base of the stairs, the tips of her fingers caressing battered gargoyle statues. Their lone eye cried agony; the mouths yearned for reprieve through their chipped fangs as they dropped to their chests. She took in the crisp country air to open her tightened lungs before becoming captive to the establishment as she reached the handle at the top.

The tall doors swung apart without force, creating a long, reverberating squeak groaning ominously in the darkened and deserted entrance hall. The old, unlit, off-white candles on the untouched chandelier were decorated with dainty cobwebs. The tips of her sneakers felt the groove of the weathered stone, with natural tiling configurations seemingly straight out of a dungeonous medieval castle. Geometric rugs covered most of the floor, contrasting their motifs in the flickering light.

To her left was a giant sliding window, revealing an office appropriate for a receptionist. Dozens of shelves held clusters of manilla folders shedding specks of papers piled over cheesy workplace décor like a stack of raked autumn leaves. A thin, middle-aged man with a faded brown comb-over that distracted from his unplucked unibrow sat behind the window brushing his feather duster over his collection of creepy ceramic gnomes with grins so wide and tight.

"Hello," greeted the receptionist in an uninterested monotone, adjusting his loose-fitting tie around the starchy collar of his wrinkled dress shirt. "My name is Sheldon. I work in admissions here at Griffwood Manor."

"Hi, Sheldon," Sonya responded, trying to be polite as he pocketed his duster before grabbing a small, gray metal lockbox.

"As part of the program's policies, we ask that you keep no electronics in your possession while participating. Any cell phones, music players, or portable games need to be locked away for the duration of the week. You'll receive them when you leave."

"Okay," said Sonya, complying as she plopped her cheap flip phone and cd player into the container.

Sheldon shut the box and placed them onto the neighboring shelf, where eight identical boxes sat above a half dozen dirty coffee mugs.

"Thank you, Ms. Frost. Now, I ask that you follow the rules and try not to take your belongings. I know how you kids can't spend ten minutes without looking at your phones. Going against the policies will be grounds for further disciplinary actions."

"Yes, sir."

"Welcome to Griffwood Manor!" said Sheldon, with his enthusiasm more vibrant. "Now, you'll proceed to the main chapel straight ahead for orientation. They're ready for you."

"Thank you," she said with esteem as she moved across the entrance hall towards the wooden chapel doors.

"And Ms. Frost, let me know if there is anything I can do for you," said Sheldon, comforting her before sliding his window shut.

Sonya accepted Sheldon's suggestion with a nod of her head. She meandered past the stone benches outside the door where two nuns sat, murmuring the day's plans. She entered the pristine brick room where the illuminated masonry walls looked similar to a castle dungeon. They contradicted the clean, blood orange carpeting as ten short rows of dark maple-stained pews lined up towards the front of the chapel. A circle of chairs stood at the end, seating the rest of her group. They whispered to each other to gather comparative clues to their whereabouts. Her calves cramped, trying to stabilize her trembling kneecaps with each unsteady step down the aisle. She stared at the large wooden cross and fresh white fabric banners hung nearby, and memories of her childhood at church echoed in her mind. The back of her t-shirt dampened with sweat as she recalled the voices of the pastor overlapping the hypocritical, judgmental remarks of the congregation, overwhelming her as her spine tingled rapidly.

"Love thy neighbor as you love thyself."

"I can't believe she had the nerve to show up at our service!"

"So now faith, hope, and love abide, these three, but the greatest of these is love."

"I heard he left his wife for another man!"

"My command is this: Love each other as I have loved you."

"I saw her the other night going out with a black man! What is she thinking?"

A familiar female voice suddenly disrupted her fast-moving thoughts.

"Sonya," said Ophelia's quavering tone, alerting her.

She peered with vacancy at the cross. Her heart raced as specks of sweat began to trickle down from her forehead. Her throat closed, trying to swallow whatever saliva remained inside her mouth.

"Sonya, honey, can you please join us for orientation?" Ophelia requested, angelically fluttering her arm to the lone empty chair.

Sonya shook off her dazed demeanor to proceed towards the circle of chairs, where teenagers conversed quietly, with three young adults alongside Ophelia. She took a seat next to a boy whose hair was red as ketchup. The madam stood up to begin her orientation, adjusting her black-pinstripe Dior-esque suit.

"I want to officially welcome you all to this week's program. My mission when I started this was to take troubled teenagers, such as yourselves, and help guide them away from continuing any further discretions," said Ophelia, followed by an enthusiastic grin. "You each possess a similar quality that I believe makes you all outstanding people, the capacity to change for the better. Therefore, I hand-chose each one of you for the week with full confidence. I ask that you all approach the process with open hearts and minds. Our approach will be as laid back as you permit it. Free time will be plentiful to reflect upon your past so that you can move forward with clarity into your future. However, there will be rules you'll all be asked to abide by. Failure to comply with them will result in your removal and be sent to a juvenile detention center to finish out your sentencing. Do you all understand?"

The entire group nodded, apprehensive of Ophelia's vague terms, except for the curly-haired girl sitting in her chair. Her arms were crossed, displaying the attitude of a petulant brat full of impatience.

"Excellent!" Ophelia said, clapping her hands repeatedly in excitement. "Now, I'd like to acquaint you with the staff assisting me with the week. Please stand and introduce yourselves?"

Craig and the other adults appeared to be in their mid-to-late thirties with their clear complexions and mature ensembles. One by one, they stood up to introduce themselves.

"I'm Craig, as you know, and I'm the nurse here to assist with any medical needs. The infirmary will be located near your rooms."

Sonya was still taken aback with why this facility needed a nursing staff. Only a small group of people, not as clumsy as children, didn't need the aid for tripping on a playground since there wasn't one.

"I'm Joseph," said the next person. The black frames of his spectacles covered most of his olive-green eyes.

Specks of salt and pepper hues sparkled from the oily slick of his generously gelled hair.

"I'm one of the counselors here. I am here to listen and observe if you need anything."

"My name is Amber," said another woman with glossy lips as she whipped her long, loosened, brown fishtail braid behind her head. "I am also a counselor here. I'm all ears for you, and approach everything with an unbiased point of view and with lots of diverse experience. So please feel free to talk with me."

Sonya smirked, feeling more at ease with the comforting warmth Amber emanated. Rising from her chair once more, Ophelia paid her respects. Her clapping hands caused an unnecessary roar for her small staff.

"Wonderful! Wonderful!" Ophelia said, full of excitement as her fuchsia oversized chiffon sleeves billowed like drifting clouds. "Now, if you would all be so kind and introduce yourselves. Tell us all why you are here. Mr. Nelson, you first!"

A blonde-haired boy stood up, his shaggy highlighted hair concealing his orangish-tan skin, which popped off his sun-yellow polo shirt. He placed his hands into the compartments of his shredded acid-washed jeans, exposing the pocket bags through a hole in his upper thigh that almost peered into the crevasse of his crotch.

"My name is Leslie Nelson," said the boy, nodding his head to flip his styled hair back. "I drank and drove."

"Thank you, Leslie," said Ophelia as he lowered into his chair.

The following person stood up. Her long black locks flowed over the illumination of her glowing, bronzed skin. She unzipped her hooded sweatshirt and discarded it like a shell and revealed her vibrant yellow floral printed dress. Her straight, white teeth were like a June sunrise. Her eyes were piercing; endearing with ease.

"I'm Isis West," said the Adonia. Her shoulders were locked, juxtaposing her goddess-like appearance with shame. "I got into a fight."

Isis's allure hypnotized Sonya. A girl who was as attractive and put together as Isis couldn't get herself in a brawl and break the law. She may have been engaged in a catfight as ordinary teenage girls do, however it hadn't ever landed her in detention.

"Thank you."

Sitting next to her, the red-headed boy stood up reclusively with his green dress shirt tucked tight into his hiked-up khaki pants. His skin glistened with desperation to wash away its oily contents. He was as white as a ghost; his build was as bony as a skeleton. The peachy hairs under his chin curled like a used up hairnet.

"Tom Sackett. I got caught hacking," he muttered, his turtle-like demeanor reflecting his silent recluse.

"Thank you."

The remaining girl didn't stand up. Instead, she remained seated, trying to keep her tough exterior. Her black, curly hair was thick that it was close to covering her defined cheekbones that framed her sharp, unkempt arched eyebrows. Her muscular arms crossed over her distressed denim vest equipped with dozens of pointy chrome spikes adding to her resistant appearance.

"Cora Martin," she said in a deep tone, her chin hiked, her thin nose huffing fiercely.

"And?" asked Ophelia.

"And what?" Cora posed with mocking sarcasm.

"Why are you here?"

"I don't know why I'm here! I don't understand why any of us are here. This is so stupid!"

"Miss Martin, you were caught vandalizing public property, among other unforgivable infractions. Now, would you care to continue making this hard and get yourself excused from this program before it even starts, or do you want to participate?"

"Whatever," she hissed back at Ophelia, her eyes rolled like marbles.

She stood up from her chair and pretended to act prim and proper, sweeping her curls behind her ears. Her tone mocked a prissy valley girl.

"It is *so* nice to meet all of you! I can't wait for us to braid each other's hair while singing 'Kumbaya!' I *so* can't wait for you to cry on my shoulder while we fix our ever-growing problems that nobody will give a shit about when this is all over!"

She hunched back down into her chair, and her eyebrows met closer to her eyelashes.

"Happy, Your Highness?!" Cora said.

"Thank you, Ms. Martin," Ophelia responded; her face was statuesque and didn't react to her antics. "What about you, honey? Go on."

She looked at Sonya, encouraging her to warm up to them. She rose from her chair, preoccupying herself with her fingernails to mask her apprehension.

"I-I'm Sonya Frost," she said, plucking a sliver from her pointer finger. "I...I got caught shoplifting."

"Pssh," Cora hissed, unimpressed. "Shoplifting what? Lip gloss?"

"No," answered Sonya. She looked to the floor, making her hair fall over her sorrowful eyes like a visor in an attempt to protect herself from Cora's intimidation and assumption since she wasn't too far off with her guess.

"Taking a pack of gum from the candy shop isn't the same as beating a bitch up or breaking into someone's computer! So what kind of shit are you running here?" Cora ranted, intimidating with her sharp tone.

"I didn't choose to come here," Sonya defended.

"What's that, smartass?"

Her hind legs hurled her chair to the ground as she stomped towards Sonya, fists clenched tight. Sonya felt the heat radiate from her face. Sonya's expression didn't change; she remained emotionless and showed no indication of cowering, hoping Cora would step back and be intimidated by her fearless stance.

Craig jumped up to usher her to her seat. He evaded her flailing arms like a 90s television show presenter exposing the adulterous father of a heartbroken mother's child. Sonya sighed in relief that she was not obligated to demonstrate any significance to this new group by vouching for herself.

"Enough!" Ophelia chimed in, raising her voice; her firmness of her stiletto was muffled from the cushioned carpet. "Miss Frost is correct. She didn't choose to be a part of this program. None of you have. I hand-selected each one of you because I know that deep down, there is a person with the strength and willingness to fight the voices that propel you to make these poor decisions. That includes you, Ms. Martin."

Daggers beamed out of Cora's gaze towards Sonya before focusing her attention back on the woman.

"Well, now that we've all gotten to know each other, you can go for the day. Joseph and Amber will direct you to your rooms upstairs. We'll reconvene for supper this evening in the dining hall, located to the left outside of the chapel. In the meantime, make yourselves at home, and take some time to reflect on what you want out of being here for the week and how far you will go to obtain it. You may go."

The kids got up from their chairs, dismissed and full of unresolved confusion. The number of questions grew instead of being answered.

"Ms. Martin," Ophelia interrupted, halting the teens. "I'm going to ask for you to stay behind. I would like to have a private word with you. The rest of you may go."

The group continued toward the entrance hall. Sonya turned to Cora in her seat, her irritation was like armor from Ophelia standing in front of her; the woman's arms leaned over the frame of Cora's chair. Ophelia's Medusa stare was mere inches from Cora's pointed nose.

"Okay," said Craig, trying to redirect their attention. "Amber will take you ladies to your rooms on the right, while Joseph will escort the boys to theirs on the left. The second set of doors will lead you to the extra chambers and private studies. I would recommend leaving those areas alone for the time being, since the nuns are resettling there after some much-needed renovations."

Sonya became disgusted as she looked at the color-coordinated doors. Her eyes rolled from the pukey, pastel hues of pink and blue nauseating her stomach.

"Behind me, as you know, is the reception office, where you all met Sheldon earlier. This was also a recent addition when we bought the building. He is still er-organizing."

Stacks of files toppled to the floor from the shelves breaking, lowering like a trap door. Sheldon's fist pounded onto his desk in annoyance, vibrating the contents of his coffee mug with a drop trickling from the rim.

"Around the corner from these areas will be offices and our meeting areas for your sessions. They'll be available if you need anything from Joseph or Amber."

The rest of the group nodded their heads in understanding.

"All right," he concluded. "Joseph and Amber will now show you to your rooms. I'll see you later for supper. Enjoy your stay and make yourself at home."

"Right this way, ladies." Amber signaled her arm toward the pink door close to Sheldon's office.

The three stepped into an empty room to an escalating spiral staircase. The weight of their luggage shook the rickety structure with each step, unsteadying their balance. They stepped into an abandoned lounge. The carpet was atypical to the rest of the unit; crisp black and well kept. The walls were sharp white, cleaner than a fresh pair of underwear. They showcased the paintings of various landscapes with sharp outlining of black antique frames. The narrow hallway closed in like a glamorous asylum with each step.

"This area is exclusively for you!" Amber said with delight, giddy like a summer camp counselor. "We had this place renovated a bit. They added space for your separate living areas. Behind me is the bathroom, which is connected to the infirmary, where Craig will be the majority of the time. Well, hopefully not, as long as you don't hurt yourselves!"

A generous gulp clicked from Sonya's neck.

"Isis, your room is on the left side and Sonya, you will stay in the space on the right. Please, get comfy! I'll be staying in the room just down the hall! Knock if you need anything!"

"Thank you," Sonya and Isis muttered, bowing their heads as they walked with caution down the corridor toward their respective rooms.

Before they parted ways, Isis nudged Sonya's arm, jolting her attention.

"That was pretty awesome that you stood up to Cora," she said with encouragement; her smile cast light from her shiny, porcelain-white teeth.

"Yeah," she sighed, clearing her bangs out of her eyes.

"If you want a hand in whooping her ass, I've got your back!" Isis proposed, guaranteeing her protection with a punctuating wink.

"Thank you."

"Seriously, us girls need to stick together. You can trust me."

She unlocked her door and slipped inside. She let go of her bag next to the charcoal-black wooden dresser before walking to the ivory cushioned armchair that sat close to her twin-sized bed. She became overwhelmed in this new and uncomfortable environment and needed to sit down to clear her mind and refocus her approach for the week. Peering out the window, she noticed the willow tree limbs leisurely swaying around the courtyard as they pulled her focus toward the ancient clock tower. She observed the cracked, wobbly construction and then beheld the face of the piece. She honed in on the arms, squinting and wondering why it was broken down or why they didn't spend the money to repair it. Her focus was pulled to the shape of a figure standing in a pane by the number six. Towering in stance, it faced her, provoking her. Rubbing her eyes to readjust her vision, she assumed it was a figment of her imagination.

The shadow was gone.

Chapter 6

June 2006

THE SHADE OF THE DECAYING trees provided reprieve from the sun's diminishing heat to the premature vegetation in the garden. The overhead announcement for five o'clock blared throughout the speaker system, notifying the participants to convene in the dining hall for supper in one hour. Sonya changed into her favorite black faux leather pants and jacket to highlight the punk rock font of her Green Day shirt; her clothing was too sweaty and wrinkled from the long drive. Stepping into the corridor, Isis shifted Sonya's attention while she attempted to tie the black laces of her worn-out red converses. Her legs teetered as she focused on Isis's bell-like hem of her sun-yellow jumpsuit swishing over the carpet.

"Hey, Sonya," said Isis, cocking her knee to show off her glossy pedicure tucked underneath her white strappy sandals.

"Hi," she replied, brushing off a speck of lint that clung onto her pants.

"How was your afternoon?"

"Fine."

"What have you done since we got here? Did you explore the place?" Isis asked.

"No," she said, letting out a yawn. "I just took a nap. The bus made me nauseous."

"I'm sorry. It *was* quite the ride."

"So, I take it you went on an adventure?"

"I did!" she responded enthusiastically, her face glowing.

"Maybe you could share with me sometime?"

"Maybe I could show you now? There are a lot of interesting finds!"

"Wouldn't we get in trouble if we wander the grounds?"

"Then why bring us here if they didn't want us to wander?"

Sonya chuckled with sarcasm, saying, "You must entertain yourself easily. How can you like it here?"

"Do we have much of a choice?" she asked, pacing from one side of the wall to the other, full of energy. "We have to make the best of it."

"True."

"Care to make the most of it with me?"

"Sure."

She showed a small half-smile in reaction to Isis's blushing cheeks and fluttering eyelashes.

"Cool! I want to show you this room I found!"

Isis walked down the hall towards the exit. Her long hair drifted like chiffon curtains blowing gracefully through an open window. Sonya trailed after, taking in the kindhearted congeniality that was so new to her. The refreshing encounter began to dissolve the toxicity of Blade and Darris' poison she was used to.

No patronizing.

No disinterest.

No ulterior motives.

The bathroom door slammed, severing Isis's allure from Sonya. The sound of a record player played in her mind, skipping a melodic harmony that instantly sucked the air out of the room.

It was Cora.

"You better stay out of my way," said Cora, radiating intimidation. Her denim vest reflected the light from her finger plucking Sonya's sternum.

"Okay," Sonya responded, her forearms shielded over her chest.

"You're lucky that bag of bones stopped me. People who mess with me don't get a second chance! Your ass would've been grass!" Cora hissed, her egotistical dominance established.

"I didn't do anything. I answered a question."

"Are you getting smart with me again?!"

Seriously? I'm just talking!

"No."

Sonya's tone remained the same, staying expressionless to conceal her fear.

"I said I didn't choose to come here."

"I don't give a shit what you said! I'm in charge here! Don't you forget that!"

So full of crap! Big talk for someone who just got here.

Cora advanced toward Sonya, only half a foot away from her. Sonya could feel her warm breath radiate diffusing off her. The stench of foul tobacco and rotting onions crept out of her curled lip, ventilating through a thin layer of hair.

Good God! Perhaps a mint would help. I'm sure we can be great friends if your spice was not burning out your mouth.

"I don't think Lady Ophelia would appreciate her first meal with us to include somebody with a bloody nose or a black eye," said Sonya, shedding an antagonizing, smug grin. "You wouldn't want to get into trouble on the first night for starting a brawl, would you?"

Cora's huffing grew more intense, like a bull preparing to charge toward a brave Spanish matador. Her cheeks flushed pink with heat, like a heating stovetop gearing up to boil a water kettle. She shoved Sonya back, thrusting her towards the wall. The watercolor-painted landscapes were no match for her stomping, even with the stability of the black antique-textured frames.

That's right...get out of my face.

"You better watch yourself!"

Cora yanked the door with rage, almost pulling it out. The light fixture above Sonya shivered from the ungodly slam that proceeded behind her.

Sonya became revitalized after breathing out a contented sigh of relief, not submitting to anyone. She remained reclusive during a confrontation and feared getting in trouble or beaten up if she crossed someone, even if they offended her. She was content with letting people say or do what they wanted to protect herself from harm. She used her newly-adopted tough exterior to keep the bullies away.

AN OBNOXIOUS SCHOOL bell rang, screeching the eardrums of hundreds of students. Gym class separated as the ninth-grade girls funneled toward the locker room with exhaustion. They were eager to shower off their sweaty bodies to prepare for their next class that required no physical demand. Sonya picked up the scattered slow-rolling volleyballs left behind to hide under the rickety bleachers in the old wooden gymnasium. One by one, she gathered the equipment, silently praying her classmates would be out before she would have her turn. She placed the final volleyball on the rack with care before being greeted by the thankful teacher.

"Thank you very much, Ms. Frost," said Ms. Thorley, patting Sonya on her back. "You didn't have to do that."

"It doesn't bother me," she responded as she strolled towards the exit.

She tucked her head between her shoulders, preparing herself to go to the locker room with silent whispering mantras of protective wishes.

"Is everything okay?" asked Ms. Thorley, concerned as she saw Sonya's bashful demeanor dragging at her feet.

"Everything's fine," Sonya said, her lips tense.

"Are you positive? You always stay behind to help put away equipment. Is there something you wanted to talk about?"

She was reluctant to express her reservations. She held back, avoiding any special accommodations.

"I-I just want to help."

Her voice shook. Her smirk trembled timidly.

She made it to the entrance and walked across the hallway towards the locker room. An overwhelming cloud of steam glazed her face. She took in the sticky perspiration and low-priced cherry blossom odor. Sports bras and gym shorts were wadded up on the cement floor, soaking up the stream of water as she fiddled with her padlock. Focused on unlocking her locker, she tried to ignore the curvaceous silhouettes shadowing in the thick air. A group of three blonde girls stepped next to her; the cushion of their soft towels nudged her backside to trip into the lockers.

"Excuse me, you're in my way!" scolded one girl as she flipped her hair behind her shoulder.

"I-I'm sorry," said Sonya, her focus remaining on her belongings.

"Yeah, you should be!" hissed another girl.

With the grace of God and aggressive turns of the knob, Sonya opened her locker. Her hands shook as she bungled with her school attire, knocking over her bottle of generic vanilla shampoo onto the floor. The slippery floor caused her tennis shoes to lose traction. She couldn't hold the bottle in her palm because of her sweaty grip. The third girl stamped her foot on the base, forcing a generous squirt of white substance from the top.

Come on, dammit!

"Why is it that you are the last one to take a shower?" she asked Sonya, picking up her shampoo with ease. "I don't believe *any* of us have ever seen you shower."

"Do you think you're special or something?" another girl asked; the towel rose to her hip bone from her hands planted atop her waist.

"Have your boobies come in yet?"

In an attempt to conceal herself, she shielded her chest with her hands, feeling self-conscious. Her chest tightened with fear as her classmate's attention drew toward her.

"Do you smell?"

"I know," said the middle girl, creeping closer to Sonya, her fist clenching the shampoo bottle tight. "You're a lesbian, aren't you?"

"No, I'm not!" said Sonya, raising her voice in disgust.

"Then what the hell is your problem?"

"I just don't feel comfortable taking showers in front of other people," she answered, a pink hue flushing her entire face.

"I knew it! Smelly Sonya! Sonya, the lesbian!"

"Don't call me that!" said Sonya, her arms trembling in fear.

"Or else what? Are you going to stink up the place with your lesbo stench? Maybe we should help you with that."

The classmate squeezed the shampoo bottle, spreading it on every inch of Sonya's face. An acidic burn stung her eyes, blurring her vision; her shoes slid on the floor as remnants of the solution oozed onto her hands and trickled off her fingers. Sonya screamed in agony as it doused her entire body; her skin became heavy, as though covered in mud.

"What's the matter, Sonya?" asked the classmate, her tone whiny as she grabbed Sonya by her lengthy locks. "We're only here to help."

She clenched the neckline of her shirt with her other arm and dragged her into the shower room. Sonya pleaded for her to let go as she detected her follicles beginning to viciously rip out of her scalp.

Hot water pelted her face, suffocating her skin with ever-growing suds. The girls in the stall joined in.

"Lesbo! Lesbo! Lesbo!" chanted the crowd of girls all together, sniggering hysterically.

They howled with laughter and included themselves in the activity by emptying their own bottles of soap onto her. Choking on the hodge-podge mixture of fruity and floral soaps, her throat gurgled on a sudden growth of bubbles. Her teeth and tongue tasted the slippery glaze that overlooked the bile vomiting away from her stomach.

"Please, stop!" Sonya begged as tears ran out her eyes, causing the soap to burn worse than it already was.

Feeling hopeless, she coughed on the chemical stench of body wash and conditioner. Her gut ached from the aggressive gagging carrying into her chest. A whistle sounded like nails on a chalkboard that rang over the laughter and torment overwhelmed the room. An older woman stood at the shower entrance. Her sweatpants and shirt sagged from the steam; her brunette hair curled as her face stabbed the adolescent fun, fuming with anger that cut their attention.

It was Ms. Thorley.

"That's enough!" she roared, shoving the half-naked students out of her way. "Everybody *out*!"

She blew the whistle to break up the group as they pelted the empty bottles at Sonya in defeat to end their bullying charade. Miss Thorley seized a pile of towels and wiped them on Sonya's writhing body, as she tried to collect herself and remove the soap suds from her swollen eyes.

"I'll have a word with all of your parents!" Ms. Thorley said to the children as she looked disgusted at the class. "I will see that every one of you gets detention! Now, get the hell out of here!"

Sonya squirmed, trying to stand up, collapsing to the floor like she was on a thick layer of ice, even with Ms. Thorley reaching for her hand to assist her.

"Are you all right?" she asked Sonya, concerned as she grabbed her with both hands to sturdy her.

"I'm fine," Sonya responded with quiet anger; bubbly wads of soap spat onto the floor like bird droppings.

"I'm going to ensure those girls don't do that again. This has got to stop!"

"It will never end," said Sonya, snatching a towel and wrapping it around her torso. "Don't you see? No matter what you do, this shit will never stop!"

Sadness weighed over Ms. Thorley as she watched Sonya storm out of the locker room. Chunks of airy bubbles drifted behind her like heavy smoke clouds of exhaust as she slammed the door.

Her soaked locks of hair froze from the chilly gusts of wind. She remained vacant with shame until she got home, ignoring every judgmental glare of the townspeople who slowed their cars down to observe her misery.

She went to her room and glared into her second-hand vanity mirror; her wails of incessancy grew with each step. Her scalp stung with pulsating vibrations mimicking each hateful tug. The nonstop sound of laughter kept ringing through her brain over the faint snaps of suds within her ears.

She wanted the pain to stop.

She wanted to be left alone.

A pair of purple crafting scissors sat on her dresser, next to her teen magazine clippings. The meticulous pile of boy band candids tipped over her vanity. She began to slash through the once long and beautiful locks of hair. Chunks fell to her feet as she shed her shy and innocent image with each dull chop, soaking up the drops of tears puddling close to her shoes. She no longer had to act tough for her classmates to avoid her. She needed to look tough. Her brush separated the speckles of hair poking her skin that was causing her face to itch. Her teeth gritted as the shape shortened into a helmet-shaped pixie cut protecting her exterior and concealed her feelings.

SONYA'S BODY TREMBLED, the echoing sounds of "lesbo" resonating in her head. The taste of mixed soap came back into her memory. Her sweaty palms moistened the slick texture of her pants; her smudged eyeliner ran as her tears of anguish replenished once again.

She took a deep breath to silence the tormenting voices before exiting the dormitories to fortify her toughness, shielding herself before joining Isis on her adventure.

Chapter 7

June 2006

THE CONFERENCE ROOM was dark and stuffy. Brick walls were barren, crying with desperation to be accessorized with artwork. Cobwebs illuminated by the lack of sunlight from the window as they covered all four corners.

The staff congregated around the small round table, pouring streams of lukewarm water into their transparent plastic cups. The sound of papers scattering across the surface relaxed Amber's mind. Her stomach fluttered with excitement as the rest of her colleagues took a seat. Joseph collapsed back into his chair while Sheldon prepared a notepad and clicked on his pen.

"Okay, well first off, I want to thank you for being a part of the program," said Ophelia, her fingers fluttering with zeal. "I am very passionate about this project, and I am invested in bettering these children."

They all gave a brief nod of acknowledgement. Craig cleared his throat before taking a generous sip from his cup.

"What are your thoughts about them?"

"It seems that this is a diverse group of kids!" Amber said, eager to help as the tapping of her foot sent ripples into the liquid.

"Yeah, diverse," Craig said with sarcasm. He swirled his cup, creating precarious waves of coffee to teeter onto the edge. "That's a good way to put it."

"Calm down, you won't have to do the bulk of the work."

"I think that Cora girl will be quite the spitfire, though," Joseph said, his eyebrow raised with trepidation. "Do you believe we are ready to manage someone like her?"

"That is a legitimate concern. Nonetheless, I do believe she will listen to us when she sheds her surliness," said Ophelia, still carefree.

"I agree," said Amber. "Most people that act that resistant are just using it as a defense mechanism. I think we can get through to her."

"We have only a week. How much time do we need?"

"I'm uncertain, but we have protocols I trust will rein in any of them," said Ophelia.

"I don't think they will be a major problem," Amber agreed confidently.

The back of Joseph's pencil tapped onto the table repeatedly, echoing into the tense air that lacked an equal amount of faith in their boss.

"All right, this is good. What about the others?" Leslie? Tom?"

"I think Leslie has potential."

"Yes, lots of potential," Craig agreed, biting his lip.

Joseph glared at Craig; the nurse's fists were clenched tight as he began to rock in his chair.

"I'm thankful his actions didn't affect anybody else."

"I agree," said Ophelia. "Sometimes, things happen for a reason and the perfect candidate falls onto our laps for us to help."

"I don't believe that Sonya fell into our laps," Amber said softly, her eyes staring into Ophelia's. "I think it's a little unfair that she's taking the bullet for her friends."

"She was the one that pulled the trigger. She could've backed out on her own free will."

Joseph's arms suddenly crossed over his chest. His feet scuffled along the floor.

"Joseph is right," Ophelia defended. "Like it or not, she decided of her own volition. We are not here to declare allegiance. We are here to prevent them from repeating their actions."

"I think we need to look past the surface of things. We can't assume everything as real. Besides, she reminds me of one of my family members—"

"Don't let your personal relationships blind you from the task at hand," Joseph interrupted, his chin rose.

The room became silent. No more squeaking chairs from the uneven balance of weight. No more heavy breathing or fidgeting with the office supplies.

"He's right again. I know you've had some difficulties with your relatives and have little exposure in the field because of the time you devoted to looking after them. You should concentrate on why you are here."

"I will."

The inside of her lip felt the piercing bite of her teeth in compliance. The weight of her head wanted to bow closer to the table. She wanted to be taken seriously in her role, so she remained frozen with her eyes glazed.

"Do I have your full cooperation? I expect you to complete the task at hand that I hired you for."

Amber took in Ophelia's authoritative stance; her eyebrow raised as she leaned over the top of her chair. The eyes of the remaining three glared at her with deep focus; their silence tensed with apprehension. The excited fluttering in her stomach she once had became leashed like an energetic dog in an open backyard. The reality set in that she wouldn't be able to accomplish her mission the way she thought she would.

"Yes, ma'am."

AS SHE MADE HER WAY down the hallway, Sonya became overwhelmed, barely being able to make out Isis's magnificence waiting for her at the other end. She ignored the multitude of bookshelves and did not acknowledge the lineup of portraits. Isis stood with her arm resting on the neighboring bookshelf; her jumpsuit tickling the light layer of dust caked on it.

"Come on, slowpoke!"

They went through the nearby door, only to be welcomed by a cramped space the size of a petite waiting area at a small-town doctor's office. The bookshelves were well kept, but the collection of toys needed an upgrade; genuine handcrafted wooden pieces sported discolored paint, the chipped corners of a jack-in-the-box needed a rub of sandpaper, and coloring books shed loose pages of pictures filled with crayon scratches etched in and out of the borders. The walls were repugnantly filthy, caked with grime as though cigarette smoke slicked over the streaks of colors that children drew.

"My god! This place is gross," Sonya said, cringing at the dried-up wads of chewed-up bubble gum splotched along the underside of the table that drooped to the floor like stalactites.

"I know. I mean, I wouldn't live here if I had a say in it."

"I'm sure you like your spaces to be tidy and neat."

She wished she were there as another cobweb was cleared by her forehead.

"Not necessarily, just controlled chaos," Isis said as she coughed a speck of dust, missing the comforts of her home.

Isis grabbed the bouncy ball; its galaxy print faded close to a black hole. She attempted to bounce it on the floor, only for it to meet her halfway to her knees. Its volume was close to empty, desiring a pump or two of fresh air to liven it up. She took a pair of dolls. Their hair was in desperate need of a good brushing, and their outfits were craving an upgrade. Their bare feet were gnawed down to nothing as the metal core fractured out of the ankles.

"What is this place?" Sonya asked, creeped out as the doll's head separated from the body.

"Hell, if I know," she said, giggling as it toppled closer to her toes.

"So, you brought me here to play with toys?"

"No, silly! I found something I wanted to show you."

She reached over to the red toy box; her biceps flexed as she yanked it away from the wall. The door behind them clicked as the knob slowly turned and they heard the muffles of conversation. It was Amber and Sheldon. The teens covered their chest with their arms crossed. They didn't know if they were allowed to venture away from their rooms.

"Hey, you two!" Amber said with comfort. "Getting settled in?"

"Yes," Sonya mumbled as she cleared her throat.

"Don't fret," Sheldon said, confiding Sonya's nerves emanating from her. "This is a safe place. You're in excellent hands."

"Thank you," Isis said, trying to contribute.

"You two found the toy room," said Sheldon.

"Yes, we have," said Sonya.

"Let me show you something special," he said gently, his eyebrow wriggled on his forehead with enthusiasm.

He placed his stack of files and notepads on the play table, neighboring it to the dirty plastic tea set. He went to the toy box and grabbed the corner separating from the wall and picked up where Isis left off. A rectangular hole began to reveal itself. Dust and plaster scattered on carpet as the gap grew; the emptiness stretched further as the visibility became greater, like a cave receiving sunlight.

The group of four crawled into a room that was different from the play area. Walls were filled with color. Red and orange spirals mesmerized the teenage girls like a room in a funhouse. Padded chairs made the playroom seats covet with envy. Three small tunnels were a part of the remaining walls. The rooms oozed mystery like a fast-food restaurant's play place.

"Wow," said Sonya, her eyes sparkled from the overabundance of color.

They took in the contrast of transition, admired by the extremes with more vibrant colors and toys being shiny and new, and not stark and disheveled.

"Right," Isis agreed as she tumbled into a tiny pit filled with multiple colors of plastic balls. "I mean, look at this place!"

"What is this?" Amber asked, grazing her hand upon the lustrous toys that were brand spanking new.

Sonya became concerned that even the staff didn't know about this place. But that was overshadowed by the beauty of the toys. The hot wheels looked as though they came straight from the mechanic. The dolls appeared to have visited a plastic surgeon. Their clothing was modern with today's fashions. The white t-shirt they wore was crisp and new and their low-rise jeans sparkled with polished rhinestones. Sheldon hunched down, cracking his lower back as he crawled into the nearby tunnel.

"From what I heard, it's a modern room that was created for the kids to withdraw to for distraction," he answered, his feet vanishing from the girls' vision.

"Why don't they show off this instead of the other one?" Sonya asked, her toe tapping the surface of a trampoline.

"It's one of Ophelia's *many* unfinished projects."

Sonya's admiration rose, feeling her childhood nostalgia take over. Her eyes sparkled with glints of innocence. Her desire to throw caution to the wind and engage herself in the fun was present. The regret for not playing with the toys at a younger age was evident and inspired her to play along.

"This is so cool!"

I wish I could've had these when I was younger.

"I know, right?" Isis said, throwing a pink ball at Sonya's back.

"Hey!"

What is she up to? Nobody has been this way towards me.

Sonya grabbed a green one, the pressure of the force of air grazing Isis's face. Their laughter grew with each throw, turning into a colorful snowball fight. Amber joined in, ganging up on Sonya as she double-fisted some balls. She dove to the corner, sheltering herself behind one of the chairs as though she were in battle. Their joy was equivalent to a daycare's recess, full of inclusivity and merriment.

The end of a petite bookshelf began to move, revealing Sheldon's penny loafer shoes. He crept out of the hidden passage, contorting his oversized limbs through the small tunnel back to normal alignment.

"Boo!" he roared, his monotone non-convincing.

"You are so believable," Isis said, laughing as she dodged another ball.

"That was kinda fun! I wanna do it again!" Sonya said, catching her breath that was full of giggles.

Sonya and Isis looked at each other, enjoying the moment. If this is what the week at Griffwood Manor would be like, then this wouldn't be half bad. They even wondered if their parents were aware of the hidden amenities of the establishment before agreeing to enlist their child. It didn't matter to them, they were here, and it was not their parent's problem.

"Sonya, check out the other tunnel," Amber insisted. "I wonder where this other slide will end."

She scoped out the room, feeling for camouflaged cracks in the wall to see if there were other hidden passages for them to explore. She caressed the oversized stuffed animals, hoping to find one. Her hand squeezed a fuzzy pink teddy bear for a button.

"Okay. You go through that one, Amber."

The three started to crawl inside their respective tunnels. Sonya's shoulders began aching as she detected the tunnel getting smaller.

Her kneecaps were begging for relief as they clapped against the hard surface.

"I don't recall this being difficult at McDonalds!"

The space became darker; she couldn't see a couple of feet in front of her. She realized the passageway had shrunk from a child's paradise to the size of a central air system before reaching a fork in her path. Which way should she go? To her left, a slight glint of light appeared, revealing the heels of some shoes.

"Where the hell is the slide?"

She turned the other way, embracing the scary darkness. With each inch she shimmied, her hopes for a declining slope of a slide grew. Her breathing shortened with the mixture of exertion and claustrophobia. Her patience withered away from the declination of her adrenaline, slowly transitioning back to her angsty teenage self. The tips of her fingers dug into the crease of the foundation. She inched them ahead, noting the uneven change in terrain.

It was the slide.

Finally! she thought, relieved.

She grasped the edge and pulled herself forward. The momentum of her thrust launched her down the chute. Her heart fluttered as the air rushed past her face. She reminisced once again in the joy of something as simple as going down a slide. She chuckled for a moment before her chest pounded against the cushioned surface ending her trajectory.

Brushing the dust off her legs, she took in the hush of the placid space. Hundreds of plastic glow-in-the-dark stars lit up the hues of navy and fuchsia. The intergalactic abyss was bigger than the original room. Spaceships were parked alongside the wall, tall enough to straddle like a quarter-operated mechanical horse outside a grocery store. Brown bean bag chairs resembled bumpy meteors.

"Far out," Sonya said, the tips of her fingers grazed the popcorn-textured walls containing hand-painted planets for realism.

The space echoed a slamming door, startling her. She knocked over a stack of *Magic Eye* books. The hybrid optical illusion of sedimentary rocks and lava lamp images came to her mind as she studied the movement of the colors.

"I-Is someone there?" she asked, her breath shaky.

There was nothing, as though she was isolated in outer space itself. She squinted her eyes to peer through the pitch darkness across the other side of the room. The stars on the other end winked in and out of their glow, as though something was obstructing them. Her muscles twitched from the tapping sound that resembled a tree branch stroking the siding of a house.

She wasn't alone.

Her hands trembled with trepidation; her knees began to buckle. She looked to her side, directly into the egg-shaped holes of the glowing alien's black eyes. Behind the figure was a small hole similar to the tunnel's entry. The sound grew louder, inching closer to her. Without hesitation, she started crawling inside the passage. Her forearms ached as she propelled herself forward with haste, using every bit of her strength. Keeping her distance from the mysterious guest, her feet slipped while she used their vigor to aid her in getting away. Grasping the edges of another incline, she dragged herself forward rapidly. The repetition of the slide made her blood rush through her system. Her stomach became nauseated from the twisting and turning, which differed from the straight shoot of the first fall.

She didn't know where she would end up next, nor did she care. All she wanted was to be surrounded by people she knew; people she could see in proper lighting. Hell, she would be content with being back in the company of her horrible classmates. As long as she could see, she would be at peace. Her anxiety peaked as the view of a small light grew once again.

Her chest felt the sudden jolt from the impact of a play mat, much less comfortable than the fluffy plush from the first drop. She got to her feet, ignoring the cartilage in her knees cracking like dry wood on a fire.

The room was deserted, much like a janitor's cupboard. Cobwebs covered the brick-lined room, apart from the solitary stool on the floor. She ran up the isolated spiral staircase, dashing as swiftly as she could. Her lungs were heavy as she trudged up each step, glancing back at the bottom of the chute, wishing it would stay empty. She pushed through the entrance, feeling the burdening resistance of something hindering it. She pounded her fists, hoping to find somebody there to assist her.

Nobody answered.

Summoning her final bit of energy, the hatch lifted. It swung over, slapping onto the carpet. The gigantic teddy bear toppled over to the floor as though it were drunk. She climbed into the main playroom, catching her breath as she looked for help. The vein in her neck beat a wicked pulse. Her forehead was clammy with spots of sweat.

Nobody was there.

She sank back into the ball pit. The weight of her muscles fatiguing made them heavy, the uneasy terrain of plastic balls curving deep into her spine. The floaters in her eyes danced atop the multiple hues of rainbow colors. Loneliness washed over her as she wondered where everyone had gone. Her fear was renewed as she realized she was alone while her stalker inched closer. She grabbed the teddy bear's paw and cradled its torso underneath her arms. She cuddled the creature, hoping it would bring her ease, praying it would come alive and protect her.

Chapter 8

June 2006

ON THE OPPOSITE WING of the entrance hall was a lone circular table, unaccompanied in the space. What could've seated an entire school for children was now left barren. Nuns swept the specks of sand from the floor as teenagers and staff conversed by the kitchen on the far end.

Tom and Leslie were absorbed in dialogue about their favorite Saturday morning cartoons. The debate on if *Doug* or *Pepper Ann* was cooler was becoming more passionate. Isis, Joseph, and Amber all displayed hints of curiosity amongst their enthralled facial expressions, recalling the pleasure from the fun room. Cora sat alone, to no surprise, glaring out the gigantic window across the room, blankly staring at the swaying willow trees. Sonya walked over to the empty chair between Isis and Amber, welcomed by the shift in their conversation about their favored vacation spots. They invited her into the chat with a wink of their eyes.

"There you are, slowpoke," Isis said, teasing, perching her arms onto the table. "What took you so long?"

Sonya refrained from admitting to Isis that she was distracted by the unknown guest intimidating her, nor did she care to report on Cora's behavior to make matters worse. She brushed her bangs behind her ears and thought of a reasonable excuse to deter her from the truth.

"I-I had to go to the bathroom."

"Well, good to see you regardless," Isis said with ease, her smile illuminated by the outdoor glares beaming through the window. "This isn't too much of a horrible place after all."

Sonya indulged in Isis's kindness. As awkward as she was with traveling to an unknown destination non-consensually with a group of strangers to get help, she felt there was at least one person she could trust.

"Good to see you, too."

Sonya shed a slight grin before their ears cringed in pain from Leslie's chair scooting closer to them. The metal legs scraped across the untreated wooden floor, announcing his presence.

"So, what brought you here?"

"I thought we talked about this earlier?" Isis said, rolling her eyes.

"Yes, we have. But I want details. Sonya, you first."

"Let's talk about something else."

Sonya's hands trembled in her lap, not necessarily comfortable talking about her past with everybody. Not voluntarily, at least, and not with these strangers, including Isis.

Not yet...

"You said you shoplifted? Didn't you?"

"Yes."

"Well then, tell us what you stole. I need all the details. Don't leave a single thing out!"

Leslie's finger twirled the split ends of his over-treated hair, disappearing into his highlights the more he pushed for answers. Nevertheless, Sonya was reluctant to come across as elitist by not saying anything and didn't want to risk being seen as above everyone. She also refrained from disclosing that she was peer pressured into committing her transgression. She couldn't be viewed as a mere pushover, which would fuel Cora's bullying. All she could do was embellish the truth to appease him.

"I stole spray paint."

Yes! Good idea! Spray paint! she thought.

"Sweet! Did you do some badass graffiti?" he asked, his interest piqued. "I could see you doing some crazy stuff!"

If only that were true.

"Well, I was going to, but I got caught," she said, winking at him with sarcasm; her left eye closed as the right side of her mouth opened with a slight click of her tongue.

"Aw, shit! I would've loved to see it!"

Cora huffed with dissatisfaction. Her dirty smirk antagonized the conversation.

"You haven't tagged shit."

"Oh really?" said Isis, leaning in, irritated. "And what makes you say that? You don't even know her."

"She's not the graffiti type," she added proudly as she leaned back in her chair, an unsteady creak cutting into the group's silence.

"That doesn't make sense," Isis defended, rolling her eyes with disbelief. "People can be whatever they want, regardless of what they look like."

"That's a load of crap!"

"So, you're telling me that those who choose to be bad appear a certain way?" Isis asked, her tone rising with agitation. "Some everyday or white-collar people can be dirty, rotten scoundrels! Not every killer prances around looking disheveled and unpolished!"

"Well then, it doesn't seem like you're the kind to go out and start fights with strangers," said Cora, her eyes blinking rapidly. "I'm sure that bothers you too. So, why not share *your* story with us? How could a pretty little dainty girl, such as yourself, beat up bitches?"

Cora kicked her feet onto the table to further lounge herself with arrogance. Her smirk stretched closer to her ears. Isis retreated to the back of her chair; her head sank towards her shoulders like Sonya's. The shameful energy weighed her down like a wet blanket.

"They weren't *bitches*," she responded defensively. "They deserved every bit of what they got."

"Of course they did," Cora snickered, placing her hands behind her head.

Her seat teetered with the back two legs to support her unsteady reclining.

"Now, now," Ophelia's voice echoed across the room, cutting into their debate. "Let's not have this bickering ruin our first meal together."

Someone disturbed her effort at superiority for a second time, and she rolled her eyes again, irritated. Ophelia's heels clattered on the floor like clunky wooden clogs.

"To celebrate togetherness within this program, I have treated you all to something you will love."

A ticket home?

"I got us some pizza!"

Ophelia walked to the kitchen counter to lift a stack of six rectangular boxes before slamming them onto the table. Wisps of steam floated from the cardboard pile; the aroma of cooked meat and vegetables steeped in garlic and oil drifted tantalizingly into the nostrils of the hungry teenagers. Leslie clapped his hands with glee. Tom perked up with excitement, licking his lips after mouthing the word "pepperoni."

"Why not have a little laid-back dinner to add to our carefree conversation?"

"Carefree?" Cora hissed, dissatisfied. "If you call little miss fancy pants over there telling us why she is so tough 'carefree,'' then count me in."

"No, I didn't say that!" said Isis, her aggravation growing. Her face radiated heat as the pizza boxes exploded with steam from Tom's eager fingers lifting the flaps.

"That's right," Cora added, "You're not tough. You're weak. You're pathetic. You're *nothing*!"

What the hell is her problem?

Isis thumped her clenched fists onto the table, shaking the boxes and making them leap an inch from the surface. She stood angrily from her chair, her backside knocking it to the floor. Leslie and Tom stopped their voracious feast as melted cheese spilled from the crust, gradually trickling down their fingers.

"You're wrong!" she yelled before storming away.

Isis's hair drifted behind her with the ends sweeping onto Amber's slice of supreme. Her breath huffed like the exhaust of an old, rusty train. Her sandals slapped the floor, the sound reverberated off the empty corners of the royal-purple curtains. The sisters scattered out of her way, scurrying towards safety as Isis slammed the door to go outside to the trees.

What a way to ruin the fun. I don't want to see this side of her.

Cora shrugged her shoulders, unbothered by Isis's dramatic departure.

"Was it something I said?" she asked, her tone high-pitched and whiny.

What a bitch.

"That will be enough," Ophelia said. "We are here to work on ourselves as a supportive community. That means we must behave as one, too!"

The paper plates spun like frisbees as they left Ophelia's hand.

"Now, let's eat!"

THE SUN SLUNK INTO the horizon; slender twigs glided past Isis's shoulders as she vanished deeper into the foliage towards a solitary cement bench. She took in the open scenery of the untilled cornfields stretching out into a never-ending patch of cultivated soil. Dry grass became moistened from tears falling from her chin. Feeling misunderstood, she reflected on her life while the soft tickle of the evening breeze slithered down her exposed neck. Chills ran down her spine, her loneliness growing deeper as darkness fell. The crackling sound of twigs breaking as the weight of footsteps pressed against the dried wood startled her.

"Are you hungry?" Sonya asked, concerned as she cradled a couple slices of lukewarm pizza on a damp, flimsy paper plate sinking away from her grasp.

"Oh, yeah, I forgot."

"You need to eat something. I would hate to see a strong person like you get all weak and frail. But, you know, they say that starvation could alter the mind and change people."

She nudged Isis's arm, trying to pass along some of her encouragement, no matter how much she didn't believe it.

"Well, none of us want that, now do we?" she agreed.

Isis obtained the plate from Sonya to allow her to sit down and join. She clutched the lukewarm slice and started stripping off toppings, her fingertips bespattered in tomato sauce with each mushroom and green pepper.

"You don't like veggies on your pizza?" said Sonya, smiling.

"Veggies don't belong on pizza!" she said, taking a chunk of dried cheese and nibbled on it like a mouse. "At least you didn't bring any slices with pineapple on it!"

Sonya cackled louder, almost losing her balance on the bench.

"Well, I was going to bring you one, but Tom and Leslie ate all of it."

"Of course they did. Lucky me."

She gazed at the final ray of sunlight shimmering off her glossy black hair as she took another bite. Sonya was distracted by the beauty beaming from Isis even while she ate, no matter how much sauce accumulated around her lips like a child playing with lipstick for the first time.

"M-May I ask you something?" Sonya asked, hesitating, trying to mask her deep breath.

"Sure."

"I understand that you wouldn't go into detail about your fight with Cora. Would you share with me?"

"If I tell you, will you be truthful about your shoplifting?"

A sliver of oregano winked from Isis's front tooth.

"What do you mean?" Sonya asked, cocking her head to the side.

"I know I just said it inside, but you *really* don't seem like the kind of person to vandalize property."

Shit! My goose is cooked! she thought. A generous gulp of saliva trudged down her throat.

"Is it that obvious?"

"You're such a nice girl. I don't take you as the rebellious type."

She's good. I don't want to give myself away too soon. I mean, I just met her.

"Well, then what kind of person do you take me for?"

"No offense, but you seem like the type who will do anything to be in good graces with the people you value."

"None taken."

"Am I on the right track? Between you and me."

But I like her. I don't want to come across as a jerk. I don't want to lose her trust.

"Actually, you're spot on," Sonya confirmed with apprehension, forcing her vulnerability to come clean with the truth. "I have been abandoned by many people based on their assumptions. I only had two friends left, if you could even call them that. I was so desperate; I would do anything to have them on my side."

Isis took a bite of her second slice of pizza. Meat lovers.

"I guess that the feelings weren't mutual."

"What do you mean?" Isis asked with her mouth full.

"Well, they pressured me to shoplift, and I got caught. All they did was shut me out in the cold, laughing at me as security escorted me to the main office."

Isis coughed, choking in disgust.

"That's messed up!" she said, trying to swallow the piece again.

"Yeah, and now I'm here."

"You shouldn't let other people control you!" said Isis, empathizing with her heartbreak. "People who make you do something in return for friendship aren't your *real* friends. Just be yourself, and those that care about you will love you for who you are no matter what."

"I know."

Isis draped her arm over Sonya's shoulders, comforting her. The warmth of her embrace sent tingles down her back, churning her stomach. Sonya started to become secure for the first time in years as Isis's hand slowly massaged her shoulders. Her heart pounded with intensity, feeling solace radiating from her beauty, affection, and understanding.

"So, are you going to tell me what happened to you?" she asked Isis, intrigued as she studied the glistening from her hazel eyes.

"It's getting dark. We should get back inside. Maybe we can talk about it sometime tomorrow?"

"Sure," she agreed, nodding before leaving the bench. "Let's go."

Isis paused, letting out another exhale. Her apprehension of saying farewell to the day held her back.

"I'll come inside in a moment. I want to be left alone a little longer, Okay?"

"Okay. But before I go, I want you to give you something."

She took off one of her many black friendship bracelets, wriggling it off her bony wrist. The tiny hairs on her arm clung tight before becoming free from entanglement.

"I want you to know how thankful I am for your kindness."

"I can't accept this," said Isis with hesitance. "We just met."

"Please, take it. It would mean a lot to me," said Sonya; a small luminous smile brightened her face. "I'll see you tomorrow."

"Goodnight."

Isis's eyelashes fluttered more rapidly, blushing with characteristic excitement.

Sonya disappeared into the cluster of branches that gently slapped the tip of her nose as she made her way to the cement stairs. She stared at the gargoyle, looking deep into its stony eyes. A tiny smirk of empowerment shed from her lips, hoping it too would not embody misery anymore.

Once she entered the building, she walked past two nuns dusting the receptionist stall. The stench of ammonia stung her brain as it invaded her nose. A concerned Joseph, who stood at the chapel entrance with his arms crossed, halted her. His face was stiff, and his eyebrow raised closer to his hairline. His sternness was full of authority.

"What do you think you're doing?" he asked, concerned.

"I was just checking in on Isis," she said, pinching the hairs on her wrist and irritating them once again.

"Well, it's time for lights out. Please head to your room."

"Yes, sir."

She rolled her eyes to acknowledge his farewell as she turned toward the spiral staircase. Her excitement grew as she drew closer to her space, knowing she had a friend to endure the unpredictable events the week will bring. Someone to trust when being broken down through therapy. Someone to have her back in the face of Cora's belittlement.

THE DARK OF NIGHT SWALLOWED up the sky, stifling the final plea of the sun's last breath. Isis took a breath to gather her composure, inhaling deeply as she stared at the twinkling glimmers of the stars assembling above. She was relieved she didn't have to confess to her crime, as her timid nature faded away. She was too ashamed by the event that transpired inside the dining hall. Her reluctance to open up prevented her from taking advantage of the moment.

Another branch broke, taking her breath away, interrupting her racing thoughts.

"Sonya, I said I'll be back in a moment," she said with a faint chuckle.

Silence overtook the darkened countryside. The nighttime fog snaked around the bases of the trees, enveloping her as she heard no response. She turned, ready to relinquish her private time. A grim, black shadow stood by the base of a nearby tree, staring directly at her. Its arms remained behind its back; its panting breath magnified between the chirping of the cricket's harmony.

"Who are you?" she asked, confused, her eyes narrowing together, trying to identify the person in the cloak.

Emerald-green jewels reflected through the creeping fog, blinking under its black hood. The figure raised an arm from behind its back, revealing an object with sharp edges intersecting toward the top like a sword.

But it wasn't a sword.

It was a cross.

Isis jumped from her bench, suddenly terrified. Feeling trapped within the tree's shadowy limbs, she couldn't escape the unfamiliar intruder. She dashed towards the nearby abandoned clock tower. Branches slapped her across her face, whipping the corners of her eyes, blinding her as she hurried to the door.

Stricken with panic, her palms were pierced by the rusted iron on the doorknob as she clenched for dear life. Her shoulders screamed in pain as she tried to yank the door open with every ounce of her strength, her hands trembling with sweat as the knob continued to slip from her grip.

It wouldn't budge.

The figure crept closer to her, its long, black train billowing in and out of her sight. Isis flinched in terror, covering her eyes, screaming at her approaching doom as the assailant raised the weapon above its hood, swinging it down toward her petrified body. Her heart raced as she crouched toward the ground, trying to shield herself. Her arms and legs tingled into numbness, and she became overwhelmed by the looming panic taking over her consciousness. She saw only a glint of the object as it smashed along the side of her head.

She thrashed back against the door; her body fell limp as it surrendered to her fate. Isis stared into the blinking jewels that brought color through the darkness as the piece was lowered again into her side.

Chapter 9

June 2006

LITTLE SONYA SAT IN the church pews, eagerly waiting for the rest of the congregation to take their seats. Comfort eased herself further with members shaking each other's hands before embracing in a casual hug. The feeling of acceptance warmed her chilled body. Children clung tightly to their parents, attempting to retreat from the unwanted attention and repetitive comments by other churchgoers about their pretty dresses and dapper junior suits. The elderly pastor signaled them to be seated, silencing their kind remarks as he started his sermon.

"Good morning!" the pastor greeted enthusiastically.

"Good morning!"

"Ladies and gentlemen of the congregation, as you all know, I will be retiring from my patronage today and will be succeeded by Pastor Ryan. May he guide you all on the path to salvation. It has been a pleasure to lead this church over the past forty years. Preaching his word and teaching his lessons by spreading his joy is not an easy task, but it's been a task worthwhile. I know that Pastor Ryan will carry the legacy of this church with love and acceptance for all."

Sonya glanced over to Paster Ryan as he rose from his throne-like chair. The velvet, chesterfield cushion creaked as he stood to greet the congregation. His middle-aged body was dressed in an expensive smokey-gray designer suit, appearing as though he came fresh from Wall Street. His hair was gelled back smooth, reeking of sheer opulence; his skin was taut and buffered out from Botox. As much as she noticed the decline in her old pastor's health, she acknowledged that life goes on. She was eager to meet the new pastor and hear what messages he would be spreading to the community by passing on the legacy.

"Today, the word of God," the senior pastor resumed.

"Romans 14:1-4. As for the one who is weak in faith, welcome him, but not to quarrel over opinions. One person believes he may eat anything, while the weak person eats only vegetables. Let not the one who eats despise the one who abstains, and let not the one who abstains pass judgment on the one who eats, for God has welcomed him. Who are you to pass judgment on the servant of another? It is before his own master that he stands or falls. And he will be upheld, for the Lord is able to make him stand."

"Amen," the congregation followed in unison.

"We all make mistakes. Nobody in this world is perfect. We must not judge our neighbors simply because they differ from us. Either by appearance, lifestyle, or even belief, we must love our neighbors just as much as we love ourselves. Even if one who commits sinful acts according to the word of God, we must not act superior to them. We embrace them with the same love as we do with those who follow his word."

Sonya embraced the lecture, grinning ear to ear while playing with her long, twisted braids. She was in a place of welcoming. A place of warmth. A place of acceptance.

ONCE THE SERMON FINISHED, she completed her normal task of making the customary coffee for the congregation as the service was ending with the collection and final gospel. The harmonizing cadence of "Amazing Grace" warmed her spirit. She went into the clean kitchen to remove the plastic wrap from the assortment of crusty cake doughnuts and cookie donations. Her tastebuds became allured from the decadent temptation. She couldn't resist snatching the pastry covered in vanilla icing topped with what appeared to be almost fifty colorful sprinkles. Euphoria danced in her stomach with each enriching bite; crumbs and sprinkles fell into flimsy filters on top of the hefty piles of cheap coffee grounds. The bitter aroma of Columbian grounds caffeinated her lungs. Once she turned the water to brew, she observed two elders carrying the golden plates piled with crumpled-up cash and checks to the nearby office. Holding her half-eaten doughnut close, she crept to the closed door; the cold wood kissed her ear as she leaned in to eavesdrop on three masculine voices.

"I will put this pile into the account. These two we can divide between the three of us," said one voice.

"I'm glad we agreed to this. All my suits are looking torn. What are you going to spend your money on?"

"The wife and I want to go on a nice vacation. We haven't taken one in six months."

"We will be able to take her in no time. Five-star treatment!"

"Only the best. She can't fly coach. It's too crowded for her."'

Sonya was in disbelief as the realization hit her. These people she looked up to were embezzling the donated funds for personal luxury. A newly-familiar voice spoke up next.

"If you need somewhere to get a great designer suit, I know of a spot for you. I go there with my wife every few months for the newest collections fresh from Fashion Week."

Pastor Ryan.

"If we keep this up, you will be able to take more trips."

"Please, help yourself," said Pastor Ryan. "There is plenty in this pile. No one will even know the difference. I don't see a problem with taking some for the people who preach His word. And now that I'm running the show, there is sure to be plenty more where that came from!"

The doughnut fell out of her hands as the multi-colored sprinkles splashed all over her feet like shattered glass. Her loud gasp echoed in the hall as the organ played its last note, followed by pure silence.

"Did you hear that?" asked one man, startled, dollar bills crumpled tight in his fist.

"I think it came from outside the door," said another, the screeching sound of metal rang in her ears as a file cabinet slammed shut.

Sonya picked up her doughnut and sprinted back to the kitchen, running through the swinging doors. Facing the pots and preparing the pitchers, she tried her best to appear busy by filling up the Styrofoam cups with coffee, her fingertips feeling the heat through the material.

Pastor Ryan walked out of the office, clutching his hand over his suit pocket. A bulging wad of cash was nurtured for safekeeping like he was nursing a heart palpitation. A crunch came from under his toes in his black dress shoes. Multiple colors of sugary powder grounded deep into the carpet below. He scoped the empty premises, noticing Sonya was the only one nearby. His smirk grew as he sauntered into the kitchen to speak with her, his predatory nature similar to a hungry shark.

"Hey there," he said, leaning onto the counter like a thirsty bar patron.

Sonya's eyes widened, and her hands trembled as hot coffee trickled out of the pitchers. She turned around to face the man, and his cocky expression cut deep into her nerves.

"H-Hi!" Sonya said, her voice shaky with intimidation.

"I've heard a lot about you. It's Sonya, right?"

"Yes, I'm Sonya."

"I heard you have been *very* helpful in preparing our coffee hour every Sunday. That is awfully kind of you to volunteer for all of us."

"Why thank you," Sonya responded, starting to let her guard down.

"I know it would be a tragedy to lose someone as supportive as you from our congregation. Don't you agree?"

"Excuse me?" said Sonya, confused as she placed the pots on the counter between them.

"I think you know what I'm capable of," Ryan threatened, his well-groomed eyebrow arching above his eye socket. "I'm in charge of this church now. I have a lot of power here. If you get in my way, I will make sure you are not welcome here ever again. Do you understand?"

Sonya stood motionless as she stared directly into his penetrating brown eyes. Her eight-year-old self respected authority, but this person was different from her parents or teachers. It was as if she was gazing right into his soul, detecting the frigid greed and biased hate he kept hidden beneath his ordinary family man façade. She said nothing as his eyebrow perched higher, cocking like the thin string of a drawn bow.

The congregation emerged from the main hall and proceeded towards them. Children sprinted with anticipation for sweet pastries. They giggled with glee as they took all the sugary treats, leaving behind a limited and less desirable assortment of oatmeal raisin and snickerdoodle cookies. Without missing a beat, Pastor Ryan's facial expression snapped from threatening narcissist to welcoming father of three.

"Now, let's get some treats and coffee for these lovely people. What do you say?" Ryan said as the pitch of his voice raised, exuding fake encouragement to her.

"Yes, sir," said Sonya, grabbing herself a tray and scuffling out into the dining hall with urgency away from him.

"That's a good girl."

The pastor shed an exaggerated grin where the dimples were close to disappearing into his ears, looking more demonic than angelic. His menacing glare reminded her of the pictures she looked at in Sunday school, the horror of their expressions made her spine tingle. The tone of his whistling paralyzed her with fear. His fingers twiddled in his pockets as he walked away, playing with the chunk of loose change that he had gotten away with taking.

What should I do? I can't lose these people. I need them.

SONYA WOKE UP FROM her deep slumber, gasping for air as the frigid chill from her unfinished thought rattled her. Clammy sweat trickled down her forehead as she wiped her cold palm across her face. She realized she had transitioned from one nightmare to the next.

She was still stuck at Griffwood Manor.

After crawling out of her sheets, she attempted to welcome a new day. Cradling her arms around her black thermal shirt to find some comfort in her unfamiliar situation, she stared at the drifting strands of the willow tree. The limbs rocked gently, mesmerizing her, rousing her determination to face the day. Beyond the wooded fringe, she noticed a white spot on the green grass. She squinted her eyes to focus on what appeared to be a saucer, and remembered the pizza she brought out to Isis after she stormed out of dinner the night before.

I know I just met her, but Isis doesn't seem like the type to litter.

The dish remained there, unmoving, as the wind was not powerful enough to push it away from its resting place.

Whatever. I hope she's doing better today.

She removed her pajamas and donned her casual black t-shirt and jeans. She left her room and headed toward the bathroom to brush her teeth, preparing to bid farewell to her nighttime plaque. As she mindlessly brushed, she daydreamed more about what adventures she and Isis would go on. She was open to exploring the grounds and peeling away the history of Griffwood Manor in between whatever Ophelia had arranged for them.

Now that her breath was minty fresh, she walked down the spiral staircase, reminding herself to keep her guard up for Cora and her antics. She had no interest in showing any vulnerability around her. Sheldon welcomed her with a warm smile and wave when she opened the door to the entrance hall.

"Hey, Sonya, top of the morning to you!" Sheldon said with zeal, placing his hands in his pockets.

"Morning," Sonya quietly responded, smiling back.

"How was your first night?"

"It was okay."

"Cheer up, champ. I understand it's difficult to be away from your family and friends with a bunch of strangers. We all do it at some point in our lives. That's part of growing up."

"It's not that. It's this place. There's something weird about it."

"Yeah, it can get a bit creepy," he said, chuckling in agreement. "It will get easier with each day as long as you allow yourself to participate."

"Sure," she agreed, her monotone apathetic.

Sonya continued to walk toward the dining hall. She immediately smelled the aroma of fried bacon and eggs mixed with doughy pancakes. She couldn't wait to eat as another wave of hunger pains rattled her stomach. Everybody was deep in conversation, already partaking in the feast. Even Cora appeared to be exchanging friendly dialogue with Tom as she flooded her plate in a pool of sticky maple syrup. Leslie took a generous bite of a banana, swallowing half its contents while winking at Craig. Craig choked as orange droplets gargled out his mouth, acknowledging his pass.

"Sonya, darling," Ophelia greeted her, gently placing her silverware down. "Good morning."

"Morning."

"We have been waiting for you," she said with fluttering passion.

She waved her arm at the empty chair next to Cora, who returned to her stubborn disposition as she gave her butter knife a sudden suffocating squeeze.

"Please have a seat, and we will get started!"

Sonya fidgeted, uneasy about sitting with her newly appointed nemesis. Sonya looked around, seeking comfort from her friend, only to realize she was missing from the group.

"Excuse me, where's Isis?"

Chapter 10

September 1986

THE SLIGHT STING OF brisk air hit Buck's nose, causing a tiny accumulation of snot to trickle over his lip. His hands were tucked deep into the pouch of his sweatshirt, his tender fingertips seeking warmth from his stomach. His breath fogged heavy like a smoker's exhale, drifting away as it thinned out with each passing second. His muscles begged for relief from the lactic acid that had built up from his adventure the night before.

"Good morning," said the sister that met him at the bottom of the stairs.

"Morning, Sister June," Buck said, his voice raspy with exhaustion.

"Another glorious day, isn't it?" she asked, taking in the beauty of the unbothered countryside.

"I guess so."

"Did somebody wake up on the wrong side of the bed?" she asked, concerned as she noticed his defeated tone.

"No, I'm not feeling well."

"What's the matter?"

Buck's stomach knotted tight; bits of pancakes churned in his gut. His apprehension heightened as he gazed upon the tree branches near the trunk from which he was ensnared. He remembered its opening groan, hungry for the satisfaction of his body to become trapped inside. He turned back to Sister June's icy blue eyes that became framed by the concerning raise of her eyebrow in concern.

"Can I ask you something?"

"Of course you can," she answered, yearning for him to open up to her.

"What happened to Mother Superior?"

"She doesn't reside here anymore. Why do you ask?"

"I was just curious."

"Curious?" she asked, also curious.

"I overheard some things that I wanted to ask about myself," he explained, his eyes gazed around to the others to check for eavesdropping.

"What kind of things?"

"Well, I heard that she's a ghost," he said softly, not wanting anyone to overhear him.

"Did you, now?"

A tiny smirk showed from the corner of her chapped lips.

"I did. And also that she roams the grounds at night to seek all the misbehaving children."

"Well," she paused with a raised eyebrow. "Have you been a bad boy?"

"Excuse me?" he asked.

"I wouldn't want any misfortune to befall you if you broke the rules."

He stood there silently, desolate and fear-stricken. His heart missed a quick beat, his breath staggered with dread.

"Relax, you're still here! If you've done nothing wrong, there will be nothing to worry about."

Regardless of her reassurance, he froze with intimidation. Maybe what his peers told him was indeed true and there was a presence.

Not only a presence, but something malevolent that would take action to cleanse the property of toxicity.

Sister June chuckled as she walked away. Her feet touched the soft grass as she skipped into the courtyard. She hummed a melodic tune resembling a children's hymn. She gave a little twirl underneath one tree, her fingers combing through the strands of the branches as though she were braiding locks of hair.

Frank appeared behind Buck, using the railing to balance his gait as he descended the steps. His hand cradled the pudginess of his bloated belly. His nausea was apparent with his skin pastier than usual and straight expression.

"Too much to eat?" Buck asked.

"I can't help it," he answered as he reached the bottom. "What's one to do when there are so many chocolate chip pancakes at their fingertips?"

Buck's mood began to brighten, separating from his apprehensions. He admired Frank as he struggled with something as simple as self control. His recollection of the prior night became only a mere coincidence of peculiar occurrences, prompting nonstop racing thoughts.

"Anyway, how'd you sleep?"

"I slept fine," Frank said, taking deep breaths to let his stomach settle. "How about you?"

"It was okay. I couldn't help but think about it."

"What about it?"

"I don't know. Isn't it strange that we haven't seen Sister Magdalena all morning?"

"Perhaps."

"Wouldn't you think she would take action after we pissed her off?"

"I don't think so."

"Oh, please! She would've revoked our breakfast privileges, and you wouldn't have gotten any of those pancakes."

"Nobody comes between me and my flapjacks!" Frank boasted, growling a fulfilled belch. "If she did that, I would kill her."

They exchanged smiles, their teeth beaming in the sunlight like polished porcelain. The rumbling in Frank's gut diminished, despite the squeezing of his abdomen every time he laughed.

"Should we go to our secret spot and hang out for a bit?" Frank asked, his eyes glared deep into Buck's. "I'm a little bummed that we didn't have our alone time in the clock tower."

"Me too. I'm just surprised the door was unlocked. The sisters always keep the building locked."

The door slammed behind them atop of the stairs, the hinges creaking bloody murder. A sister walked out, her breath short, her face filled with panic.

"Boys, come here please," Sister Alice requested, her tone pointed with seriousness.

The two looked at each other, their confusion making their eyebrows raise. Their arms tingled as the hairs stood up like porcupine quills. Their knees shook as they hoisted their weight up each stair. Frank's stomach felt as though it was going to hurl out of his mouth.

"Y-Yes, Sister Alice?" they both asked.

Their guilt was evident; they knew they were caught. Their night of escape had become public, and their parents would be filled with disappointment. They envisioned the looks on their mothers' faces as they received the news that they were not only disobeying the rules, but doing so as a couple? The sadness of their fathers as they drank generous amounts of hard liquor in silence at the realization that their sons would not grow up to be the men they imagined.

"It's Sister Magdalena. Have either of you seen her?"

Chapter 11

June 2006

"WHAT ARE YOU IMPLYING, dear?" Ophelia asked before pouring herself a generous glass of orange juice. Beads of condensation growing as it filled to the top.

"Isis isn't here," Sonya replied, confused. "Where is she?"

"Oh," she said with sincere regret. "I'm afraid she will no longer be with us for the duration of the program."

"What do you mean?"

"Well, darling," said Ophelia, cutting her small pancake into minuscule pieces fit for a toddler. "I found her file on my desk this morning. It appears that our poor little Isis has broken the rules and was transferred out."

"What has she done to get kicked out of your stupid program?!" Sonya asked in disbelief, flinging her hands in the air in desperation for an explanation.

"Yeah," Cora said, placing her two cents in addition to several bacon crumbs spitting out of her mouth. "What did the princess do to get her dainty ass out of this castle?"

Sonya looked back at Cora, her fists clenching as her knuckles cracked like bubble wrap, tuning out Cora's loud and unmannered chewing. Leslie's open mouth excused a bite of fruit, toppling it onto the table.

"I'm not sure what she did to get herself removed. But I trust in my colleagues' ability to make decisions for the best." Ophelia said, dabbing the corners of her lips with her crunchy napkin.

"So, whose choice was it to remove her? I want to know what happened."

Joseph and Amber hunched their heads closer to their meals, digging their faces into the fortress of flapjacks. Feeling the awkward tension, they focused on filling their stomachs to avoid Sonya's brewing angst.

"Please, Miss Frost, let's not get ourselves into any sort of trouble. You are a special child that I believe will benefit from this program. Now please take your seat and have some breakfast. We have a long day ahead of us."

Sonya kept her cool, huffing her breath, and ambled to the empty chair in defeat next to Cora, who was hiccupping chuckles. She ignored her and focused on her pancake, showing no mercy as she stabbed it with her knife. Syrup oozed out of its surface like blood from a fresh wound. No matter how the sweet maple substance tried to lighten her mood, it didn't distract her from her anger toward losing Isis for unexplainable reasons. She shoveled a generous amount into her mouth, filling her cheeks like a squirrel as she fought to contain her frustration.

"Now that I have all of you here, we will spend the morning to give thanks to the women of the establishment who have generously shared their space with us."

The entire table went silent. They were uneasy about the unknown possibilities of the project they were about to be assigned.

"I would love for us to assist the sisters with the revitalization of their vegetable garden."

The teenagers groaned with disgust. The last thing they wanted to do was manual labor. The only saving grace of leaving their families to come here was getting out of the never-ending lists of chores.

"Do we have to?" Leslie and Cora whined in unison.

"Yes, you do," Ophelia answered with confidence. "This place was once abundant in the growth of produce. The sisters barely had to leave the establishment for groceries. It is the least we can do for them."

The teenagers went silent, staring at their half-consumed plates of food in misery. Their defeat was evident. Even Cora had nothing to say. Her lips tensed as she held back her snarky remarks.

"Fabulous!" said Ophelia, ignoring Sonya's sharp stare. "Then later, we will proceed with our trained therapists for some sessions."

"Therapists?" asked Cora. "You think a stupid therapy session is going to fix little miss sneaky fingers, sir drinks-a-lot, and mister no-personality?"

"Please do not speak of others that way," she said with a slight hiss. "We need to know who you are and where you came from in order for us to get to the root of your indiscretions before working on letting the true healing begin."

"What a crock of shit," Cora said under her breath as she chomped into another fistful of bacon.

"Miss Martin, it seems to me that you've had a lot to say about this program." Ophelia's tone rose more directly, as though she were a mother scolding her toddler for drawing on the walls with permanent markers. "It also appears that you are still here, with the same bratty attitude since your arrival. I don't have to help you. By all means, I can make the call to have you transferred to corrections. From what I've heard, your peers there have an affinity for dealing with behavior like yours and take care of it accordingly."

Cora's head snapped to attention. Her face turned pink, embarrassed by Ophelia's authority. Sonya could feel the heat radiating off Cora's sweaty forehead, and was entertained by somebody putting her in her place.

"I know that deep down, there is a better version of you just pleading to come out," Ophelia resumed as she hunched over the table, bracing her frail body. "If you were this tough person who you try to lead others to believe that you are, your actions would follow suit. All I hear is a bunch of talk and no substance. Now, I suggest you keep your whiny comments to yourself and allow yourself to take part in this program!"

"Fuck you!" Cora yelled, pounding her fist on the table. Orange juice sloshed over the rims of everyone's cups as liquid puddled around her plate.

She turned her chair to face away from the group, using the trees as a distraction while rubbing her hands over her forehead, clearing the heaping load of accumulated sweat. Sonya leaned over to find out what she was doing.

She was crying.

Not wanting to involve herself further, she took in the small victory before forking in another sausage link. The savory saltiness negated her nerves as she enjoyed Cora squirming with vulnerability.

"Now, where were we?" Ophelia asked, refocusing the conversation to the rest of the group, all staring with fear and vacancy, their stomachs turned off from her resistance. "Oh yes! We'll take a couple of hours for reflection and reconvene at precisely eleven o'clock. Miss Martin, I seriously recommend you take this time to reflect."

Cora didn't respond, but released a small, shaky exhale. She picked at her fingers as tiny flakes of cuticles fell to the floor.

"We'll be starting this session in pairs, followed by a fabulous afternoon exercise."

"Pairs?" Leslie asked before taking another bite from his banana. "How are we supposed to have a breakthrough with our personal problems if we have somebody with us? Some of us don't want others to know our past."

Exactly! I don't want these people to know about me. I just met them! And I definitely don't want anything to do with Cora. Sonya thought in agreement.

"We'll have our individual sessions later on. The first session will focus on empathy. You may share something important with your partner that could benefit your journey toward healing."

"I...I'm not the best at talking in front of strangers," Tom said.

He mumbled into the dry crumbs of his toast, barely understood by the rest of the group.

"Well, this will be a good chance for you to be better at socializing with other people, Mr. Sackett."

Sonya's nerves took over her once again. She in no way wanted to be matched up with Cora, nor did she desire for her to know her intimate secrets and insecurities. She envisioned a session filled with eye rolls and mocking, stabbing judgment. In her head, she prayed in desperation, hoping a higher power, or even Ophelia, would answer.

Please pair me up with one of the boys.

Like a woodpecker drilling its beak onto the base of a thick tree, her foot tapped nervously on the floor. Each passing second felt longer with the anxious crescendo that beat into her eardrums.

Please pair me up with one of the boys.

"Miss Frost, I'm going to pair you up with...."

Eek! Please pair me up with one of the boys.

"Mr. Nelson," she said feverishly. Her arms glided in a circular motion as if she was telling her she had won a substantial prize on a cheesy game show.

Sonya expelled a vast sigh of relief, the painful tension released in her back. The hallelujah chorus belted in her ears as the visualization of light illuminated from behind him. Leslie let out a gracious smile as his pearly white teeth glowed against his tan skin. His arms jiggled up and down as he gave her a sassy wink, exuding mutual relief.

"Which means that Mr. Sackett will be with Miss Martin!"

"My name is Cora!"

My apologies, but your birth certificate and juvenile record indicates your name as 'Cora Jean Martin, isn't that correct?'"

She had nothing to say, only pursing her lips.

"I believe I'm asking you a question. It would be in your best interest to answer it."

"Yes," she answered, her voice raspy.

"Okay, that's what I thought. Any other objections, Miss Martin?"

She started to shake her head, her face becoming pink again.

"Stupendous!" she clamored with glee. "Now, off you go. Be ready to assist the sisters in about one hour."

Cora didn't wait to propel herself out of her chair and charged toward the door; her feet stomped with fury that the orange juice shook again. Puddles rippled onto the table like a scene out of *Jurassic Park*, causing Sonya to expel a small giggle. The jet-black feathers on Ophelia's circle skirt swiftly coated the floor's surface as she exited to the kitchen, pausing at each nun to recognize their existence with a tender tap of her gloved hand upon their cheek.

"Sheldon!" she barked with authority. "Give me a hand in the kitchen, darling!"

He opened the door and dashed across the dining hall, dragging his feet as he passed the group of teenagers. Joseph and Amber walked out together, dismissing the tension as they started their day's work run-through.

"I'm sorry you're stuck with that monster!" Sonya apologized to Tom, who remained seated in defeat. His pancakes became mutilated from the repetitive stabbing of his fork.

"It's okay," he said, somber. "She doesn't scare me."

"No offense," said Leslie. "But it seems like everything scares you!"

"Well, I'm not."

"Then why are you so damn quiet? You could say *something*."

"I'm observant. Just because I don't possess a flashy personality doesn't suggest I'm scared."

"That sounds like you're scared to me."

"No, he isn't." Sonya defended. "I get it. You observe people before you open up to them. I'm like that, too."

"Yes," Tom agreed, shedding a slight grin.

"You're an introvert. There's nothing wrong with that. You shouldn't be so hard on him, Leslie."

"Yeah," Tom said, walking away. "I'm going to go back to bed. I'll see you around."

"You're going back to sleep?" Leslie asked. "You're sleeping your life away."

"There's nothing else to do here. I can't even be on my computer, so I'll just play their game here and snooze my time away. I'm not hurting anybody."

"Don't say that too loudly in front of Ophelia," said Sonya, her warning dripping with sarcasm. "She won't believe that you're taking the program seriously and send you away like she did with Isis."

"I'm not scared of her."

"Well, what about you, Leslie?" Sonya asked. "What are you going to do while we await our punishment?"

"I think I'll find something to do," Leslie said, his gaze focusing across the hall toward the door. "Or should I say, someone?"

She stared at the entrance where Craig was leaning against the wall behind him like a rugged high school rebel against a locker. His eyes drilled into Leslie, full of desire.

"Isn't it illegal for an adult to have sex with a minor?" Sonya asked, unimpressed by Craig's titillation.

"I'll be eighteen in the fall. I can do whatever I want. If it wasn't for my closed-minded parents, I wouldn't be in this dump in the first place!"

He strutted toward Craig with his hips swaying back and forth without a care in the world as he unapologetically perpetuated his desires.

Craig threw his arm around Leslie's shoulder as the door secured behind them, leaving Sonya in the dining hall alone in peace. She grabbed a piece of bacon and walked over to the window overlooking the serene sway of the drifting willow twigs. Nature's simplistic beauty began to hypnotize her. The thought of Isis was the only thing that popped in her head, still perplexed by her removal. Gloom settled with the realization of her plans halting. As the crows circled the trees, one stopped to perch itself close to the clock tower. The animal dismounted onto an embedded wooden instrument with pointed edges, like a small sword securely standing in the ground. Her eyes squinted, straining to focus on the object further. It wasn't a sword.

It was a cross.

"Ms. Frost, could you please help us with the dishes?" asked Sheldon, his head peeking out the door behind her.

Sonya remained silent, nodding her chin, taking one last view at the item before walking back to the table to comply with his demand.

AFTER TWENTY MINUTES of hand washing plates to clean up after the messy teenager's buffet, Sonya went out the back door. Her wrinkled, water-logged hands expanded from the much-needed revitalizing air. She moved her fingers through her greasy hair as the heated rays hit her bare forearms. Air invigorated her lungs as she walked down the stairs to greet the gargoyle statues before venturing into the trees.

The clustered sea of branches caressed the front of her body like a beaded fringe curtain. The delicate leaves drifted away from her shoulders with every step. As the last bunch coasted away, she stood at the entrance of the clock tower. Doubt crept in with one discrepancy she discovered.

The wooden cross was missing, nowhere to be found.

Visible through the trees was a small view of Griffwood Manor's dining-room window. The sisters' mousy silence shed pity on the poor child when they stopped their wheelbarrow and stared at her perplexity. She refocused her gaze on the custodian sauntering up the stairs to the front entrance, stopping halfway to take a break from the painful exertion on his arthritic knees. Scoping the rest of the premises, her eyes rested on the colorful stained glass of the oversized window as it glimmered like rhinestones in the beating sunlight. A dark shadow stood by the drapery, too far away for Sonya to decipher their face. All she saw was an arm raising closer to their hood with the wooden cross. They took the short end of the head and placed it over its mouth, kissing the base with a quieting gesture, shushing her. Sonya's spine tingled as it crawled up with the realization hitting her. Somebody else was on the property, and it wasn't Isis.

Chapter 12

June 2006

THE HEAT OF THE SUN scorched the back of Sonya's neck as she made her way down the stairs. Birds chirped while they played a game of tag, weaving through the branches. The fragrance of sheared grass invigorated her, reminding her of when her father would trim the lawn while she sat in her chair and listened to her cd player. Screams from the lungs of Ronnie Winter tuned out the roaring hum coming from the old mower as it passed close by. Except this time, the custodian was the one pruning the foliage, and there was no music to bring serenity.

She approached the garden, where a cluster of sisters exited the shed. One by one, they burst out of the structure like a clown car. They each held assortments of gardening tools as they lined up, staring at her like a mob of housewives.

"Hi," Sonya said, her tentativeness reflected off one shovel.

They stood there, each perching their eyebrows, unimpressed with the delinquent's mousy demeanor.

"I'm Sonya."

Still nothing.

"Okaaaay," she said. The shears couldn't prune the tension from their lack of response.

She approached the less decrepit sister and attempted to draw upon her knowledge of manners toward the senior members of her former congregation, reminding herself to stay polite. Her fingers connected with the handle of a small shovel and rake. She looked into the eyes of the sister; the ease brought comfort out of her jade-green irises.

"May I use these?"

The sister smiled before she nodded. Her grasp loosened to allow Sonya to take possession of the tools.

"Thank you. You have such pretty eyes."

No sound came out of the sister's mouth. She mouthed the words *thank you* and nudged Sonya's elbow, ushering her toward the flowerbed.

She squinted at the sun as it seared her retinas, wishing she had a pair of sunglasses. She walked over to the farthest corner of the garden, away from the others. The pebble-filled dirt poked her knees. Her range of motion was limited from the constricting skinny jeans that clung tight around her legs, almost cutting into her circulation. Sweat dampened the back of her shirt as the black fabrics selfishly absorbed the sun's heat.

The sister nodded, acknowledging her task as her gloves dug into the surface of the garden. Remembering her childhood when she used to assist her mother, she knew she had to till the ground. Her rake penetrated the top; the dry dirt began to break down, desperately in need of a rainy day. The earth packed along the underpart of her fingernails.

"How long have you been a nun?" Sonya asked, awkward with not knowing what to ask, but desperate for socialization.

She said nothing at first. Her focus was more on pulling out the stubborn weed peeking close to her knee.

"Too long to remember."

"You *can* talk!"

"Shhh! Be careful. Mother Superior doesn't like it when we talk during work."

"Oh, I'm sorry."

Sonya cringed as her eye shot over to the other sisters greeting Tom and Joseph with the same silence she faced.

"It's all right, my child. You didn't know."

"I'm Sonya," she said with discretion. "What's yours?"

"I'm Sister Alice," she said.

The wrinkles in her cheeks became more defined as she let out a small smile.

"Nice to meet you."

"Likewise."

The two worked together, synonymously trying to pull on a stubborn root that was as thick as a small garter snake. The root was so long that the more the two pulled on it, a small mound was created around them as it kept revealing itself out of the ground.

"Come on, you little sucker," Sister Alice said with a grunt as the two kept battling the strength of the ground clinging onto its bastard child.

"Damn, this one's tough," Sonya said, her teeth gritting as her grip slipped away.

"Got a stubborn one?" Amber said as she approached the two, dropping her hoe nearby to her unclaimed station.

"Yes," Sonya mumbled, repositioning her feet in front of her, using her back to pull like she was rowing a boat.

"Here, let me help you."

Amber tied the hemmed corners of her periwinkle blue flannel together before loosening the top button to showcase her pastel pink tank top underneath. She kneeled down to join the two, grabbing the root. Her forearms flexed as she yanked with force. The remainder of the root eased itself out of the ground; their bodies flung back from the tension of the ground letting go, causing a small pileup of women.

The three giggled as they took in a deep sigh of relief, celebrating the battle of the garden. They admired the length of their nemesis of about twelve feet, looking similar to one branch of the willow tree.

"Can we just go for one of the smaller roots next time?" Sonya joked, wiping the beads of sweat from her upper lip.

Their laughter got louder, causing the lineup of sisters to disperse closer to them. Mother Superior marched onto the loosened dirt, her shoes crunching upon the dried curdles of land. Her arms were cradled around her chest, concealing her hands into her black robes as though she didn't have arms to begin with. She cleared her throat as she stood above them, blocking the sun from their eyes. The shade concealed part of her stern expression, but was clear to Sister Alice, who retreated back into silence. Mother Superior pointed back toward the manor, signaling her excuse. Sister Alice got onto her feet with haste, brushing the spackles of dirt off her knees and elbows. She trudged away from the group, her head bowed in shame, knowing her infraction. She turned around to face Sonya and Amber, shedding one last grin to acknowledge her gratitude of enjoyment before disappearing into the trees.

"We are here to work," Joseph said, scolding them as he launched some roots into the neighboring wheelbarrow.

Amber and Sonya snorted silently, reminiscing in the joy before resuming their work. They grabbed their tools and resumed their task.

"So, Joseph and Amber, what made you two interested in working for Ophelia?" Sonya asked.

"I like helping people," Amber answered with pride. "My uncle had a lot of problems growing up."

"Really?"

"Yes. He suffered from an identity crisis and lashed out at my parents all the time. I saw how it affected my cousins and it broke my heart to see them endure his pain."

Sonya yanked another root from the ground, a smaller and easier one this time.

"What happened to your uncle?"

"I don't know," she said. "He packed all of his belongings and took off. My cousins struggled with drinking and drug problems due to their deep emotional distress caused by his abandonment. One of them got so sick that they died of a broken heart."

"A broken heart? How can someone die of a broken heart? I thought that was something you only saw in movies."

Amber didn't respond; not right away, at least. The hum of the lawnmower grew louder as it weaved its way through the trunks of the trees.

"You'd be surprised by how much depression can affect your physical health."

Her head bowed closer to her chest as her lip quivered. Her hand clenched the tool tight as it jabbed it harder and faster into the dirt.

"Well, I'm sorry."

"It's okay. He's in a better place. I'd like to think that he is still with me everywhere I go."

Sonya grinned, acknowledging her inspiration. She became encouraged by Amber's mission to follow in her path toward healing.

"Ever since he died, I wanted to do everything in my power to help kids with their struggles," she said with hope. "Nobody deserves to live in misery."

"That's amazing."

"Thank you!"

"Joseph, what about you?"

Joseph got to his feet, his hands full of weeds draping out of his palms like small tracks of hair. His response was not as warm as Amber's. His seriousness cut cold into their warm exchange.

"I just don't want kids to fall into the pressures of getting into trouble," he responded, tossing the strands into the wheelbarrow once again. "I think that kids have more ahead of them than they think they do. I want them to see their lives as delicate, and I want to prevent them from ruining their futures by doing something they will regret later."

Sonya gulped. Her connection with him lessened, disconnecting from his lack of nurture.

"Don't worry, Sonya. I'm here to help you. It's that I have a different approach to healing, right Amber?"

"Right," she said, her response lukewarm.

She walked over to the wheelbarrow, her arms flexing as she lifted the back to allow the momentum of the front to move. Joseph joined her as the two walked into the trees; their voices bickering at one another as they debated the summary of their conversation.

Joseph's interjection was awkward. Sonya used her frustration to stab the ground. Each jab let out a bit of anger that she needed. Her biceps strained as she tilled the soil, her breath huffing as the ground succumbed to the softening of her labor. The thoughts of her pent up frustration with Blade and Darris and her pastor left her mind with each stab.

Sonya took a break from her anger management, and the crew stared at her with wide eyes. Leslie's rake barely grazed the top of the surface. Cora's eyes rolled to the back of her head as she took a break from plucking individual strands of grass to justify her labor with the least amount of effort. The sisters glared at her, nervous as they regarded Sonya's one spot was as deep as a tiny crater. Behind the sisters was another person staring at her. Its dark shadow was unnoticeable through the blur in the brush of the trees. The silhouette leaned against the base of the willow, its pose full of comfort with relishing in the fury coming from Sonya's hands.

Chapter 13

June 2006

TWO HOURS PASSED WHILE Sonya laid on her bed, recovering from the toll of the heat that exerted a majority of her strength. She stared at the ceiling to pass the time, attempting to piece together why someone had sent Isis home. She also was pensive, trying to process why the unknown guests were tormenting her. First in the clock tower, then the dining hall, then the garden. Who is this person? And why were they here?

She slipped on her red Converses before heading out the door. Cora stood by the bathroom. Her puffy eyelids barely showed through her head that drooped low to her shoulders. Defeat oozed from her demeanor as she combated tears crying for release.

"Everything all right?" Sonya asked her with concern, her humanity was erasing her entertainment.

She rested her hand on her arm to comfort her, hoping for the beginning of a peace treaty. Cora's body heat transferred into Sonya's fingertips. Without hesitation, Cora returned to her usual intimidating persona, dismissing Sonya's warmth. Her jawbone tensed, and her eyebrows lowered deeper toward her brown eyes.

"Who the hell asked you to come to me?" she snapped, retracting away from Sonya's callused hand.

"I'm just checking in on you. I know what Ophelia said was upsetting. I wanted to reach out to you."

"Well, I don't need your help! You don't know me, and I don't want you to know me."

"Okay, I'm sorry."

"I don't want to hear it. I'll whoop your ass if you try that shit again!"

The door slammed behind her in typical fashion that followed with the room shaking. Sonya became distraught with disbelief. How could somebody switch their attitude within seconds like a deranged sociopath? Exiting the nearby hallway to find Leslie, she tried not to let this bother her before her therapy session. She needed to keep her cool and remained focused, no matter what.

The corridor was empty and quiet. Nobody in sight but cobblestone floors and a long, fraying scarlet carpet guiding her. Mod, minimalist paintings of many shapes and lines covering the stale walls caught her admonishment. A maroon Escher-esque painting transfixed her, but every entryway confused her focus like a tunneling maze. Neighboring the artistic anxiety was a soothing cluster of swirling strokes, mimicking a Van Gogh night sky. Her heartbeat became interrupted by the next piece, a portrait of a woman.

A nun.

It was as if she was painted for a high school yearbook. Her intimidating expression scared Sonya, staring deep into her soul. Her piercing, jewel-like green eyes beamed through her pasty-pale skin, transparent enough to see directly into her. Rage and retribution snarled from the slight curl in her lip, judging her with each passing second of being observed.

A sudden slam of a door from one of the study rooms interrupted her focus. Craig shed a cocky, smug expression as he zipped up his white pants, with Leslie following behind him.

"I'll see you later," said Craig before exchanging a kiss and giving Sonya a hard stare.

"I can't wait," Leslie responded with enthusiasm, tucking his watermelon pink polo into his ripped jeans.

As Craig vanished around the corner, Leslie looked back toward Sonya, composed and yearning for the treat of a cigarette.

Oh, for heaven's sake! she thought, irritated that she caught a glimpse of Craig's hand adjusting his genitals through the crotch of his pants.

"So, are we ready to do this session?"

"The toy room, really?"

"Yes!" he boasted. "Did you know that there's a secret passage?"

"I do. Please tell me you didn't canoodle in there?"

"Right on top of the teddy bear!"

"Ew! Why the bear?"

"Why not?" he said, catching the last bits of his breath. "Besides, why not a third? I'm sure that bear hasn't had any action."

"I don't think that fraternizing with the staff is part of the rules," Sonya said as she placed her hands upon her hips. She tried to combat her feelings of repulsion and not imagine the stuffed animal's personal space being violated. "Whatever the damn rules are."

"Well, it'll be our little secret," said Leslie, winking at her. "Right?"

Sonya was apprehensive about keeping secrets and being an accomplice in breaking Ophelia's rules. However, she was not keen to make enemies and undoubtedly didn't wish to lose any more trust in people since Isis became a casualty of whatever regulation she violated.

"Right. Should we go now?"

"Let's!"

Leslie led the way toward the entrance to the spiral staircase. He halted as he opened the door, brightened with a sudden idea.

"We should find somebody for you!" he said with rising interest. "Maybe you'll find Mr. Right when you're here for the week. Or miss! Whatever floats your boat!"

Well, you're taken, so my only options are Tom and Joseph. One is too old for me, and the other is too quiet.

"Fat chance."

"Just out of curiosity, what is your type anyway?" he asked as they made it into the main entrance hall, being greeted by the rush of the scurrying sisters.

"I don't know."

"Well, what are you into?"

Sonya didn't want to respond to that question. They only met a day ago and she wasn't sure if he was a gossip queen based on his nosy persona. Self-conscious that he would spill the beans, she answered conservatively.

"I have a type. Nobody here fits it, that's all."

They walked to the other side of the hall, exchanging a friendly wave with Sheldon. He acknowledged them with a glimmering smile before bending over to reach inside his unorganized filing cabinet where papers were on the verge of explosion. Amber waited for the two of them, her foot tapping with irritation.

"You're late," said Amber, disappointed, crossing her arms like a blind date had stood her up.

"I'm sorry," said Leslie. "We were just—"

"I-I had cramps! I-I had to take care of business. It won't happen again, I promise!"

"Very well," said Amber, which she proceeded with a defeated and empathic sigh. "It will cut our session short because of your tardiness. So, let's get started."

She guided the two adolescents into her tiny, cubicle-sized office. The walls were darkened in stark plum-purple. She directed them toward the mustard-yellow chesterfield chairs as she ventured to the other side of her black desk.

Sonya's hand hid under her other arm as it crossed over it, pinching her skin while taking in the stale scent of the lit pumpkin-spiced candles burning in the corner. Its flickering flame danced a dim light, illuminating her fake, plastic sunflower plant.

"Okay, this session is designed to focus on one of the darkest days you have ever experienced. I want you to describe what you consider the worst day of your life."

Sonya froze in fear, like a scarecrow in a bitterly cold cornfield without expression. She didn't know what she would say, especially with Leslie in her company. He leaned closer to her, perked with intrigue.

"Since you were late, we will only have time to hear from Sonya. What was the darkest day of your life?"

That's not fair! Why can't he do his? she thought with irritation.

Sonya stuttered, not knowing what to say, not knowing how to act. Her stomach knotted like a balloon animal succumbing to the grasp of a clown, kicking her pelvis and giving her *actual* cramps.

"I-I don't feel comfortable talking about this with another person in the room," Sonya responded, her voice crackling, her throat thickening as though she were going into anaphylaxis.

Leslie reached over, tenderly placing his hand onto her lap.

"Don't worry. I won't tell anybody. You have my word. You can trust me."

Sincerity beamed from his face, and his genuine self manifested through his nosy demeanor. His subtle grin gave promising gratitude for not selling him out.

"See, Sonya?" said Amber, clasping her hands before putting them onto her desk. "Let's hear it. Anything said within these four walls will remain in here, right, Leslie?"

"I promise."

"Okay," said Sonya, wary. "Did you want me to talk about the day I got caught at the mall?"

"Honey, I want darker. I know all about what got you here. I examined your file and noticed that you don't have many friends. It's also reported that you were active in the church. Is that correct?"

"Yes."

"Well, let's dig into that. What made you stop going? The church is a great community to reach out to for support."

"It was."

"Then tell me what happened that made you stop?"

Sonya's hands continued to shake as though she were buried in snow. She had no choice but to take in a gasping, deep breath. Suffocating under the pressure, she began to explain to them what went down at her church that caused her to leave.

IT WAS THE FOURTH OF July three years ago. The establishment was sponsoring an event in partnership with the town. The overwhelming stench of charred meat filled the air; smoke engulfed the newly mowed turf, dismissing the famished mosquitoes urgently seeking a bloody treat. Everybody was welcome, no matter who in the community showed up. It was their way of raising funds and welcoming potential members while having a casual, fun time.

Sonya was fifteen when she walked with a cluster of teenage girls from her youth group who settled themselves on the dry, green grass, glimpsing at the kids playing tag. The adults jammed out to the uppity beat from the catchy rock band reminiscing in their P.O.D. fantasies. Others laid out their picnic blankets in preparation to indulge in the never-ending supply of hotdogs and hamburgers paired with dozens of assortments of pasta salad beautifully presented in multi-colored Tupperware containers. A man tripped on his shoes, face planting into his plate of potato salad and coleslaw that cushioned his fall. Sonya conversed with her two church mates, braiding each other's hair with pleasure.

"This is the best summer ever!" said Sonya, exhilarated as she wrapped a strand of her friend's hair around another.

"I know!" one girl agreed with glee, admiring the tight accuracy of her tracks.

"I've had the best time with you two at Sunday school and camp this summer! I know this is a little cheesy, but I look at you as my best friends," said another girl.

"You mean so much to me too," said Sonya, professing her pride beaming over the patron's enthusiasm. "I hope nothing will ever change between us."

"He may challenge our friendship, but our love will keep us strong. Nothing will tear us apart."

"Amen!" the three cheered in unison, followed by jubilant giggles that warmed their hearts.

Sonya's joy and adoration of their faith coursed through her veins. Despite her terrible experiences with her classmates in school, such as being dragged around the locker room by the hair and facing hateful slurs often, she was certain that the church's unconditional love and support would always keep her spirit strong. Her friends were her rock and supported her even when they were cognizant of her dark secrets.

All her secrets, except one.

"Oh, my goodness," said one girl with disgust, pointing to the edge of the stage. "Look who showed up!"

Sonya followed her friend's finger. The perspired band took a quick intermission to grab a drink of water at the left of the bandstand as members of the town caught their breath from joyous dancing. At the bottom of the stairs stood two girls in identical black schoolgirl ensembles except with their hair colors opposite a vibrant blue and pink.

"Who invited *them*?" asked the other girl; her upper lip curled close to her nose.

"Who are they hurting?" Sonya asked, confused by their abhorrence. Sonya saw nothing wrong in the two girls' presence. "They're here to have a good time."

"So? They're *freaks!"*

"I think they are both stunning," she defended, her tone high and full of conviction as she plucked a dandelion from the grass.

"Wait? You think they are pretty?"

"Of course. They look gorgeous!"

The two retracted with revolting apprehension, cringing as if they found a spider crawling on her forehead.

"What's wrong?" Sonya asked, noticing the change in her friend's demeanor. The distance between them was growing slowly. "Is there a problem with finding somebody pretty?"

"If a man lies with a man as one lies with a woman, both of them have done what is detestable. They must be put to death; their blood will be on their own heads," the girls said in unison, like groaning zombies. They furthered themselves away as though they were avoiding the plague.

"Why are you quoting Leviticus?" Sonya asked, puzzled by their accusation. "I'm not a lesbian."

Sonya wasn't comfortable coming out to her friends as a lesbian, as it wasn't her identity. She knew that some of the verses read at church services growing up were an impediment to her happiness if interpreted that way. When she was ready to come out and live her fullest life open and authentically, she would have to take that up with the higher power, as she remembered reading in the book.

"You are going to burn for this!" her friend hissed, sprinting behind the other toward Pastor Ryan, who was conversing with his wife and another couple close by.

"Wait!" Sonya shouted with desperation; the strain of her breaking heart took her breath away. "I thought we were friends, no matter what!"

Her friends got one last peek at Sonya before selling her out. They took in the sadness evoking from her, hopeful that she could be removed from the premises. Pastor Ryan focused with intrigue. His smile broadened the more he took in the girls' intense tattling, not even taking a breath between their drawn-out sentences strung with dramatic exaggeration. Ryan gazed at her, knowing that he and Sonya hadn't had the best relationship since she caught him becoming familiar with the offering funds years ago. Ryan's grin grew bleak, finally finding a reason to expel her from the church.

"Gotcha," he mouthed menacingly, relishing every second of Sonya's discomfort.

Tears formed as she began to leave the party, desperate to find safety as she brushed spackles of dirt from her jeans. She felt suffocated, trapped while she tried to swim through the tightened crowd of people.

"Excuse me," said a male voice on the microphone from the bandstand. "May I have everybody's attention? Before anybody leaves, I want one last message before we begin the fireworks."

Sonya paused her exit to give her attention to the center stage. She wiped her rapidly falling tears as the voice was none other than Pastor Ryan. His dictator-like presence commanded the consideration of the event as he stood tall with his chest out.

"I want to thank you all for coming. I want to thank everybody who provided the food and entertainment to make this evening a possibility to rejoice."

The only people who clapped along were the loyal members of the congregation. The rest of the patrons acknowledged his gratitude before resuming the consumption of their free meal with no interest in participating in the religion.

"I also want to shed some sorrow for those who choose to live in sin. I pray for all of them to find salvation as they struggle to live with themselves through their devious acts."

His tone became more direct. His head turned, meeting Sonya's gaze through the crowd of people.

"I ask to pray for one *special* soul in particular. Our beloved Sonya Frost. I want us all to pray with me and cast out the demons that are consuming her at this very moment, as they have overtaken this sweet, innocent little girl. If a man lies with a man as one lies with a woman, both of them have done what is detestable. They must be put to death; their blood will be on their own heads."

The congregation gasped in shock as Sonya became repulsed by Ryan's public exploitation. Every person she once bonded with turned in sickly disgust, breaking her heart with each disappointing gesture of dismissal. The exit became blockaded by the ever-growing cluster of members. People she had close interactions with now placed their arms out toward her as if they were performing an exorcism. Their over-the-top wailing of sadness stung her spirit, crippling her as she felt stuck. Panic mixed with embarrassment, creating a toxic cocktail that flowed through her stiffened body.

"Ms. Frost. Or do you not know that wrongdoers will not inherit the kingdom? Do not be deceived: Neither the sexually immoral nor idolaters nor adulterers nor men who have sex with men nor thieves nor the greedy nor drunkards nor slanderers nor swindlers will inherit the kingdom of God."

Sonya had enough of using scripture as a means of personal attack. She raised her middle finger toward Pastor Ryan, saying one last phrase she had held onto since meeting him.

"Fuck you!"

"Sonya, may God have mercy on your soul."

His cocky grin grew, knowing he used his influence to kick out somebody aware of his behavior, threatening to expose his unethical choices.

"Let us pray for her demons to be released."

Sonya detected the howl of the congregation build as they moved closer to her. Their arms were still raised, speaking an unknown language of randomized syllables and chanted prayers. She felt stuck and overwhelmed by the humiliation of Pastor Ryan's remarks and the use of manipulation, as though he were a cult leader. Her body collapsed onto the ground; her hands pooling controlled puddles of tears that rushed from the shame of this once enjoyable crowd. The saddening disgust grew the more her community turned their backs on her from a single manipulating command. She had hope that the people would be better than their leader, knowing right from wrong. She looked past the people who practiced their judgment throughout the years and saw the potential for change, which broke her heart even more now that it is on her.

A small hand planted softly upon her shoulder, gathering her heartbroken attention. Sonya looked at what appeared to be a six-year-old. The innocent face of an angel with black hair smiled at her. The sparkle of a little mole glistened from the sunset like a singular sequin on his lower cheek. What tuned out the roaring prayers was a child. His toothless smile made her feel welcome and loved once again as though she were in the presence of blissful salvation.

"Go on, give her the gift," commanded this firm voice behind the kid.

Sonya peeped over the kid to a young adult with a full head of hair. His ungroomed beard gave relaxed vibes, shedding hope from his laid-back appearance.

The child giggled as his innocence made Sonya ease with the situation. She smiled at them and felt the presence of an actual angel, eliminating her reservations, encouraging forgiveness from her peers' extreme actions. The father lifted the kid and brought him into his arms. Frustrated, the father took the note out of his child's hand and shoved it into Sonya's lap before disappearing into the sea of chanting people. She opened the folded piece of paper, her hope for humanity normalizing.

"YOU ARE GOING TO DIE a slow, painful, sinful death. You will burn in hell!"

SONYA'S RAGE FLOODED through her body; her temperature rose so high it could ignite the nearby fireworks. Another hand grabbed the top of her head, digging into her scalp as it turned her around. This time it was Pastor Ryan, continuing to pray words of nonsense, antagonizing her with a bullying wink. Her senses rapidly faded into a blackout, she did the one thing she had been waiting to do since he threatened her years ago. She spun like a ballerina in a music box. His hand gave her the total force she needed to slam a full-blown strike into his nose and shove him back to the ground.

The prayers stopped instantly as they all aided their injured leader's side, trying to stop the excessive bleeding from his breaking nose. Sonya panted, able to breathe again from the overwhelming mumbles of nonsense. She walked to the exit toward freedom enjoying the pastor's wailing pain that was desperately fishing for sympathy with his victimizing over-the-top cries.

"Maybe you should use all the stolen offering money from these innocent people to pay for a new nose! And may he have mercy on *your* fucking soul!"

Sonya disappeared into the lot of parked cars. She cried, collapsing next to the muffler of a gigantic black truck. A group preaching so much about love and acceptance could be twisted to benefit their own views. Her peers humiliated her for not stopping him, who acted immorally as he used religion as a weapon to demonize people he didn't like.

"Hey!" said two girls' voices.

The first firework blinded her; its clapping bang stunned her.

"What you did back there was awesome!" said one of them, twirling her pink hair with intrigue.

"Yeah!" said the other, agreeing in fascination. "I'm Darris, and this is my friend Blade. Did you want to hang out?"

Wiping the tears away, she picked herself up. Their relaxing ease brought acceptance. She faced the church again, full of revulsion as the congregation continued their festive activities, unaware of what had just occurred. It was as though the betrayal never happened since they exiled her from their community.

SONYA WEPT, RELIVING the hate and anguish. Leslie scooted his chair closer to her and rubbed his hand between her shoulder blades, astounded from the pain pouring from her damaged soul.

"I'm so sorry that happened to you, Sonya," said Amber, solemnly, her pen jotting copious notes onto her small pad of paper to hide the sparkle of a tear forming.

A vacant expression of shock and disgust was clear across her face, attempting to hold back her own tears.

"That is inexcusable."

"Yeah," Leslie said, angry. "Those people are the worst. A church close to mine did the same thing to people of color! They profiled them as a means of leverage to make them feel unwelcome. I'm not involved in the church, but those who twist their beliefs with the book are the biggest hypocrites."

"Yes, they are."

Sonya sniffled her leaking snot droplets back inside her nose.

"And, hey, I'm glad you came out to me as a lesbian. We have something in common now!"

Sonya sat straight as she composed herself, trying to shake off her discomfort.

"I'm not a lesbian. I'm bisexual."

"Very good, Sonya," said Amber, reaching her hand out, comforting her. "May I ask what your parents thought of all of this?"

"When I got home, my mom and dad were waiting for me. Somebody called them and filled them in on the details. My actions disappointed them. It was as if they had nothing to say about how the church acted that caused me to defend myself."

"And how did that make you feel?"

"Unloved. Unappreciated. Lost," Sonya answered, crying again. "It was Blade and Darris that had my back and supported me unconditionally. If it wasn't for them, I would go through high school alone and with nobody to care about me."

"The same people who left you when you got caught shoplifting?"

Sonya looked at Amber with disgust, not toward her particularly, but with the reality that her two closest friends abandoned her when they were done with her. The same behavior of disposing of friendships when they were no longer a benefit to them.

The phone rang on Amber's desk, jolting the three's attention.

"This is Amber," she said into the receiver, silencing the obnoxious tone.

Amber listened intently at the other end of the call. Sonya looked at Leslie as he flashed a warm and thankful grin. His eyes glistened from the accumulating moisture that sprung. His gratitude grew as his hand squeezed hers tight.

"Thank you for sharing."

Sonya peeked a small smirk through her tears. The security of being supported and cared for eased her.

"Okay, see you soon."

Amber took in a breath to eclipse her personal heartbreak with her professionalism.

"That was Ophelia. We are to meet her in the dining hall for our activity. Let's go!"

Chapter 14

August 1986

A MASS OF PERPLEXED youngsters walked toward the cement stairs of Griffwood Manor off the orange school bus. The young kids became distracted by the collections of leaves filling the dry ground. Older youth scoped out the vibrancy of weeping willow trees with waving branches, welcoming them. A rake scratched the grassy surface of the lawn, clawing for leaves by the hands of the gardener listening intently at their fear.

"Okay, children," said the eldest nun, who commanded their attention as she stood in the center of the cluster of sisters. "Let's line up."

The teenagers went in formation with absolute intimidation, matching the military lineup of black robes. Their arms crossed close together, and they remained silent in compliance with the leader's stern demeanors.

"I am Sister Magdalena."

The head nun introduced herself, staring at the kids with rigid authority, her left eyebrow raising higher.

"You've been brought here because you are all sick and infected with sin. For the next couple of months, myself and the sisters of Griffwood Manor are here to assist with healing and growth. We have rules you are all required to follow. Any infractions of those rules will result in immediate punishment. Do I make myself clear?"

She glared at them, pacing back and forth to assert her dominance. Her eyes pierced into the depths of their innocent and frightened souls expelling sadness.

"Yes, ma'am," said the adolescents, their nerves shaky in harmony.

Sister Magdalena paused with disgust, placing her hands on her hips as she scoped their weaknesses like an assassinating robot.

"You shall address myself as Sister Magdalena. Not ma'am!"

Her breath huffed with disdain.

"Yes, Sister Magdalena."

The group corrected themselves with trepidation, their heads bowed in shame, staring at the multiple hues of dusty gray on the gravel.

"Very good," she said, more relaxed with egocentric satisfaction. "Our Heavenly Father wanted all of us to learn and grow. You will all have classes with our sisters, along with prayer and worship. Curfew policies are to be up at seven o'clock every morning and into bed by nine. Do you all understand?"

"Yes, Sister Magdalena."

"Don't be frightened, my children," said Sister Magdalena, her tone softening. Her unconvincing nurture shed a tiny smile. "This is a place where you shall feel safe. We're all on his grounds. I understand it's hard to be distant from your parents with many people you don't know. But just know that the sisters of Griffwood Manor are here to help and support you, not to make you feel out of place."

Half of the children became convinced as a sense of calming relief encouraged them. Their tensed shoulders sank back to their normal position, following an exhaled sigh of contentment. The other half remained guarded, apprehensive about what was to come without shedding a relaxing blink.

"Let's get you all to your rooms. Sister June and Sister Roberts will show the boys to their rooms, while Sister Clarice and Sister

Meredith will show the girls to theirs. Before that, however, we'll convene in the chapel."

The children marched back into the bus to seize their belongings, scattering over each other to scramble for their bags. The group left a thin, pale boy with red, shaggy hair behind. The acne on his face boiled, surfacing his skin's bacterial oils. Apprehensive to clasp his blue backpack and a black duffel bag that was overly filled, he wrestled to adjust the weight on his shoulders like an ant bearing a bit of cheese. One of the sisters caught him as he stumbled down the stairs. Her firm grip secured his stance while he brushed the dust off his chest.

"Did you need some help?" asked the nun, her soft tone gentle and welcoming with care.

"No, thank you."

His clasp quaked while cinching the straps of his possessions up his arm to stabilize the load.

"I insist."

She contended with a reach of her arm out to ground his balance. The muscles in his face relaxed, lightening the pressure in the back of his head.

"Okay. Thank you."

"My pleasure. I'm Sister Tate."

The lad gave a pleased grin as she effortlessly lifted his bag over her shoulder once again. The beaming sunlight gave her an angelic glow. Her tenderness lowered his heartbeat.

"Let's catch up to the group. We don't want to fall behind."

They ascended the long stairs; the rest of the children disappeared through the two enormous wooden doors. He took in one last defeated breath of the fresh air before suffocating into the confining supervision of the unknown inside.

"Aren't you a little young to be a nun?" the boy asked, his raspy tone jabbed innocently at her image.

"Don't be silly," she said, chuckling. "You don't have to be old to become a nun. You just have to be committed to giving your life to serving."

"Is there anything you wanted to do before committing?"

Sister Tate froze from the boy's question. His curiosity offended her lightheartedness. She shed a vacant sadness across her face, her smile straightening flat.

"I'm sorry," he said, the weight of remorse veiling over him. "I didn't mean to say that. I-I was curious."

She nodded, her ease diminishing away as her professionalism crept back.

"Right. Let's keep going."

The Gothic architecture of the interior took the boy by surprise as they entered. An excessive number of lit candles allured him; the cold, chipped cement floors and walls became less noticeable. The stuffy air tightened as the door closed behind them, trapping it again in the windowless room. An identical set of open wooden doors aired out the starchy church where the remainder of the children were waiting for them, their luggage piled underneath the giant cross.

"Before we take you all to your rooms, we'll need to inspect your belongings. I will confiscate anything not approved by Griffwood Manor standards," said Sister Tate, guiding her free hand toward the empty garbage bucket like an eager tour guide.

The boy froze with trepidation about what could happen. He could have been with someone who brought a gun or knife. Did somebody sneak a bottle of alcohol to take the edge off an unpredictable fun night? He became nervous about finding out what people he would be stuck with for the next couple of months based on what was packed.

"Come on, now," urged Sister Tate, walking back to the child and beginning to guide him into the chapel with the press of her hand on his shoulder.

He stepped inside the sanctuary, the vibrant red carpet covered most of the floor; his eyes became overloaded from the extreme transition away from cement as though he saw a colored television for the first time. With each step, he took in every detail of the old renaissance paintings depicting well-known stories. From David using his slingshot to defeat the giant Goliath, to Samson getting his haircut and losing all his strength. Noah ushered pairs of elephants and bears as unforgiving storm clouds congregated over the gigantic arc to begin its forty days and nights of nonstop torrential rain.

I wish I was as strong as them.

Each story deluged his mind. The pointed guidance of another voice abruptly ended his attention.

"Young man," said Sister Magdalena, steadfast, waving her hand to signal him to step forward like a sheep to the slaughter. "Come on up."

The boy nervously moved toward her, who stood at the center of the front of the chapel. A giant wooden cross was fastened on the wall, highlighting her garbed silhouette. His head perched down, fearful as he approached her to set down his baggage by her shoes.

"Young man, what is your name?"

He paused, the group of young eyes behind him stared with glazed curiosity.

"Are you going to answer me?" she asked again, her impatience growing fiercer.

"F-Frank."

Please don't hurt me.

His tongue was getting thicker. His throat was in desperate need of moisture. The pale skin has now flushed with red like a tiny ember to charcoal.

"Okay, Frank," Sister Magdalena said, stepping toward him, her bony hand caressing his shoulder. "I will be going through your belongings and making sure they are up to standards. Is there anything you would like to confess before I do so?"

He shook his head slowly, focusing on a rainbow tie-dye backpack in the pile.

She unzipped the first duffel bag. Heaps of clothes exploded out of it like a bomb. She patted down the excessive amounts of solid-colored t-shirts and starchy blue jeans, then resumed grasping every black sock and pair of plaid boxer shorts as though she were a prison guard. She then continued with the second compartment, tipping it upside down to ensure they thoroughly examined all the contents before giving Frank the final clearance.

Not my favorite boxers. I don't want anyone to see those!

"Very good."

Frank looked at her smile. Her satisfaction brought relief that there was nothing concerning that could've gotten him into any sort of trouble by their standards. His lungs emptied out the breath that clawed for an escape, and he turned around to walk back to the rest of the children, his body filling with ease.

"Wait!"

"Yes, Sister Magdalena?"

"The backpack."

"What about my backpack?"

"I need to look through that as well."

Frank's palms quivered again as he loosened the straps from his shoulders. The nun unzipped the bag. Objects cascaded onto the floor as she tipped them out. She braced herself on the floor with her knees and ran her fingers over the spiral-bound notebook and two dozen Crayola-colored pencils spread over his disheveled clothes. The orange notebook's spine shook, surrendering a booklet. Its colorful exterior appeared to be a comic book. Grabbing the publication, a young man on the cover had dazzling blue eyes with his arms locked over his knees in his crimson and ivory plaid shirt. The red, lowercase letters spelled "Blueboy" over his shaggy blonde hair.

Uh-oh.

Sniggers brewed behind Frank as the head nun looked perplexed more and more with each turn of the magazine's pages. Her eyes opened wider, appalled by the mature content leaking from the binding that included sweaty muscles glistening and soaked, white underwear outlining girth.

"Frank, this magazine has nude men inside!" she said, disgusted, throwing it to the floor as though there was a giant bug between the covers.

Yes, that would be correct. I don't see a problem with it.

The pages opened to the center to reveal a not-so-tasteful pose of a man pleasuring himself on his bed. His hands were tucked under the waistband of his loose jeans while he stared with lustful desire at the camera; the bottom of his lip was pressed from the bite of his jaw to entice the reader.

Frank's face flushed with spotty red hues, his embarrassment matching the chapel's carpet.

"This dirty smut is unacceptable and full of filthy sin!"

That's just your opinion.

Sister Magdalena huffed while she struggled with getting back onto her feet, stomping as she stabilized herself.

Frank became overwhelmed and shamed as tears began cascading from his face, moistening the carpet below him.

Please don't hurt me!

"Get over here now!"

Her feet shook the arches of Frank's shoes from the ungodly wrath she exuded.

The hairs on Frank's head tightened like they were getting pulled from his scalp as her brittle fingernails dug deep into his scalp. His throat scratched as he screamed with fear over to the center of the chapel. His kneecaps cracked when she vehemently pushed him down, almost twisting his weakened ankles.

"I need you to pray for forgiveness!" she commanded, shoving his head lower to the floor.

The enamel of his teeth brushed against the loose fibers of the carpet. A string of beads left her pockets with an iron cross at the end, slapping into his tiny fingers with brute force.

"Take the rosary! I need you to pray!"

Frank could barely hear the commands of Sister Magdalena as his humiliating cries jabbed into his ears with the throbbing agony of the children's laughter.

"I need you to pray! Pray for forgiveness!"

Ouch! You're hurting me!

Frank's head became forced lower to the floor repeatedly. Tears continued to spout with haste from his eyes, more and more with each painful shove of her hand on the back of his head. He bowed at the foot of the crucifix, enduring the wave of judgment from behind. Blood trickled from his palms, cutting deeper into his extremities while drops blended into the red carpet from the anxious grip of the sharpened ends of the pendant.

"PRAY!"

Chapter 15

June 2006

SONYA AND LESLIE LIFTED themselves out of their chairs, her chilly body becoming blanketed with warmth as they embraced each other with a long and caring hug. Leslie comforted her, throwing his skinny arms around her bony shoulders with security, erasing her melancholy disposition. Her bones crackled in his firm grasp before she planted a small, gracious peck onto his oily cheek.

"Thank you so much," she whispered, her breath shaky with gratifying relief. The weight of her internal struggle with judgment becoming lifted off her shoulders was invigorating.

"You're welcome."

Walking toward the door, she glanced at the fake sunflower plant one last time before the distraction of a washed-out silhouette of an oversized cross appeared. The staining on the door was different. It looked like it had taken over an eighth of the space.

"Amber, what happened to the door?" she asked, turning to Amber with curiosity.

"What do you mean, Sonya? It looks like any other door."

"It looks like something was once here. The staining on the door has faded."

Amber glided the back of her hand across the faded stain. The differences in the wood grain roughened upon the back of her knuckles.

"Oh, you're right. When I first moved into this office, there was a large wooden cross that hung there."

"A cross?" Leslie asked.

"Yes. If you recall, this facility was once a home for dozens of nuns. When Ophelia hired me to be a part of the staff, she told me she would redecorate the rooms to make them more personalized. I guess she finally arranged some changes here."

"I see," Sonya said.

"It could use more work," Leslie said. His sass caused a small chortle in Sonya's ribcage.

The three passed into the waiting room, glimpsing Cora's backside as she grunted. Her feet stomped like a whiny toddler. She stormed past Craig, who guarded the dining-room door. His stance was stoic with his arms crossed, his muscles flexed like a security guard, allowing no trespassers at the VIP entrance backstage.

"You two wait here," Amber said. "I'm going to check in with Ophelia to ensure everything is ready."

"Yes, ma'am," they said in acknowledgment.

"Please, don't call me ma'am," Amber said, snapping back with irritation. "Call me Amber."

The two nodded, and their smirks began to show.

Amber disappeared into the dining room, leaving Craig alone. His smirk grew cocky toward Leslie while his arms twitched with tiny flexes. Leslie's pupils grew with each vein that bulged. His mouth watered with thirst.

"So," said Leslie, his finger caressed up and down the middle of his chest like a paintbrush, highlighting the canyon-like crevasses of his chiseled pecs. "Are you going to tell us what...activities we will do there?"

Craig's half-smile grew further with an accompanied huff that was shaky coming out of his nostrils.

"You are going to get me into trouble, little boy," he said, his cold professionalism slipping away with each gentle caress of Leslie's hand.

"I hope you will stick around after this *activity*," Leslie said, his palm creeping down Craig's abdomen, his fingertips sliding in and out of the waistband of Craig's pants. "I can imagine a few activities of our own."

Leslie's fingers were digging more into Craig's pants, and his lips reached up to Craig's ear, whispering as each syllable pulsated with Craig's eardrum with desire. His professional demeanor has faded with each twitch of Leslie's enticing gestures.

"I hear there's a basement. Perhaps we can check out the rooms? *All* the rooms?"

Craig's abs twitched, tightening closer to his stomach as his back arched toward him. A short, pleasuring breath grumbled as his eyes relaxed from Leslie's lustful passes. He gave into Leslie's touch as it continued closer toward his privates through the prickly stubble of his hair that led to his solid and firm erection.

"Hem-hem!" Sonya cleared her throat, annoyed. Her foot tapped loud in the empty room.

Craig and Leslie's euphoric attention cut off and returned to Sonya's presence. Leslie removed his hand from Craig's pants, rolling his eyes in aggravation matching Craig's frustrated blue balls.

"Don't you think it's a little weird that you're hooking up with one of the patients?" she asked him as she tried to erase the soft-core porn she witnessed.

"It's not like I do this with *every* patient," he groaned, desperate to reestablish his masculine façade.

"He's also seventeen."

"Soon to be eighteen. Besides, he came on to me."

"And then *you* can—" Leslie said, his invitation stirring the frustration further.

"Stop it!"

Leslie laughed at his joke. Craig huffed a chuckle in agreement, knowing the payout for his compliance.

"Just don't get yourselves in any trouble," Sonya said, her eyes meeting the back of her skull as they rolled in defeat.

"As you wish, ma'am," Leslie said, patronizing her with a limp salute of his right hand.

"And Craig, you might want to adjust your pants. If Ophelia catches you with your tent pitched from an under-aged delinquent, she might end your guys' camping trip before you get to slumber in the entire basement."

Craig looked down. The placket of his jeans rose at a ninety-degree angle. With his hands cuffed, he guarded the button that barely lifted off the skin of his gut.

"I can fix it for you," said Leslie, his two fingers walking on Craig's clavicle.

"Enough!"

THIRTY MINUTES PASSED, and Sonya finished counting the nine hundred and eighty-seven cement blocks that made up the interior of the entrance hall, minus the cheap, mismatched rugs covering part of the floor. A generous amount of air expelled from her lungs, with no choice but to take in the sheer boredom of waiting impatiently. Leslie remained collapsed on the floor, taking a nap as he snoozed like a limp skeleton with nothing better to do. Craig studied Leslie's slender figure snoozing; his lower lip pierced from his insatiable biting fantasizing about what he would do to him in the basement after hours. The dining hall doors swung open, and out came Ophelia, gliding and clapping her hands like she was about to summon a servant.

"All right, children," she said, her velvet green gloves muffling the loud slamming of her palms. "Time to resume our activity!"

"About time!" Sonya groaned as she hoisted herself up from the cold floor, her muscles straining with each stretch. "What took you all so long?"

"It appears that one of your fellow peers had some difficulty with the exercise and destroyed the entire activity. So, we had to recreate it from scratch," Ophelia responded, her brittle teeth gritting with irritation.

"So, Cora got frustrated and wrecked shit up?"

"Cool it with the language, Miss Frost. You don't have to worry about the problem anymore, they resolved it. So, come along! Walk straight ahead, and nothing more!"

Sonya met with Leslie and walked next to him, entering the dimly lit dining hall. The table where the group once ate was gone. All but one window was beaming light as Sheldon caressed the black, braided rope and tassel to prepare to diminish it. They spread several poles out around the empty room, allowing Sonya to catch the hint of a silhouette of hovering red lines entangling like a gigantic spider web toward the center. Sonya became nervous as Craig and Joseph waited for her, illuminated by a pathway of candlelight that felt like a virgin sacrifice. Her anxiety grew, knowing Leslie was not a virgin. So, by default, she would be the one killed in the center.

"What's going on here?" Sonya asked, her fingertips caressing the red lines; tight, sharp fibers of what she now has realized was wire was scratching the surface of her skin.

"Today's activity will be all about trust," said Ophelia, her voice carried loud after the door shut behind her. "Soon, I will ask you to find your way out of the room by navigating this makeshift maze we have created for you. You will start at opposite ends of the room. Leslie, you will start at the kitchen side. Sonya, the opposite from there. You can help each other out if you make contact. This is no race, so take all the time you need. All you need to do is trust in yourself that you will make it out of these doors behind me."

"Sounds easy enough," Sonya said with a chuckle, unimpressed by the childish activity.

"Yeah. I think we will get out of here in less than five minutes by seeing everything right in front of us!"

"Well, that's the thing, my dear," Ophelia said, huffing with impatience. "You will both be blindfolded. We'll also be making it as dark as possible so if you choose to cheat, you can still try this exercise."

"Blindfolded?" Leslie asked.

"Yes, blindfolded. You must trust yourself with your other senses to make it out of any situation. Nobody else will be in here but you. You will be free from distraction. All the other doors have been secured so you won't get lost."

"Now I know why Cora had a tantrum," Leslie said, causing Sonya to laugh as she envisioned her tripping on every turn over every wire.

"Well, I have more faith that you two will not get frustrated with this exercise. Am I right?"

Ophelia's tone became more direct, hoping to at least have one successful attempt with her activity.

"Yes, ma'am," they both replied, removing their sarcasm as they sensed her seriousness.

"It's Lady Ophelia!"

"Yes, Lady Ophelia."

"Right."

She exhaled, her hands clapping again like beaten erasers.

"Excuse me," Sonya interrupted, concerned. "If you leave us all by ourselves, we could remove our blindfolds and cheat our way out of this room."

"This is where I'll be trusting the two of *you* to comply with the exercise. You have to receive a little trust for you to thrive."

"Okay...."

"Right. Joseph, could you escort Miss Frost over to the window and prepare her? Craig, take Mister Nelson to the kitchen side to prepare him."

"Yes, Craig," Leslie said, excessively licking his lips. "Prepare me."

"Shhh!"

Craig shook his head to combat his desires.

The two employees walked them around the outer parameters of the wire maze. A yellowish-brown blindfold wrapped snugly around Sonya's head, the outsides looped together taut around her skull, causing a tight throb to drum around her temples.

"Too tight?"

"Uh...yes."

He ignored her and pulled apart the ends, fastening the knot tighter. Craig repeated the same action with his blindfold and tied it around Leslie's head.

"Are you going to save that blindfold for later, stud?" Leslie asked Craig. His hand reached for his leg, tingling the upper part of his thigh. "Because I have a few surprises for you, too."

Craig slapped his hand off him, shooing him away to keep on task. Joseph and Craig grabbed the two from behind, ushering them to their starting positions.

"Are we ready to go?" Ophelia asked with vigor.

"Do we have much of a choice?" Sonya asked, her sarcasm reflected from her flailing hands surrendering in helplessness.

A chuckle left Ophelia's lips and then escalated into a fainter and more distinguished maniacal laugh.

"No."

Silence overtook the room as Sheldon walked behind Sonya, dragging the rope behind him to close the curtain, smoldering their last bit of visibility. Craig and Joseph walked around the outskirts as darkness overtook the room like a darkening cloud following the shrinking light. Ophelia opened the door, allowing the staff to exit, leaving the two alone in quiet, solitude, and darkness.

"Remember to trust in yourselves," Ophelia cheered them on as Sheldon followed behind Craig and Joseph. "I believe in both of you!"

The last speck of light disappeared underneath the muffling blindfold covering the rest of Sonya's vision. Dead silence overtook the space, sharpening the tense silence that grew. The nerves in her hand perked to full awakening, hovering over the empty air, hoping to find a connection to guide her to the finish. Her breath became heavy, shaking with nerves. The space became stuffy in an abyss of darkness. Hopelessness crept over her loss of control. Paranoia barged into her judgment, feeling alone with nobody to help her.

Nobody to guide her.

Nobody to save her.

The space around her became smaller, causing the air to tighten in Sonya's lungs. Her hands swerved frantically like a lone castaway signaling an S.O.S., hoping to find a wire to navigate out of the entangled maze. Her fingernail plucked one wire, causing them to vibrate like the string on a guitar. She took a few more steps before her other hand reached the parallel wire. Hope rekindled as she ventured to the finish. Remembering one of her childhood books, she kept her right hand on the labyrinth to follow the trail, knowing she would eventually find her way out no matter how many dead ends she faced. She delicately waddled to avoid stumbling onto the floor and hurting herself. Worry sleeted inside her brain; her curiosity for Leslie muddled her mind.

"Are you getting this?"

A DEAD END SLAPPED her stomach, teetering her balance.

Sonya's voice muffled through Leslie's blindfold. His arms wagged in front of him, hunching over to try his best to find his way through the maze. His breath staggered with each passing second that filled his eagerness to bask in the fruits of his labor in the form of Craig's physique. The poles holding up the wires were being moved, causing a grinding movement that vibrated the soles of his feet. His lack of awareness, not knowing the braces, scoots his rerouting path toward the finish.

"Is someone there?" he asked, his throat dry.

There was no response.

"Craig, is that you?" he asked, smirking with heightened anticipation.

He continued to move forward at a more rapid pace, scooting through the web. His heart raced quicker, playing along with his urge to find him.

"I know you're there."

His tone softened with a long hum. "When I find you, we are going to have some *real* fun."

His arms halted at the hint of cloth; the thick polyester alluded to hopes of a curtain. The fabric pressed against the abdominals of a body. His desires intensified to a raging peak as his thumb pressed the firming throb of a hardened nipple. Massaging the connecting pectoral muscle, his hands twitched with anticipation.

"I found you," he said, a submissive glee broke through her chuckle. "Now help me out of here so I can give you a prize."

The body caressed his arm, guiding him like a boy scout escorting an elder across the street. Zigging and zagging around each obstacle, they swerved through the nearby corner to the following straight line. An easing sense of reprieve lightened like a sheltering veil, knowing he was close to freedom. Feeling a sudden stop, the clinging of a grasping fist made him alone in complete silence. Leslie's heart rate increased more, ready to explode with lustful desire as the pressing subsided, leaving him greeted once again with loneliness.

"Have we made it to the finish line? Can I take this damn blindfold off now?"

Still nothing.

The lack of response annoyed Leslie, his knuckles crunching as dead air crept around him. Feeling the abandoned loneliness stalk, he reached his hands toward the back of his head, fiddling with the thick knot. A steel-toed boot pelted his tailbone, and his body became thrust into the unknown. He found out his heightened senses were working; his hands didn't break his fall, but that the ninety-degree angle grew to more of an obtuse pit. His legs arched back closer to his shoulders like a scorpion tail; the temple of his head knocked the rigid ends of the wooden planks. His ankle shouted in sharpened pain as it pivoted behind him. His stomach tumbled ferociously as though it would eject from his mouth.

The surface scratched his cheek and halted his tumble; the harsh taste of iron filled his mouth with the sudden ejection of a broken tooth. Disoriented, his shaky hands fumbled up his tender neck. The tips of his fingers squished into the forming gashes on his face before the blindfold loosened over his eyes. The room's spinning eased with the visibility of the top of the staircase containing a shadow. Its draped fabric billowed down the stairs as a hand closed the door behind it to lock the two of them inside the deserted basement.

Chapter 16

June 2006

CASH REGISTERS BELTED an annoying screech while underpaid clerks hovered merchandise over their scanners and the late-night rush of anxious customers flooding the grocery store. An employee dragged the mop over a massive spill of shattered spaghetti jars, grumbling profanities as the red sauce stained the floor like a crime scene. A trio of teenagers walked around, their eyes scoping the shelves for groceries through the obnoxious squeal of children. The overshadow of bloody murder interrupted the chaos, tantrums growing from not getting the product they desire. Shelves of candy emptied from the hands of embarrassed parents giving in to the waves of screaming, trying to contain their little one's wrath and deter the gawking attention away from them.

"Can you believe some of these people?" asked one teenager, annoyed. His eardrum felt the ease when the child opened the chocolate. "Why do parents give their kids whatever they want for throwing a fit?"

"I know, Hal," Leslie said as he took off his headphones, the pressure lifting like suction cups. "If that was me, my mom would leave the cart and take me to the car to beat my ass."

"Mine too!" said Tony. "We would never do that again once we drove the *long* way home."

Leslie rolled his eyes in disgust, walking toward the neighboring aisle. His fingers caressed the assortment of liquor bottles. The texture and girth of each bottle distracted him from the corporate disarray.

"What're we even doing here in the first place? We're not old enough to buy this."

"Shhh! I got it under control. Do you want to have fun at Anderson's party or not?"

"I do, but this is wrong," said Tony with apprehension, crossing his arms uncomfortably.

"Don't worry," Leslie said, a small bottle of vodka tightening in his grip. "I have somebody that will pay for all the goods we need."

He pointed to the end of the aisle. A college-aged male winked at them, his beefy fists tucked deep inside his letterman's jacket.

"He owes me a favor for some fun we had last week. Maybe I'll call him later tonight after I'm a little sauced, and we can have our own after-party!"

"Are you sure you're going to drive? It sounds like you're going to have more than you should."

Their cart caused a traffic jam and frustrated an elderly woman who double-fisted bottles of gin and tonic water. The gray curls wisped away from her head like fuming smoke.

"I'll be fine. I know my limits."

THE ACOUSTICS OF POP music vibrated the linoleum floors. Glass trembled within the wooden grasp of picture frames that teetered on the wall. High-pitched catcalls whistled from the football team as over-primped girls stumbled in their six-inch heels. The vulnerability from their incessant cries from the drama of receiving the news of their cheating boyfriends inspired them to take advantage of their bodies. Lightweight drinkers vomited their leftovers into one of the nearby bushes on the side of the house as the porch took on more guests.

"This party is bitchin'!"

"Right?!" Leslie with enthusiasm, his feet tripping on one another. "Too bad you're missing out on the after-party. We're going to have tons of fun!"

"Woah. Are you sure you want to leave, cowboy? I don't think you are in a good enough state to be driving."

"I need this! He owes me," said Leslie, his hand brushed on the backside of his jeans, his fingertips peeking through the frayed holes of his pocket.

"I'm not comfortable with you driving. This isn't safe," said Hal, blocking his path with their entire body.

"I don't care how comfortable you are with my needs," Leslie said, snapping back, his irritation growing. "I didn't ask for a third to join us for the evening. But if you want to watch, I won't stop you!"

Leslie forcefully shoved his friend to the side before marching over to his car; its red color stood out in the darkness only illuminated by a lone street lamp. The chirping crickets chimed in to finish the rest of their song, with the music fading with each step. The cluster of excessive keychain decorations tangled in his fingertips before falling off his hand and falling to the street's curb. The clap of shoes pelted onto the pavement over his sighs of frustration as he picked up his keys.

He saw nothing.

The key stumbled over the ignition before securing itself into the hole. His radio blasted the beat Britney Spears' "Stronger." He placed the car into gear to swerve out of his parking spot, his heart fluttering, eager to pay back his buyer. The engine accelerated, passing a couple of blocks with no care that his singing was off tune. The synchronized bopping of his drifting head to the upbeat empowerment of the song's chorus made his pulse tick.

Red and blue lights reflected from the mirror, dancing in his pupils taking his imagination into a techno nightclub. The craving for pills made him regret not asking the jocks for one of theirs. Sirens blared over the next verse, causing his attention to halt. He looked behind his car and found the reflection of a police vehicle attempting to pull him over. Their bumpers were on the verge of a kiss, mere inches apart as he slowed to the side of the road. His nerves overtook his bearings as his confidence became diminished. The sweat on his palms proliferated.

The officer walked over to Leslie's car, tucking his hands deep inside the pocket of his pants before tapping his knuckle on the car's window. Leslie's heart jolted at the sound of the radio as he cranked the window's handle.

"Evening, officer," Leslie said to the man, his teeth gritting tight, his green eyes floating within the bloodshot veins.

"Do you know why I pulled you over?"

"Because you aren't a fan of Britney Spears?" he responded. His nervous laughter gave no effect to crack the officer's stoney glare.

"Are you getting smart with me?"

"No, sir."

Leslie collapsed further into his seat, retreating to shame. He couldn't think of any other tactics to weasel himself out of trouble.

"You were swerving in and out of the lane!"

"I was?"

Leslie's eyes winced from the blinding jab of the officer's flashlight that discovered his oversized, saucer-like pupils.

"Have you been drinking?"

"No, sir," Leslie said, his tongue swelling his speech into a sloppy slur.

The officer stepped back with disappointment, knowing that Leslie was lying to him before presuming to signal him to get out of the vehicle.

"Step out of the car, please."

Leslie crept out of the car, placing his hands behind his back. The rotator cuffs of his shoulders winced from contorting as the metal links dug deep into his bony wrists. The sound of stilettos took over their attention once again, growing in sound as it clapped on the asphalt.

"Hem-hem," coughed a gentle, feminine voice.

The two looked over, and a woman's Dior dress changed colors from red to blue by the policeman's vehicle. A black parasol concealed her cinched-in figure.

"I don't think that keeping him overnight in jail would be best. Perhaps I could be of assistance."

"I beg your pardon?"

A black lace and mesh veil was revealed under the parasol to show the tightened face of a put-together woman. Her thin eyebrow perched high along her forehead.

"My name is Lady Ophelia. May I have a word with you in private?"

LESLIE HYPERVENTILATED after the basement door shut, unable to make out the shadowy figure in the darkness of the unlit room. The string dangled above the black gloves before being yanked to illuminate the human.

"Oh, my god!" Leslie said, squealing in fear.

A black, tattered cloak with a white patch collaring its neck and most of its shoulders brightened from the sepia-shaded bulb. With eyes hollowed out, a shiny blood orange mask glistened. Black mesh muffled the heavy breaths out of its gaping open mouth.

They cradled a wooden cross, identical to the washed-out spot from Amber's office door, nurturing its sharp points. The nun slunk down the stairs, the backside of Leslie's jeans ripping wider onto the floor's crevasse as he choked in terror. Ignoring the painful screams from his stomach, he flipped over, paddling his limbs like a turtle.

Leslie screamed at the top of his lungs. A sharp pain pierced from the base of his scalp succumbing to the nun's grasp as it dragged him into a nearby closet.

Leslie continued to squirm, his chin bracing upon the end of the stick. His head stabilized between the nun's boot and the cross, the sharp point poking under his chin. Pain radiated under his tongue. He squealed in distress while the wood perforated into his flesh. The taste of iron mixed with the earthy garnish of splinters became heavy as the wood jabbed into his teeth. His throat gurgled the fauceting blood filling his lungs. His biceps twitched as his grip slipped from the shaft he pushed desperately to repel from him. The nun's mask muffled its angry, distorted groan as Leslie pleaded for salvation.

"PRAY!"

Leslie's head thrust deeper down the cross, impaling through the top of his jaw. His body collapsed as the pointed edge jammed deeper into the frontal lobe of his brain. The grasp of his hands slipped from the weapon. His eyes wept painful tears of blood that pooled a growing puddle from the trickle of the weapon's base, forming a splash of red, hot, unforgiven death.

SONYA'S COMPETITIVE nature took over as she crossed the last corners of her side of the maze. The last bit of wire left her perspiring grasp, introducing an open patch of unclaimed space. Her arms wagged, searching for the door to escape to visual freedom. Her palms caressed the door's wood grain until she grazed the cold and satisfying iron knob along the center. Muffled light brightened from under her blindfold; satisfaction grew with knowing that she made it out of the maze by trusting her instincts and committing to the confinements of the exercise. An overwhelming swarm of applause startled her attention, satisfying her isolated mind with an abrupt rapid sound.

"Bravo! Bravo!" Ophelia cheered, her pride showcasing above the clapping muffle from her gloves. "Well done!"

Craig loosened the knot and hiked down the drenched piece of sweaty fabric toward her neck.

"Wonderful! You see? If you trust yourself, you can accomplish anything! I am so proud of you, my darling!"

"Thank you," Sonya said, her smile beginning to form. "Has Leslie finished yet?"

"I'm afraid he hasn't. We will patiently wait for him. I'm sure he will stick his neck out to ensure the task is complete, no matter what. You're dismissed."

Chapter 17

June 2006

OUTSIDE THE COMMON area, the stale congestion of mold and mildew ventured into Sonya's lungs. She studied the fraying threads on the warped corners of the withering rugs in the hallway.

Three hundred and eighty-seven.

She then observed the dust-coated bookcases; hundreds of hardcover spines sheltering torn pages screaming desperately to be read. She acknowledged the tease of socialization of the nun's faces as their portraits rotted. The menacing gaze from the most prominent portrait framed in oak was a look unlike the others; her headpiece was three dimensional on top of the veil, angular like a visor. Her jewel-green eyes beamed into Sonya's soul, following her as she moved around the corridor. A neighboring photograph inclined away as she recoiled from the startling hand clasping her shoulder, fingers dipping into her tense muscles.

"Holy shit!"

Sonya gasped as she placed her hand on her chest. Her heart thrusted rapid beats in the way of a drummer boy.

"Jesus," Tom said, retreating with a defensive jolt. "It's only me. Why are you so jumpy?"

Relieved, Sonya took a deep breath. Her shoulders lowered to a more calmed disposition.

"It's nothing. Have you seen Leslie?"

The glow of ghostly pale skin flushed from the dim candlelight. His red hair flickered with the dancing flames as his freckles became highlighted like bright embers.

"I thought he was with you doing that stupid activity," he said with a chuckle.

"No, they separated us. Did you two do the same thing?"

"Well, yeah. It didn't even take five minutes. All I heard was Cora swearing up a storm and tearing apart the entire maze. I wish I could've seen it."

"Really?" said Sonya, her face frozen with no surprise to perk it.

"Yeah, I took off my blindfold after I heard the poles fall to the floor and saw every piece of wire torn out!"

"I swear, that girl has some serious issues."

She flung her hands above her waist, disheartened for Cora. Her disbelief that she was still there and Isis wasn't boiled her blood.

"Right? I heard she was only here because she organized the crime. She didn't even commit it!"

"Yet, she judges people for how badass they are."

Their eyes rolled like a cat eye marble, and a pitiful snarl left her lips.

"You'd think that Leslie would be done by now. He's smarter than he appears," Sonya said, refocused.

"You would think."

"We should check and see if he's finished. I'm sure dinner would be any minute. Ophelia wouldn't cancel over this crap."

The two walked down the hall again, passing by the assortment of nuns in their paintings. She took one more curious glance at the green eyes following her to the other end of the room. The nun's smirk was crooked; the yearning plea on her face shook Sonya's nerves as the door shut behind them.

THE WIRES WERE WIPED away as if they had never existed. Nuns polished the dining hall to the best it ever looked, free of rampant dust bunnies and tangled cobwebs. The large circular table sat in the center of the room as it once did, with Amber, Joseph, and Ophelia on one end and Cora on the other with her angered and unwelcoming aura. Her head rested upon her crossed arms in defeat as though the group had scolded a toddler for scribbling nonsense on the walls with crayons. Her curls frizzed out more than before as steam continued to leave her head to turn it into an electrocuted afro. Cora's intrusive stare vanished as Ophelia sprang from her chair with her arms fluttering, as if she was about to drift with joy for Sonya and Tom's presence.

"My darlings!" said Ophelia, her vibrato more prominent than ever. "Come on in! Join us!"

Sonya and Tom's arms folded in front of them because of Ophelia's overbearing glee. Their steps slowed with apprehension from her frantic ushering, trying to use one another as a shield for protection.

"Come on. We've been waiting for you two so that we can eat."

Sonya pulled on Tom's arm, nudging him as she noticed the presence appearing strange and not like normal with one chair absent from the circle.

"Aren't we waiting for Leslie?" asked Sonya solemnly. Ophelia showed no spark of concern.

Ophelia's fluttering arms stopped. She signaled a disappointing sigh; her gloves disappeared into the billowing drapery of her skirt.

"Honey, I'm sorry to say this, but Mr. Nelson won't be joining us for the remainder of the program," she said, her tone lowered with peeking rasps.

"What?" Sonya asked, shocked, squinting her glare toward her. "Where'd he go?"

"He's been removed. Like Ms. West, It appears Mr. Nelson has broken the rules. With deep consideration, his case is better suited outside Griffwood Manor."

"What the hell does that mean?"

Sonya's tone rose higher. Tom's hand strained as he cautiously held Sonya back to prevent another outburst.

"Ms. Frost, I will kindly ask you to watch the language," Ophelia scolded, ignoring the empty and sorrowful glaze coating their faces.

"Sonya, I need you to cool it for us," Tom whispered to her, his knees shaking.

Sonya took a deep breath and let her racing heart slow down. Her mind combated the contradicting thoughts of rational focus and exploding outbursts of frustration. Her feverish body slipped down a few degrees, trying to ignore the muted laughter that Cora was barely suppressing with her hand. Joining the group, hot air tickled the back of her neck that came from Cora's decaying teeth. Tom locked into his reclusive nature, worse than ever since his arrival, praying that the domino effect of Cora taunting Sonya would end, holding back on Ophelia.

"I'm sorry for my outburst, Lady Ophelia."

Her piercing blue eyes stared into her; her aloofness unconvincing with feigned patience.

"Is it possible that you could tell us what happened to Leslie?" she asked, her voice shaky.

The kitchen door swung open. Steam trailed off their carts like train exhaust with Craig and Sheldon pushing. The wheels screamed in dehydration, with dry rust scratching everyone's ears.

"Did somebody order dinner?" Sheldon said, chipper, marching happily behind Craig to overshadow the struggle of the heavy haul.

Sonya's anger minimized her hunger pains. Her stomach churned only a little from taking in the mixed smells of sauteed vegetables.

"Okay, everyone, enough of all this sad news about our dear friend Mr. Nelson," said Ophelia, rising from her chair, eager to assist.

"No," Sonya said, the cloth napkin clenched firmly in her hand.

Ophelia's eyebrows lowered close to her bony eye sockets. Tom's shoulders tensed further as they rose to his droopy earlobes. The taste of blood spackled on his tongue from the sharp bite on his lower lip.

"I'm sorry, Lady Ophelia. Can you please just tell me what happened to Leslie?" said Sonya, her hands shaking with her forced tone, shielding her anger.

Ophelia's lip curled, her fair skin flushing into a light pink hue as she leaned over the table. She placed her arms upon it as though she was about to flip it over like an angry New Jersey housewife.

"Mr. Nelson has broken the rules!" she said, growling firmly, demonically. "Rules that have been set in place the minute you all arrived. I'm not going to elaborate on the matter any further."

An intimidating wave of fear coursed through the teenager's arteries, including Cora's. Amber's jaw lowered closer to her plate in surprise as she never saw this aggressive side of her boss. The veins in her loose skin bulged as though the wrath of God itself took over her, and this once frail-looking woman became ready to raise hell.

"I will not have this talk again. Understand?!"

"Y-Yes," the children answered, stuttering in fear.

"Yes, what?"

"Yes, Lady Ophelia."

"Very good."

Ophelia softened as the god-like presence left her body. Craig and Sheldon's guilt clouded the diminished light that once perked their energy. Their heads bowed somberly at the pots below them, nervous to even change the subject for their feast.

She shielded her glove with a tattered-brown oven mitt before grasping the pot's lid.

"Now, who's ready to eat?!"

SONYA EXITED THE DINING hall, her stomach heavy with chicken and mushrooms. Bright yellow hues to darker blood orange greeted the courtyard as she took a refreshing breath of desert-like air. She crossed her arms from the tingling in her spine while strolling through the dangling willow tree branches with sadness. Her feet dampened from the greeting dew along the long shreds of grass as she shuffled through. She approached the bench where she once bonded with Isis the previous night. Tears formed, helpless and alone, without the two people she trusted the most out here, collapsing on the cement in defeat.

"I miss you, Isis," she mouthed to herself, gazing longingly toward the clock tower's gritty panels. "Why did you break the rules?"

The wind whistled over her lonely temperament. Branches rustled together, shaking like the tiny nudge of a maraca. Her meal was filling, but she didn't know that she was getting a second course. One that wasn't food. This one was a tall order of suspicion with a growing list of questions.

Why would Isis be sent home on the first night for breaking the rules, as *lovely* and *innocent* as she is?

Why would *Ophelia* not disclose any sort of reasoning for Leslie's departure?

The logic of the regulations wasn't lining up. She had to search for some answers. And since nobody was willing to help her, she needed to find out herself, no matter how many rules had to be broken.

Chapter 18

August 1986

ROASTED PORK AND ASPARAGUS permeated the well-lit entrance hall as its doors opened. The once congested dining room emptied with enthusiastic kids getting acquainted on their first day. Their stomachs indulged from their never-ending dinner of every cooked meat and vegetable plausible. Having consumed the overabundance of entrees, a husky child waddled with pastries and hot dish stuffed in his stomach. Leaving the two long tables, a boy shuffled his feet, his pale skin adjusting luminescence from the transition of candlelight. He felt alone after being humiliated in front of his new peers. Being weighed down in depression, Frank recessed outside, envious of the cluster of teenage girls who giggled as they watched boys running around on the blend of brownish-green grass. A hopeless sigh was expelled as he glanced at them, tackling each other on the unshaded turf.

He strolled through the slew of branches that swayed languidly like cheerleader's pom-poms. Each flexible piece of foliage drifted away from his fingertips while he ventured further into the deep, cooling shade. An implanted cement bench overlooked the expansive countryside. Sitting down to give himself some alone time, he took in the crisp air. He fixated on the hairy fibers fried from the warm summer heat.

No TV.

No parents.

No friends.

Unstoppable droplets formed from the underpart of his eyelid. His stomach turned into multiple knots, and loneliness clouded his innocence as he yearned to be back home. A soft hand grabbed his shoulder, startling him and halting his moment of reflection. The taste of salt gargled in his throat as he choked on his tears.

"You look like you need some company," said a brown-haired boy similar in age. "Mind if I join you?"

"I'd rather be left alone."

His shoulders deflated closer to his chest. He couldn't muster the bravery to look into the stranger's eyes.

"Oh, nonsense! You need a friend."

Frank sighed a deep breath of annoyance as he forced himself onto the bench, his butt dangling over the edge. His pale, freckled hands ran through his shaggy hair from the slow bow of his head toward his lap.

"What's wrong?" the boy asked. His fair-skinned hand glazed the back of Frank's shoulder which made his muscles tense.

"It's nothing."

"Bullshit," said the young man. His black tennis shoes let a soft crinkle on the grass. "I can sense trouble when I see it! Now spill!"

"You saw what happened earlier in the chapel. Do I need to say more?"

His eyelids fluttered as he relived the trauma from the chapel. The muscles in his chin trembled a mean quiver.

"Yeah, that was quite humiliating."

Frank inhaled a congested sniffle that created a deep growl from his nostrils.

"How am I supposed to make friends here if I'm looked at as somebody different?" Frank explained, sadness resuming down his cheek with the moistening reflection accenting his spotty blemishes.

"Well, you have a friend now, me! The names Buck."

"Frank."

"See. Now you made a friend. I have your back, and you have mine. We can watch out for each other until this crap ends."

A glint of his two front teeth appeared on his lips, smiling from the warmth of Buck's sincerity. His optimism became contagious, allowing Frank's insecurities to lift away.

"Can I ask you a question, Buck?"

His body leaned closer to Buck. His straight, white teeth glistened off the setting sun like iridescent sequins.

"Sure."

"You don't care that I'm gay, do you?"

"Why would you ask me that?" Buck said, his hip brushing his as he shifted nearer to him, his well-being becoming paramount with worry.

"Well, I just haven't had the best of luck with guy friends," said Frank, a heavy sense of defeat weighing down on him like a thick wool blanket suffocating his nerves. "The minute people find out who I am, they throw it all away and start hating me."

Buck's smile enclosed his lips, and his dimples grew closer to his ears.

"Well, you don't have to worry about that with me," Buck said, his arm swinging around Frank's shoulders. "I'm bisexual. I understand what it's like to have everyone view you as a freak."

Frank gazed into Buck's glistening brown eyes as the comforting embrace relaxed his body. His irises reflected a heavenly glow, like a clean and refreshing swimming pool. Frank rested his head on Buck's shoulder. Solace oozed from his cheeks, bringing a generous smile.

"Thank you," Frank whispered into Buck's chest.

Buck's security protected him as if it were an impenetrable suit of armor. His senseless body settled down its tremorous shake, believing for the first time since he arrived he had made a friend he could trust.

It was then he thought he might make it out of Griffwood Manor alive.

Chapter 19

June 2006

EXTINGUISHED SMOKE danced into the shadowy, hushed air as the candles were put out for the evening. Sheldon locked the door to his office before zipping up his light blue color-blocked windbreaker to head home. Joseph and Amber accompanied the three teenagers up the spiral stairs and into the main hallway, each clutching a lit candelabra. They glared the innocence of the adolescent souls into the pictorial assortment of nuns.

"Do any of you know about these nuns?" Sonya asked the adults, curious.

"No," Amber said, expelling a grand yawn. "I'm sorry, but I don't know."

"Ophelia probably got them at some church estate sale!" said Tom.

"They look stupid," Cora hissed, her eyes rolling.

Joseph remained silent, the candlelight shadowing the deep wrinkles on his forehead.

"Come on, we must be getting to bed," he commanded, his arm continuing to usher their attention toward their lounges.

"I just think it's strange that a castle in the middle of nowhere has all these rooms with nobody to fill them. Plus, these pictures creep me out."

"Let's go."

"It's unusual that nobody knows anything about this place."

He stopped, his chest inhaling deep with impatience.

"Griffwood Manor was a location for misbehaved children, run and funded by the church."

His tone changed ghoulishly, the sockets of his eyes hollowing out in the darkened shadows. Sonya stepped away from their terror that crept closer to them. Her eyes blinked quicker, flinching with fear; the candlelight became a strobe in her vision.

"The sisters helped run Griffwood Manor in hopes of helping shape and mold children to better themselves, filled with kids eager to learn and grow. They loved interacting with them, and they would let them be free and partake in activities while learning the importance of faith. Mother Superior believed every child had the ability to change if they dug deep inside to allow healing to begin."

Sonya knew who he was talking about. Her vision bounced to the portrait of her, the nun she had been observing earlier in the day. Its vibrant green eyes pierced into her mind once again. The authoritative, severe expression on her face gave her the heebie-jeebies.

"One night back in the seventies, Mother Superior went missing."

"Missing?" Tom asked, inquisitive.

"You guys, this is all ridiculous," Cora said. "Who would ever believe in this ghost story shit?"

"This all is true," Joseph said. "This all happened."

"If you want to keep telling stupid fairy tales, I'll leave you all to it," Cora continued as she stomped away from the group. "Goodnight, morons!"

The door slammed behind her. The thrust of air shoved close to Amber's candle. Her flame danced precariously, almost toppling close to extinguishment. She cradled her hand around it to keep its life going, the heat pelting her palm.

"Joseph, what happened to Mother Superior?" Sonya asked, her interest unsatisfied and eager for more.

"To this day, nobody knows what happened to Mother Superior. They say, though, at the stroke of midnight at the clock tower outside, her ghost walks the grounds of Griffwood Manor to steal the souls of the misbehaved children. Children who didn't show any desire for change, leaving only the open-minded the chance to heal and grow on her land."

Sonya's heart fluttered. Her breathing became heavier as a chilly hand grabbed her shoulder from behind. Her candelabra toppled to the floor; hot wax coated the decayed carpet away from the growing embers singing its frays.

"Muahahaha!" Amber groaned in a deep, ghoulish tone.

She and Joseph laughed hysterically, celebrating with a high-five.

"It never fails!" Joseph said, chuckling, his enjoyment filled. "Every time we get a new batch of kids here!"

Sonya rolled her eyes, her disappointment concluded her beliefs.

"So, the story isn't true then?" Tom asked, his arms now crossed tight.

"I don't know!" said Joseph, shrugging. "It's a stupid ghost story I heard when I was your age!"

Their upper lips curled before proceeding to their separate ways toward their rooms, unenthused by their joke. The adult's echoing laughter resonated further into the corridor, bouncing off the empty acoustics. The audible chuckle had yet to muffle lower as the door opened, annoying her even more.

"Eat shit," Sonya said, slamming it behind her.

She couldn't believe Amber. Why couldn't she give Sonya an honest answer? The grounds were too eerie, and she needed the truth. Sauntering toward her room, she passed Cora. The bristles of her worn-down toothbrush swept her pastel-yellow teeth. Her antagonizing laughter whistled ghoulishly. Sonya ignored her until she closed the door behind her.

She collapsed onto her bed, planting her face into the soft pillow. The sound of a small, pebble-like drop crept into her ears. Concerned for a loosened screw, she dangled over to her side, swinging her head under. A chunk of metal nestled around a giant wad of dust bunnies. Straining her back, she reached for the item, pinching the piece with her two fingers to grasp a long, morphed paper clip. She placed it on her windowsill, questioning why this would be hidden under her bed in the first place. She resumed staring at the ceiling, waiting for everybody to go to sleep.

THE KITCHEN DOOR SWUNG open as Joseph and Amber cruised inside. The moonlight illuminated off the chrome stations as they went to turn on the light. Fans hummed dully while they inhaled the remnants of the cooked stench from their dinner. They both chuckled in reminiscence about their practical joke.

"Did you see the looks on their faces?" Joseph said, walking over to the refrigerator that was caked in streaks of multiple handprints from dried up flour mixtures.

"They ate that up!" said Amber, light-heartedly.

"Kids will buy anything if you terrify them."

"They do! I remember my cousin would cry when we would scare the shit out of her."

"I thought Sonya was going to lose it!"

"I don't think she was buying it. She's a tough one to crack."

"Oh, please," he huffed as he removed a container from the freezer. "We'll get her in no time."

Amber reflected upon her actions, allowing the small sense of guilt to take over her since her connection with the teenager reminded her of her family. She retrieved a pair of spoons, and her reflection on the metal grossed her out like a child that has regret for how they treated their younger siblings when they finally grew out of their antics. Her stomach started to queeze as she reminisced about her time in the garden. The sweet innocence of Sonya's playfulness left a sour taste in her mouth.

"Maybe we should lighten up a bit," she said with seriousness before jumping onto the table to take a seat.

"Why would you want to do that?"

"Well, these kids are pretty damaged. The last thing we need is to not have them trust us because of a stupid ghost story."

"It's not just a stupid ghost story."

"Yes it is. There's no such thing as ghosts."

"Yes, there is," moaned a deep voice from the other side.

The therapists' hearts stopped, and their muscles tensed as they turned to the back corner. Nothing but a dark abyss concealing the countertops and stoves winking a tiny glint of moonlight that brought a bit of visibility. Breaths huffed into the air like gasping asthmatic smokers. The bottoms of a stark-gray jumpsuit walked closer to them, revealing its ghostly pale skin and stringy hair glistening with grease.

"He's right," the custodian said, bearing his weight upon the broomstick as though it were a cane.

"Gary, you scared us," Amber said with relief, cranking open the lid to the tub of ice cream.

"What're you even doing here?" Joseph asked before taking a generous heap of the rocky road. "Your shift ended hours ago."

"The filth never ends."

"You need to get some rest," said Joseph.

"It'll be here for you tomorrow." Amber agreed.

"So much to do. So much to clean."

"Again, it will be here tomorrow."

"Blood. It takes so much elbow grease to get it out," said the custodian.

"Blood?"

"Blood." he repeated softly.

"Bullshit," Joseph said, his eyes rolling as he took another bite that muffled his hiss.

"Mother Superior is here. She's here to finish what she started."

"This is more than a ghost story?" Amber asked, her eyebrow raised closer to her hairline.

"Please, his memory is messed up. He's been imagining things."

"Let him speak, Joseph!" Amber hissed.

"No, he really is. Just the other day, he kept telling me I was covered in sparkles."

Nervous, Amber walked closer to the janitor. Her hand cradled the crook of his back to guide him to the table. His jaw unhinged to readjust his dentures.

"Gary, is everything okay? Who is this Mother Superior?"

He looked into her eyes; her eyelashes fluttered as she stared deep into his wandering soul.

"Ask her yourself. She's right behind you."

She slowly turned around; her heart sprinted as her breath got shorter. She squinted to decipher any sort of movement within the darkness. The air oozed silence as she searched the perimeters of the room, ignoring Joseph's constant eye rolling in between each bite.

"Gary, there isn't anybody," she said more directly, her tone becoming impatient.

He blinked, trying to refocus his vision as he stared at the same spot he hadn't taken his eyes off of. The basin beside the windows was vacant, only exhibiting a microscopic indication of life with every minor trickle of water escaping the lime coated faucet of the spigot.

"She's here to right the wrong."

"See, what did I tell you, Amber?" Joseph said, jumping off the table. "I think it's time to go home."

Similar to her, he directed Gary's movements. His arm cradled Gary's shoulders to guide him out the door. The two disappeared into the darkness, leaving Amber alone with her thoughts.

Confusion overtook her mind, not knowing how to process what had happened. Her spoon stabbed the top of the bucket, digging a deep hole into the surface of her snack. The roof of her mouth became numb as the treat woke her; her brain felt the freeze from her generous serving, trying to awaken her grogginess.

Perhaps it was just a ghost, she thought. *Or maybe it's nothing.*

CLOUDS COVERED THE moonlit sky as hours passed. Sonya glanced into the courtyard. The willow tree branches stood still in the windless heat. Black crow feathers reflected holographically off the flickering clock tower lights.

It was time.

Trusting her instincts, she tip-toed to the hallway; a loud, monstrous snore groaned underneath Cora's door.

Get a CPAP machine, Sonya thought to herself. *Geez!*

She clutched the cold iron knob at the end of the corridor.

The door wouldn't budge.

Shit!

Wooden slivers pricked her forehead as she leaned upon the frame, the feeling of despair trapping her inside. She didn't have a key to open the lock, and wasn't strong enough to bust open the door.

Wait a minute.

Her eyes perched open with a bright idea, her genius empowering her not to give up. Ignoring Cora's snoring again, she went back to her windowsill to grab the paperclip. Her lips muttered a silent prayer as the clip penetrated the keyhole. The metal tap dancing made her perspire as she tinkered with the lock, hoping she could find a way out.

"Please work," she muttered, sweat forming on her forehead. "Please work."

Click!

Sonya's anxiety increased, and her chest constricted with no desire to inhale, wishing the opening would yield to her makeshift implement. The knob moved along with her grasp.

The door opened.

Yes! Thank God. My fingers were starting to give out from pinching this damn thing.

Her hands were not visible as they waved through the pitch-black hallway. She placed her fingers on the bookcases to help guide her along the room. The accumulation of dust built up from her knuckles as she passed by the portraits and stared at her slow movements like a surveillance camera. She turned to the painting of Mother Superior, and chills welcomed themselves while they multiplied down her spine. A rectangular box poked at the tip of her fingers before she grazed the base of a rusty candelabra. As the door drifted behind her, all she could perceive was the glint of Mother Superior's green eyes winking behind her. The painting's eyes followed Sonya once again with every meandering step toward the door to the spiral staircase.

Creep. I can't stand looking at her.

She grabbed a pinch full of matches and stuffed them into the pocket of her black jeans, keeping one to strike against the cement walls to ignite it. She glared at the open flame, studying it while it shimmied down the stick closer to her fingers before tapping the candle's wick. Her footsteps echoed with the tap of her toes onto the steel surface of the stairs. The noise caused her to cringe with every step, hoping it didn't wake anybody up.

Reaching the main level, she opened the door to the entrance hall. Rust creaked as she crept out into the space, looking both ways to study her surroundings, ensuring that she was, in fact, alone. The candle's light enveloped the chapel. The luminescence glimmered off the red carpet, illustrating a massive shadow of the cross to overpower its environment.

She resumed into the dining area, the smell of dinner still engulfing the premises, taking in an aromatic second course. Hoping to retrace her steps, she walked over to the window, where she began her maze, trying to find any clue to answer her questions about Leslie's dismissal. The slow drifting of the willow tree branches hypnotized her again, swaying from left to right with no suspicion in sight. Her adrenaline was rushing frantically all over her body, making her composure more challenging to control. Her mental jukebox couldn't compose any random song to ease her tension.

Bowling for Soup became a gutter ball.

Yellowcard was declined.

Dashboard Confessional got silent.

Sonya never snuck out and broke the rules of anything, except for her shoplifting experience that got her at Griffwood Manor. All of this was new to her.

Creak!

Sonya's pupils dilated to saucers. She was too frightened to turn around, but knew she had to if she wanted to find some solutions. Her breath staggered, almost extinguishing her candle. After mustering up the courage, she found nothing in front of her, nothing out of place. She returned to the noise again; it stopped her heart.

Creak!

The kitchen's neighboring door had swung open. Dead air enveloped her and was full the closer she walked toward it. The candle shook horribly from her hand trembling with the pain of scolding hot wax burning her fist. She stood at the entryway; the wooden stairs were empty, only to be congregated by clusters of filth. Biting her lip, she combated her cowardice. She made her way down, avoiding every thick cobweb that grew in quantity as she drew closer to the bottom.

At the base of the stairs, Sonya observed the exposed corridor, a lengthy passageway of a dozen sealed doors. Overwhelmed, she didn't know where she should start investigating. She saw a shadow pop through the dim candlelight at the end. The dark hole surrounded by the frame was open. She strolled down the passageway, and each metal door contained a small peephole in the middle and one at the bottom. The door looked as if it came straight from an old insane asylum, hungry for a plate to slide underneath. Red streaks of a dried-up substance faded on the pathway.

What the hell happened here?

She allowed her candle to guide the light to decipher the large room at the end of the long stretch. Dirty glass cabinets blended in chipped, bone-white wooden frames surrounding the room's perimeter. Silhouettes of medicine bottles drowned in wads of cobwebs that were thickened by a blanket of dust. At the center sat an old metal table, bigger than the workstations in the kitchen.

She shifted the flame further, and a wandering rat on the counter shrieked. Sonya's heart stopped like her body slammed on the brakes. Metal clunked on the floor, clapping audibly with a noise that bounced off the walls. The candle's light vanished, rolling on the cement and splashing hot wax around Sonya's shoes.

"Shit!" Sonya said, her voice echoing as she dropped to her knees.

Sonya's heart raced with every pat of her hand onto the cold floor. She was despondent at being lost in the dark abyss of the pitch-black basement. The wax, now lukewarm, squished on the tips of her fingers, was guiding her one step closer to visibility. She exhaled a gratifying sigh of relief, stroking the cold candelabra's loop, grasping the squishy candle with every ounce of her crippled strength.

She pulled another match from her pocket. She muttered a small, reassuring promise to the candle to not drop it again. The spark ignited from the floor, and she lit the wick, her eyes more thankful to see again. She shook the stick to put it out, throwing it to the ground. A faint hiss came from below, sounding like water suffocating a fire. Puzzled, she glanced to observe a murky puddle to her left, stroking the smooth, gritty material as hues of red lit up in the fire. She moved the light closer to her damp, fingertips. The slimy substance warmed up from the heat.

Is that...blood?

Experiencing the queasy revolt from the pit of her stomach, she was ready to withdraw for the night. She looked at the door, her body quivering from the silhouette of a shadow blocking the entryway.

"Holy shit! You scared me!" said Sonya, her hand detecting her rapid heartbeat rumbling like a car's engine.

The shadow remained silent. It didn't speak. It didn't move.

"Okay, cut the shit."

Still nothing.

"I get it, Joseph, Amber, whoever the hell you are. Let's go back up before we get in trouble with Ophelia."

The figure crept inside the room, making her path more difficult to exit. The shadow's orange face became more distinct with the candlelight, revealing the white top of its headdress.

"Nice! You even got a costume of Mother Superior to scare all the kids. Very professional."

Over the shenanigans, Sonya tried to walk around the nun, stomping with heightened annoyance. Its arm raised to halt her from moving past it; its wooden cross clenched tight in its fist. Sonya's patience wore thin as she glared into the nun's darkened eyes.

Nothing but a wink of vibrant green sparkling in and out of the darkness.

"What the fuck?"

The nun whapped Sonya across her cheekbone as the base of the cross shoved her onto the metal table. The candle dropped to the floor again, its surviving flame roaring a tiny bit of light. Her windpipe began to close, shutting out the oxygen as the weapon pressed tight against her throat. The air deflated from her lungs as she struggled to get out of the grasp of the nun's predatory nature. She felt hopeless, her sweaty fingers slipping on the chrome as she stared into the orange, lifeless mask. Her figure shook, requesting ease with the last bits of air fleeing from her. The face doubled in quantity; her vision became fuzzy.

Her trembling fist thrust into the nun's gut, sucker-punching it away from her. She gasped, desperate for relief as the cross's weight lightened from her body. Her balance teetered like she were on a ship during a horrendous storm; vertigo rushed into her brain, seeing the nun lunging at her again. With her unsteadiness as her guide, she spun herself into a roundhouse kick. Her shin sharpened in pain as the assailant tripped to the floor, allowing her the perfect opportunity to flee from her untimely demise.

Neglecting the throbbing ache throughout her body, Sonya sprinted out the door, running through pure darkness. Coughing for air, she crawled up the stairs, using the aid of the railing to crutch her. A forceful tug pulled the back of her shirt, slowing her down. The nun tried to pull her down, ruining the Good Charlotte tour schedule screen printed on the back side. She turned around, introducing the ball of her foot before thrusting it into its chest.

The stomping of her massive footsteps reverberated loud through the dining room, not caring who caught her wandering the corridors after hours. In fact, she wanted everybody to know so that she wasn't alone in the fight for her life. She wanted to be safe, and most importantly, she wanted to be alive.

Moving into the entrance hall, her vision blurred, and her fingertips tingled. Defined edges now became sloppy and blended. Her legs became loose, her muscles weighing like stones.

"Don't kill me," she kept saying. Her words slurred deeper, her head becoming lighter.

Her arms strained in wincing pain as she crawled up the winding staircase. Every step was like a mile of walking with feet encased in cement as exhaustion overtook her abused body. Entering the dark corridor, she stumbled as the room spun in front of her like she was in a funhouse with distorting mirrors. A loud scream shook two people emerging from the corner with her last full breath.

It was Joseph and Ophelia.

"Sonya, what are you doing out of bed at this time of the night?" Joseph asked, annoyed as he placed his hands on the hips of his blue striped pajamas.

Sonya exhaled a tremendous sigh, safe as she tried to maintain her balance, now swaying in every direction as though she had been heavily intoxicated.

"Thank God, you're here!" she said, her speech muffled from her thickened tongue craving water.

"Sweetie, you don't look so good," said Ophelia as she reached toward Sonya, concerned. "Are you okay?"

"It's the nun! The nun!"

Sonya swayed toward the wall to steady her wobbly balance. Her fingers clutched onto the frame of a painting. Her eyes were fixated on the piercing glance of Mother Superior that multiplied like a kaleidoscope. Remembering the mask, she gasped for air with fright as her body collapsed to the floor. She fell into a panicked, blacked-out faint, seeing only the speckle of jewel-like green irises floating in thin air.

Chapter 20

September 1986

A DAY OF STUDYING HAS ended at nightfall. The eclipse of creation has erased the memory of the theory of evolution. The knowledge of the big bang has faded from the first seven days as told by Genesis. Youngsters dragged their feet as they walked to the dining hall to take a break from learning. Review packets waited to test the kids' recollection by etching it into their memory.

The smell of honey intermixing within the pores of baked ham engulfed the area, teasing the appetites of the children. Their sluggish motivation fought hard as their mood became more depressed with the realization that the sisters were not playing around. Molding the little ones to be the best versions of themselves was the sisters' mission, and it exhausted them like they were moving underwater with the weight of chain mail slowing them down.

"I can't believe that they are pushing so much of their beliefs on us!" said one kid, struggling to balance a small stack of books under their arm.

"And what will this stuff do to make us better?" said another.

A cluster of kids took a seat at the nearest table containing the most open spots with two seats occupied; two boys, one with red hair and one with brown.

Frank and Buck.

The children's heads were dozing closer to their sheets, their grogginess becoming more victorious as their minds lost grip of their focus. Their breaths became heavy, their sinuses snorting light.

"What's the matter?" said one girl. "Too much for you?"

"I don't know why they are subjecting us to this shit," another whined in agreement.

The two shook off their exhaustion, their mouths dropped open wide to let out a roaring yawn.

"No," Frank answered, his voice dragging. "I just wasn't prepared for this."

"I'd rather take hours of algebra than go through this again," Buck said. "Are we going to survive this?"

They all groaned in defeat, their agony moaning.

Two sisters walked by the group, their focus staring deep into observation at the children's misery. Their hands were tucked underneath their heavy draped sleeves, making their fingers invisible.

"Good afternoon," Sister Alice greeted with jubilance, her enthusiasm higher than all the kids combined. "Lovely day we're having."

"Meh," half of them replied, trying to stray her concern away.

The light thump of trinkets sprinkled atop their table like hail pelting over a car's windshield. Their blurred vision tried to focus on the items spread over their homework. The sun danced its reflection off of the metallic foil of their wrappers.

"You guys look like you could use some sugar," said Sister June, her dull muttering barely audible.

They unwrapped the chocolate candies with trepidation, scoping out the rest of the room in hopes their peers didn't catch onto their treats.

"Thank you," Frank whispered with innocence as he allowed the sweets to coat his lips.

The surge of sugar roused the kids' focus like a shot of black coffee. Their motivation was back on track with the relativity of their home life and teased the accessibility of their diet. The deprivation of sweets had dried them out like a potted plant without water or sunlight. Their guard slowly lowered for the two women like a castle's drawbridge.

"Thank you so much," said Buck, his finger pinching the wrapper to wad it into a tiny ball. "We should get back to our homework."

"Wait," Sister June interjected. "We have something else we want to show you."

"We do?" Sister Alice asked, concerned.

"Yes, we do. Follow us."

Their gowns drifted across the ground, covering their feet like they were sailing. Their mischievous invitation unnerved the children. Hands gestured a small nudge to encourage them to go along. Glances of concern was exchanged; their eyes were bigger as they gathered their belongings. Papers crinkled and hardcovers slammed, creating a faint echo in the room. Their feet barely made contact with the ground, trying to not add to the disturbances as their shoulders slumped forward.

Their venture into the great hall was heavy with nervousness, passing by the custodian concentrating on their walk that was more awkward than usual, as their balance was uneven. The bristles of his broomstick scratched loud on the cement floors, grinding into the crevasses of the grout. The neighboring sisters observed their lineup, taken aback by their departure since the study period doesn't end for another thirty minutes. The children's remaining peers paused their devoted studies, dropping their pencils onto the floor.

After going up the winding staircase, they enter the grand hallway. The bright lights accentuated the intense colors of hardcover spines that were set neat on the well-maintained bookcases. The children could hear each others' hearts beating with rapid strums like a marching band drum. The portraits and murals were free of cobwebs, pristine like an art show; their textured frames were glossy with polish. A lone door was guarded by two chairs and occupied by a pair of kids snoozing heavily, their heads perched against the cushioned frame for stability.

They entered inside the petite room. The selection of preschool toys was laid out haphazardly on the faded carpet and miniature crafted table. The group became disappointed as they watched the equipment bring back their childhood memories. The custom-made dollhouse could use a fresh remodel with peeling wallpaper and warping timber floors as thin as cardboard. The chipped teacups on the ledge were in desperate need of retirement with grime caked around the rim from tiny lips pretending to drink their concoctions.

"What the hell is this?" asked one of the kids.

Sister Alice and Sister June stared daggers into the child, disappointed by the use of their language.

"I'm sorry. I mean that this room isn't really age-appropriate for us."

"Well, we're not at our destination just yet," Sister Alice said, her hands grasping the toy box. Her fingers seized the hinges.

"Are you sure you want to do this?" Sister Jude whispered, still apprehensive.

"Why not? I think we need to be as flexible as they are."

A small groan left her mouth as her body thrusted into the chest. The box advanced across the carpet and a tiny hole appeared. The opening was black with minimal visibility, creating interest in the children as their heads perched closer into the abyss. Their eyebrows ascended bit by bit to their hairlines, captivated as they began to explore.

"What is this?" Frank asked, looking back into the space to where the sisters joined them inside.

The click of a light switch ignited the space. Rainbow colored hues of plush stuffed animals greeted them; the plastic ball pit winked its reflection. The multiple pastel colors splashed along the walls that framed three tunneled openings.

"Is this heaven?" asked the girl with admiration.

"No, my child." said Sister June, chuckling. "But close enough!"

"What is this place?" asked Buck, his eyes focused on the assortment of army action figures he envied from his childhood.

"It's a little project we worked on," said Sister Alice. "We agree that the other room desperately needs some updates. The Mother Superior before wanted to create an atmosphere that is enjoyable and inviting while still ensuring the children want to learn."

"Cool!"

"You all can hang out here for a bit," said Sister June. "Don't mention this to Sister Magdalena. She put a kibosh on this when she took over."

"Why doesn't she want this?"

"She has more of a traditional approach to healing. She believes that hard work and discipline will keep you focused, while most of us believe that a short break here and there would be better."

"Why don't you speak up?"

"Whatever Mother Superior says, goes. That's the way it is."

All five of the kids shook their heads, acknowledging the fact.

Their lungs expelled a small gust of breath with defeat as their eyebrows furrowed, knowing that matters won't alter while they are there. The realization of following their required daily torment made their limbs heavier like they were attached to sandbags.

"There, there. Now, there's no need for that. Let's have a little fun for now!"

"Yes, come on! Enjoy yourselves!"

Without hesitation, the children dove right into the toys. One girl collapsed onto the pile of stuffed animals, burying herself into the cotton-candy shades of teddy bears. The two boys jumped into the ball pit, causing a colorful splash of primary colors pelting onto the floor before rolling closer to the bookshelves of assorted Berenstain Bears and Boxcar Children. The Hardy Boys caught a glimpse of the running of red, unsuccessful in breaking the focus of their investigations.

Frank chased Buck through the closest tunnel. The skin of their elbows burned from the rubbing of the plastic. Joints cramped in their fingers from grasping the connecting crevasse of each connecting piece to pull them forward. Their peer's laughter muffled quieter the further the pair got away from them.

They launched themselves out into the open room. The sponged splashes of five different shades of green upon the walls was grounded by angular brushstrokes of textured brown. It surrounded their forest fantasy by a cardboard fort of gray, guarded by two statues with their chrome armor reflecting the dim fluorescent light.

A tiny prick nudged in Buck's back. Frank chuckled, dodging another plastic arrow before the flimsy bow dropped to the floor.

"Gotcha!" he giggled as he walked over to the table of assorted princess dolls.

"This is amazing!"

"I know. Why would they not use this?"

"I mean, I know we are a little old for these toys. But I'll take this over all the constant reading!"

"Me too!"

Frank ran over to the stuffed animal, a size similar to the teddy bear they met when they entered the initial room. His fingertips caught the bumpy texture of the dragon's scales, its underbelly felt like pleats on fabric.

"I shall call you Fluffy!"

"Why the hell would you call it Fluffy?"

"I don't know. It seems fitting."

Buck's heart fluttered with excitement as he took in the contagious happiness. Frank's laughter stretched Buck's grin further. He didn't want to stop watching the glee flooding from him like a princess being freed from a castle, frolicking in the flowery meadow for the first time. His stomach turned; something that he only explored further with the girls in his class. It was then that he had wanted something more than just a buddy during their time at the manor. Perhaps this would be something to pursue further and try something new for the first time.

Chapter 21

June 2006

SONYA'S BODY FLOATED; her mind drifted as she fell down a bottomless pit. Her arms and legs flailed hopelessly, reaching toward the light as she sank further and further into a dark abyss of loneliness. Control descended terribly into utter abandonment. The continuous reverberation of her congregation she once loved chanted crucifixion that has now defied her loyalty. Her face cringed at the sheer immorality of Ryan's manipulation.

Burn in hell!

You don't belong here!

Rotten filth!

People like you shouldn't be here!

Sonya froze, locked tense from the ridicule taking over the remaining ounce of confidence she had within her. Weeping, she fell further into the darkest place in her mind, her inner saboteur celebrating victoriously while the voices got louder, magnifying her defeat.

What happened to loving your neighbor as you would love yourself?

Why won't you let him be the one to judge?

I don't judge you for the choices you make! So, why judge me?

Tears raced down Sonya's face, shame gliding down her rosy cheeks before drifting off her jawbone. The ridicule replayed from the crowd she once loved and respected, only to turn their backs on her. Their hallucination of the light above ignored the emptiness as she vanished with each conjoining rejection. She reached out for salvation with her arms, fingers stretching for acceptance, her grasp longing for love. The members walked out of sight, abandoning her to a pit of darkened judgment wrapping around her body like ensnaring quicksand.

The last peer disappeared, being replaced by one more person. A fancy suit beamed in the light. Their slicked-back hair glossed in the brightness. It was Pastor Ryan, smugly surveying as she drifted further away into sadness. His smile grew maniacal, his overly porcelain-white teeth shining bright. The corners of his lips crept closer to the lobes of his ears. His arm raised over her, summoning forces from the heavens to reinforce his reasoning.

"Don't you realize that those who do wrong will not inherit the Kingdom? Don't fool yourselves. Those who indulge in sexual sin, or who worship idols, or commit adultery, or are male prostitutes, or practice homosexuality, or are thieves, or greedy people, or drunkards, or are abusive, or cheat people—none of these will inherit the Kingdom. Some of you were once like that. But you were cleansed. You were made holy. You were made right with him by calling on the name of the Lord and by the Spirit."

Sonya's heart grew heavier, and her chest contracted as if they were tied to cinder blocks.

"The book is about loving and accepting everyone. What about only allowing him to make the final judgment?!" she yelled with desperation, pleading for reassurance to her counterclaim. "You're twisting what *you* want the people to hear. The rest are your personal feelings."

Ryan placed his arms back to his side, unimpressed by her case. A gruesome laugh huffed from his lips. A malevolent tone hardened by his tightened diaphragm.

"Now you know that if you cross me, I'll make you disappear, no matter what!"

The blackness swallowed Sonya's gasp. Her head became the only thing visible in the minuscule shed of fading light.

"We'll never disappear! You can't erase love!"

Ryan's laugh deepened, echoing boisterously in the void, penetrating her brain like a sickle.

"Yes, we can!" he responded, his eyebrow perched cocky. "And may God have mercy on your soul!"

The last glimmer disappeared as he walked away. The heavy concealment of thrusting darkness disoriented her. She experienced the last breath leave from her chest, desperate from the escalating confusion abandoning her in icy solitude.

TAKING A DEEP BREATH, her body begged for a reprieve from her turmoil. Clammy drops were spotted from a tattered-up washcloth upon her forehead. Bright fluorescent lights blurred into the white-paneled ceiling. She felt disoriented, confused about taking in the clean aesthetic of the room that was uncharacteristic of the rest of Griffwood Manor. The modern kitchen-tiled wall threw Sonya off, bringing back memories of her elementary school nurse's office. Her abs tightened as she hoisted herself up, experiencing the dizziness roiling her stomach. Being greeted by three people, their silhouettes blurry, she tried to refocus her consciousness.

"Oh, darling!" said Ophelia, the silk of her nightgown reflecting emerald green. "Are you all right?"

"Where am I?" asked Sonya, whimpering as the aches surfaced across her lower back. Her neck screamed in anguish.

"The infirmary, of course."

"This doesn't look like it's part of the manor."

"This was where a chunk of the budget had gone when we took over the establishment, dear. A lot of work needed to be done in this room. It was repulsive."

"Yeah, after you remodeled your bedroom and office into a lavish dump!" Craig said, his crankiness jolting his mood.

"Well, it isn't relevant now, is it?" she hissed back at Craig, who ignored her reasoning by unraveling gauze bandages.

"We should discuss what you were doing out of bed after hours," said Joseph.

He leaned over the foot of the exam table. His stern demeanor stood out through his misbuttoned pajamas. His glare peeked through his shaggy, gel-free hair.

"I'm sorry, sir. I-I couldn't sleep," she stuttered, not wanting to reveal her intentions.

"More importantly, how did you get hurt, my dear?" said Ophelia. The ostrich feathers of her wizard sleeves ushered him behind her. "What happened?"

"I heard a noise coming from the basement, so I went to check it out."

"You went to the basement?" Ophelia asked, gasping in shock.

"I did. What are hospital rooms doing down there?"

Ophelia turned to Joseph, hesitant as their eyes widened with concern, trying to calculate their rationale properly.

"I'm not sure, darling."

"You bought a place and didn't know what was inside it?" Craig asked, chuckling pathetically as gauze patted Sonya's cheek.

"This project is a work in process," Ophelia said, her impatience fueling her angst toward her employee. "Please, go on, my child."

"I was followed."

"Followed?" Joseph asked. "Followed by who?"

"I don't know," she said, wincing from the sudden pain screaming from the acidic burn of rubbing alcohol cleansing her shoulder. "It was someone in a nun's outfit."

"A nun?" Ophelia asked.

"Yes. They wore a black robe, with a white headdress."

"I knew those sisters were trouble," Craig hissed. "They aren't what they used to be."

"Did you see their face at all?"

"No. They wore a shiny, plastic orange mask. It looked like a ghost with its eyes and blackened mouth."

Her body retreated close to her, sheltering her discomfort like a turtle. Her muscles quivered like a vibrating cell phone as her trauma replayed its encore.

"A mask?" Ophelia asked, concerned.

"This is ridiculous," Craig said with impatience. "I can't believe you guys woke me up to take care of some crazy little shit that is imagining some fantasy of one sister trying to spook her in a dollar store mask!"

"I saw what I saw!" Sonya said, her clenched fist banging fiercely on the exam table.

"Do you believe this crap?" Craig asked, slamming the bandages onto the counter. "I don't think she should be here anymore. She has broken the rules in the same way Isis and Leslie did, and now she's concocting this preposterous tale to cover up her misstep!"

Sonya's lips tightened. Her nostrils flared like floodgates to let out perfuse breaths. Her teeth felt as though they were going to crack inside her mouth from her stiffened gritting. Desperate for someone to believe her, she turned to Ophelia, but her arms were crossed. Her patchy, unpencilled eyebrow was barely visible as it raised.

"You're right, Craig. Rules *have* been broken, and accountability *must* happen."

"Did you want me to take her back tonight?" he asked, a smug grin growing.

"That won't be necessary. Ms. Frost isn't going anywhere."

In disbelief, Sonya's jaw dropped to the floor. A fly was close to creeping inside; the corner of her mouth tingled a vibration from its wings.

"What?" Sonya asked, gasping.

"I do believe I've informed you of the rules when I hired you, Craig," Ophelia continued, her tone forceful. "It has come to my attention that you have been having affairs with some of our residents."

"From whom?" his voice pitched higher.

"Oh, don't act all innocent *now*, darling! These corridors are very empty. I could hear you moaning from the other side of the manor!"

"Don't you know it is illegal to have sex with minors?" Joseph asked. "I've seen you sneak off with these teens so many times. It sickens me you have no self-control!"

"T-They came onto me!" he said, his voice cracking from the sheer defense. "Plus, they would've been legal in a few months!"

"Way to be professional," Sonya hissed toward him, her bumptiousness beaming with security.

"You shut up, you little brat!"

She stayed composed, piercing through his finger pointing into her humble soul.

"ENOUGH!" Ophelia said, hollering at the top of her lungs.

Ophelia's skin shaded close to a dusty rose. Feathers shed onto the floor like a sick pet.

"When I hired you, I know you were struggling with your recent breakup with your girlfriend and losing your job, being fired for your homosexuality—"

"I'm not gay!"

"Is that why your girlfriend left you, too?" Joseph teased, his voice snotty.

"No, we just had a different approach to love."

"And what would that be? Any hole is a goal?"

"That will be enough, Joseph! Head back to your room this instant!"

Joseph's nose pointed to the ceiling fan, and his cocky snub dismissed his unemployed colleague.

"But Ophelia," Craig said, pleading with desperation as his eyes glossed with tears, "I don't have anywhere to go. This is my home! What about our past together?"

"I'm sorry, son. You have evaded these mishaps for too long. It's time to take accountability for your actions and move on. I shall expect you to be gone by morning."

"But Ophelia!"

"That is final," she concluded. The train of her nightgown filled the room as she walked away from him. "Best of luck to you. I do wish that this would've ended differently."

The hem of feathers lagged behind her, and Craig's head fell into his hands. His merciful weeps punched Sonya's conscience as he cleaned up his workstation before storming out. His clogs scuffed against the tiled floor from his defeating drag. She trailed after him into the hallway; the soreness of her muscles was no longer a pain compared to Craig's broken heart.

"Craig, wait!"

He stopped and turned around slowly, his loud snort making an effort to stop the flow of mucus from his nostrils. The muscles of his chin tightened as he quivered in defeat.

"I truly am sorry."

Craig thrust his fist to his side as though he was flicking the snot off his arm. His chest rose and fell rapidly as he attempted to catch his breath.

"Be careful," he said, his tone serious with caution. "And watch out for Ophelia."

The door swung open, and he disappeared into the dark passage. The obscurity incapacitated her while she limped back into her room, gradually being received again by the growing noise of Cora's snores. Once within, she slumped into the chair next to the windowsill and tucked the paperclip deep into the cushion. Exhausted, her heavy muscles have made themselves at home, forcing her to ponder Craig's advice without strain.

Watch out for Ophelia.

Sonya knew peculiar things were happening within Griffwood Manor. She may not have gotten the answers she was searching for, but at this moment, she had a launching point to figure out what was going on with the place. She not only had to be concerned about a crazed nun strolling the grounds, but she must now be concerned about Ophelia. Or perhaps they were one in the same?

Sonya leaned her noggin back to the apex of the chair, perched herself to stare off at the lone clock tower, hoping time would not freeze at this moment.

A STUFFED BROWN LEATHER suitcase clattered down the steps as Craig hauled his excessive luggage inventory. Drops of tears drizzled on the cement as he descended. His hair fluttered from the wind greeting him, whispering sweet nothings. They triggered his ex-girlfriend and former employers to remind him of his heart-crushing rejection.

You're *bi? Oh my god! That's gross!*

Our company has strict policies about employing people of your lifestyle. There is no room for our clients to be forced to allow your tendencies to coincide with their needs. It is with full regret to inform you that your contract will be terminated as of today.

The gravel grounded from his heavy steps as he trudged toward his car parked next to the bus. The rejection mixed with the wind sending chills down his spine; his keys jingled as he struggled to maintain his composure.

You come to me for a job? Ophelia's voice fluttered in his mind.

Yes, he said, full of shame. *I have nowhere else to go.*

I haven't seen you since you were a teenager. What makes me believe that you'll be responsible and take your position here seriously?

I'm desperate. I have no job. No home. Nobody to care for me.

Very well. I remember you as one that didn't follow the rules back when I first met you. I'll only allow you to work for me if you abide by the program's standards. Do you understand?

Yes, ma'am.

I mean it. You are grown up now, and I need you to put these urges behind you.

The door slammed on the driver's side of the car. Another round of uncontrollable sobs pooled in shame, letting out all his anger and frustrations.

"You can do this, Craig," he whispered to himself. The shakiness in his voice kept steering his confidence. "You can do this. You have to."

He grabbed the keys and directed them toward the ignition. His trembling hands impeded his focus as he fumbled it into the hole. With each attempt, he became more frustrated.

What the hell?

He took his free hand to navigate in the barely-illuminated darkness. His fingertips caressed the dashboard's worn leather interior along the steering wheel's underside. A cold metal chunk lodged inside the ignition like cement on a pothole.

"Huh?"

Pricking his finger, he pulled out the piece to decipher what it was, leaning closer to the moonlit-glossed windshield. His fingertips felt divides like they were vines sporadically engraved around the cross-like shape. Cutting into his nail was a small loop at the top, loosened from the separation of the necklace. Confused, he threw the charm behind him, his eagerness to leave growing.

From the backseat of his car swung a bunch of glistening beads looping over his head and draped over his chest; his body locked with tension. The beads were black as night, reflecting lusciously with inscribed crosses. It was then he comprehended that the metal piece was part of the necklace.

The strand slid up his shirt and tightened around his neck. The cartilage of his Adam's apple crunched. He gasped for oxygen; the constriction of the jewelry crushed his trachea like a vicious anaconda. Blood drew from his skin as it dug deeper into its purple-hued surface. Blood engulfed the whites of his eyes. His vision blurred with every ounce of air squeezing out like an emptying tube of toothpaste. His arm flailed, knocking the rear-view mirror, adjusting the reflection toward the backseat. The glint of a shiny orange mask reflected the wink of green through its blackened eyes.

"PRAY!" the distorted voice grunted.

The beads crushed the last undamaged fiber of his windpipe. The temples of his head boiled as it pleaded for blood flow from its blocked carotid artery. His mouth was wide open in disbelief, unable to grasp as his strength faded to nothing. He collapsed to the side with his arms heavy. His hands dangled over the edge of his seat as the nurse's existence drifted out of his corpse, signing the unemployment papers for his life.

Chapter 22

June 2006

OVERCAST CLOUDS CONGREGATED over the willow trees, branches swaying more energetically to the winds in a manner similar to a long head of hair swishing at a hard-rock show. Birds ducked for cover while droplets of rain pummeled mercilessly into their intricately crafted nests. The insides of Sheldon's suit coat flopped open, his brown lapels slapping his face. He attempted to clean up the array of gardening tools toppling over like a precarious Jenga stack. Eerie whistles gusted a ghostly command into his ear; he placed a rake into the shed. The sting of icy rain tightened his flinching cheeks.

Sonya rose from her chair. The soreness in her neck strained horribly from leaning against the windowsill and passing out minutes after she sat. She reached to wipe the small amount of saliva from her chin with her arm. Breaths of relaxation tried to ease the thoughts of the horrific nun the night before. She cracked her back as she removed her shirt. The gash below her hairline ached from the cotton ribbed neckline dragging over it. She delved into her duffel bag to take out an identical but fresh shirt and put it on cautiously. After changing into a fresh pair of dark pants and tying her sneakers, she walked out the door and down to the common area, avoiding Cora as best as she could.

Going into the hallway unnoticed, she observed the nuns' portraits. More specifically, Mother Superior, whose green eyes glared animosity into her soul.

"I hate you!"

She looked at the rows of bookshelves, discovering the bulky-spined publications blanketed in a substantial coat of taupe-colored dust. The ricochet of dirt from her forceful breath caused her chest to let out sharp coughs. Her stomach became queasy from her airways expelling every unwelcome particle. Her teary eyes refocused on the assortment of versions of the Bible, combating the sting in the pit of her stomach that relieved her pain from her church's rejection. Next to the religious context was a plethora of textbooks. From all grades of mathematics to civics, the shelves were filled with knowledge to create envy in any boarding school.

Law and Order: Rules and Regulations.

Elementary Algebra.

From Crime to Christ.

Tantrums and Entitlement: Using Discipline to Eliminate Toxic Behavior.

Pray the Gay Away.

Disgust came over her as she stopped her finger over the last publication. How could someone even write about taking advantage of belief to someone's core? And what kind of person would want to read it? Every new question horrified her more and more.

Cora's footsteps thumped louder, drawing closer to her. Sonya fled like a startled doe that listened to a broken tree branch under a hiker's heavy foot. She pushed the books back into their designated slots before running downstairs.

"My child," a voice said, halting her before she reached the door.

A cloaked woman stood dead center in the hallway. The shadow of her silhouette stroked the portrait of the nun as though the image jumped out into reality. Sonya's anxiety grew. The stress of another attack looming on her made her guarded. Her grasp continued to slip along the handle of the door as the window's light revealed her face.

Sister Alice.

"Yes, Sister?" Sonya said, catching her breath with relief.

"I heard about what happened last night."

"You did?"

"Yes, all of us," she said, placing her hand upon Sonya's injured shoulder.

"News must travel fast around here, doesn't it?"

"It does. I've been praying for you."

"Thank you, but I don't think that's necessary."

"Oh, but it is, dear."

"Why?"

"Terrible things are happening here. I fear for your safety. I fear for all of your safety."

Sonya gulped a larger wad of saliva. Her nerves tensed from the nun's warning.

"I've been praying for you. The corridors of this establishment are filled with darkness."

"Darkness?" Sonya asked. "You mean the nun?"

A slamming door echoed throughout the rest of the space behind them. The two jolted with fear, locking with tension as they cradled closer to one another. Sister Alice's outstretched sleeves provided Sonya with a thin layer of comfort. She pinched the guardian's fabric, petting the top of her skin.

A slew of dark shadows floated in the darkened passage, multiplying with each second. Their necks craned to display the faint glimmer of the crowns of their headdresses. Sonya took another breath of relief once again, noticing the remainder of the convent. She could barely make sense of the sternness as they glared at their colleague. Their disappointment showed with the slight shake of their heads as they crossed into the neighboring door.

"I-I should go," Sister Alice said with trembling lips, her eyes looking sharply into every corner of the space. "I will continue to pray for your safety. In the meantime, just be careful."

"Okay."

The nun gave one last intense stare at her before she caught up to the rest of the group. Her sorrow pierced into Sonya's mind as she focused on the image of Mother Superior. The portrait's withering gaze kept her back in line as she bowed her head to join everyone else. The hem of her garb swished as her silhouette became more concealed into darkness.

HER HAND GRIPPED THE railing of the spiral staircase. Befuddled, she didn't know how to process Sister Alice's proclamation. As she relived the trauma from the previous night, her muscles screamed with desperation. Her knees buckled as they took on the weight of her balance, and her vision was cloudy from the beginnings of blacking out.

After making it to the main level, Sheldon, who removed his suit coat, greeted Sonya. His arm struggled as it wriggled out of its soaked sleeve like a vacuum-packed plastic sack, glacially peeling. The drenched locks of his receded-chestnut hair flicked the drops of water onto the entrance hall floor puddling around his penny loafers.

"Dreadful storm out there, huh?" Sonya said, blending herself away from suspicion.

"Cats and dogs got nothing on this!" Sheldon said with sarcasm, his hands slapping his pants that clung to his slender legs.

She was reluctant to ask more and research the past of her living space. Her hand moved uncomfortably onto her right bicep, gliding up and down her untoned muscles.

"Can I ask you a question?"

"Fire away!" he said, his breath catching as he walked to his office door.

"How long have you worked here?"

"I've been here for nearly five years," he answered with pride, like he was being interviewed for a promotion.

"What do you know of this place?"

"I'm sorry. What do you mean?"

"The nuns. Did you know what happened to the owners before Ophelia took over?"

"All I know is that they lost their financial support before she took over."

"Funding for what?"

"This place was used as a safe haven for dozens of troubled teenagers needing to reflect on their infractions. It had so many children at a certain point, they almost had nowhere to put them."

"Even the basement?"

"The basement?" he asked, suddenly bewildered, his eyebrow perched.

"Yes."

"Ms. Frost, nobody has been in the basement. Only Ophelia has access to that part of the manor."

"Really?"

"Yes. I have never even been given permission to clean it out for storage. There's no room for all these old files. This tiny office can only accommodate so much!"

Sheldon glanced over his watch to check the time. Feeling the tardiness, he removed the keys with haste from his pocket to unlock the door.

"I'm sorry to cut this short, but I must get to work. Ophelia will strangle me if I'm not on time!"

"Okay," she said, turning toward the dining hall, unsatisfied. "Thank you for your time."

"Not a problem. Oh, and breakfast will be pretty meager today. I left cereal and milk out for you all."

"Where will the others be?"

"Everyone has to finish their work. They advised me to let you know that they'll meet up with you guys later."

"Okay. Thanks. I'll see you around."

Sonya paced past the chapel. The vibrant, red carpet caught her eyes as the rumble of thunder shook the chandelier above, making it tremble from the ungodly stomps. The tumultuous roaring of the breeze made her skin quiver with hesitation. Upon entering the dining hall, she acknowledged Tom's presence as he was eating a bowl of cereal by himself. He gawked at the tree branches as they waved back and forth like an inflatable tube man from the heavy breeze.

"Sonya," Tom said, a mouthful of multicolored cereal followed by milk rushing down his chin. "Good morning!"

"Morning."

"About time somebody joined."

Sonya sat next to him, sliding a white porcelain bowl and silver spoon closer to her, unimpressed by the sugarless flaky bran cereal.

"What kind of place grants their inmates as many hours of free time as we do?" Tom asked sardonically, his hands stretched out casually.

"I know, right? So much for a punishment," said Sonya as she fiddled with the bag inside the cereal box.

"Maybe we should get in deep shit more often. I could use a vacation from my shitty parents!"

"Yeah," Sonya said solemnly.

"Are your parents as bad as mine?"

"They're okay," she said, hesitant, without conviction.

"Really?"

"They love me as their kid. They just don't appreciate certain parts of me."

"You being gay?"

"Excuse me?" she asked, taken back from his accusation.

"I may not be as over the top as Leslie, but I do have a gaydar. And it works quite well for me," he said, munching on another bite.

She didn't know where else to deter his accusations from. She had to admit the truth.

"They don't acknowledge that part of me," she said, full of shame.

"Well, they either love you or don't. There should be no gray area for loving your child."

"True. But they're the only parents I have. So I either embrace them as they are, or I don't have any at all."

"Then why can't they do the same for you?"

The validity behind Tom's logic struck her nerves. She stared at the kernels of rainbow-colored cereal trickle into her bowl, tuning out Tom's loud munching with the melodious sounds tumbling onto the vacant ceramic. Grabbing the milk carton, she slowly tilted it over her food; the small stream of dairy distracted her.

Her attention was interrupted from the outside view, beyond the foliage. Back and forth, the twigs swayed vigorously to counter the ferocity of the gale-force winds like wet hair to a robust hairdryer. As the branches took a subtle break, the shadow of a figure appeared at the base of the clock tower.

"Sonya," Tom's voice rose. "Sonya!"

Her arm stung as it became pinched from his attention.

"Are you okay?" Tom asked, dropping his spoon into his bowl.

"Yes. Why?"

"You're still pouring the milk," he said, laughing as he pointed to the giant puddle of white liquid beginning to overtake the table, flowing toward the edge before splashing onto the floor.

"Oh shit!"

She jumped up from her chair, frantically reaching for the paper towels. Her fist looked like a wrinkled boxing glove, wadding the entire fresh roll before soaking the mess with angry dabs.

"Next time, you should just milk the cow over the dish," he said, laughing hysterically. "At least each udder has a small amount, so you won't overdo it!"

"I'm sorry. I jus—"

Her attention paused again, glimpsing back outside and noticing the silhouette of the black-robed nun once more. Its tattered train drifted with the gust of heavy wind. She tossed the dripping towel on the table, flinging the milk onto the front of Tom's shirt while she raced toward the kitchen.

"What the fuck, dude?" he said, hissing while he wiped the ricochet of liquid off his face.

"I'm sorry!"

Her sneakers reverberated audibly on the floor as she sprinted toward the exit. Her muscles awakened from the stern direction of her movement.

"I gotta go!"

"Well, I can see that!"

She disappeared through the swinging door that hypnotically swung like a pendulum.

"This is why I don't date girls," Tom said, shaking his head.

SONYA OPENED THE BACK exit on the other side of the room. She was welcomed by strong winds as her shoes splashed onto plentiful puddles of rainwater, creating a waterlogged mess. Blistering cold rain stung her cheeks like sewing needles. Hair fluttered in every direction with the quickly changing direction of the whistling wind. The endless blinding of the torrential downpour whipping into her eyes disoriented her. She didn't slow down, ignoring the numbness in her hands that guided her through the entangling willow tree branches. Her panting breath became more visible in the chilly, fall-like air, numbing her exposed skin. Experiencing despair, she avoided the relentless branches and made it to the clearing on the other side.

No nun in sight.

Hovering her hand over her eyes, she observed every inch of the wooded parameter to find her assailant. Nothing was out of the ordinary. Frustration flooded over her hypothermic demeanor which overwhelmed her thoughts of clarity and rationality. She stomped her feet onto the ground like a child playing in puddles.

"Fuck!"

As she surveyed the manor, the first tree in front of her stood out. A dark, hollow opening was visible like a tiny cave. Her curiosity brought her closer to peep further. Reaching the base, her hands grazed the chipped, earthy trunk, big enough for her to fit inside. She took refuge inside for a desperate need of a break, a slight reprieve from the merciless stormy wind formed. Her arms encircled her chest, magnifying the conflicting pain that increased in her hurting core. The space was roomy; she sprawled around for relaxation; her feet tucked under the large roots for stability. She sat at the foundation to keep herself warm, cradling herself. Her declining warmth overwhelmed her. Her jaw chattered like a jackhammer drilling the back of her head, and her shivering body distracted her from the gray-scale clouds outside. Atop the entrance, she detected scratches, the penmanship appearing different from wildlife markings. She tried to make sense of the faded, neanderthal-looking writing.

Buck + Frank.

Chapter 23

September 1986

A LOUD BELL CLANG FROM the clock tower struck three o'clock, excusing the children to go outside into the crisp, overcast weather for their long-awaited recess. Brown and orange autumn leaves danced merrily to the song of the gusty wind. They weaved through the stripping willow trees, navigating in all directions around their thick, sturdy trunks. In the courtyard, light jackets of all colors raced with jubilance, scattering like a dumped bag of skittles. A lot of energy was being drained after an exhausting day of learning. Hours were spent focusing hard on studying and challenging their minds to improve themselves.

A trio of nuns followed behind the children, scrutinizing them from the top of the cement stairs of Griffwood Manor. Their stance blended with the gargoyles as they prey with their yardsticks grasped tight. Two teenage boys chased each other; their identical mustard-yellow hooded sweatshirts, swerving in and out of the dangling, loose-leaved vine branches and disappearing from the nun's sight.

"Oh, man!" Buck said, sighing as he caught his breath. "This is the dumbest program I've ever been a part of!"

"I know! What were our parents thinking with signing us up for this shit?"

"What good does 'banishing your evil demons' do for somebody?" Buck asked, unimpressed by the curriculum.

"Praying doesn't change the quality of one's character," Frank said, the hem of his hood gathered closer into puckers as the strings further from his face.

"And why do they keep using specific issues as an excuse to torment people? These are the same people who drink too much and wear mixed textiles."

"Right?" Frank nodded in agreement as the two approached the cement bench by the clock tower. "I'm so sick of these hypocrites choosing and using vague passages written by a white male and using them as a weapon against others! I bet they don't see them selling their daughter into slavery like it also reads."

"I know."

"Don't people know that inspiration is using one point of departure and interpreting through their own mind?"

"Why don't they feel inspired to be better people instead of judgmental cows?"

The softened grass crunched softly under Buck's stomping feet.

"It's not cute to judge when you don't have permission!"

"Now *that's* something I will agree to!"

The two boys laughed as they stopped to admire the view of the field. The wind blew the tall grass, and the air containing the scent of decayed dirt calmed their angst. Buck's knuckles were chapped as they wrapped around Frank's, squeezing his fingers tight in reminiscence.

"Promise me we'll still have each other no matter what happens here?" Frank asked, his request full of sorrow.

Buck turned his head to face him, his watery irises reflecting the dull sunlight, his grin as long as the branches, full of pure happiness.

"Of course," Buck reassured, squeezing Frank's fingers tight, the pulsating sensation beating through his fingertips.

"No matter what these nuns do to try to brainwash us, our feelings will always be there."

Frank continued to take Buck's hand toward his lips. Frank's warm breath heated the blonde hairs on his wrist as his cracked mouth planted a kiss on the top of Buck's clenched fist.

"We only have a few months left," Buck said. "We can do this!"

"And once we're old enough, we can move out of our rotten parents' houses and live together."

"Like we're meant to."

Buck's heart beat faster, warmth radiating from inside his chest. His stomach knotted with his devotion, abounding eagerly for their future side by side. The two crept in closer, peering straight into each other's eyes. Their hearts pulsated rapidly, like a woodpecker's beak to the chipped bark of a tree. The tips of their cold noses tapped like toasting champagne glasses, and their lips locked together with no desire to separate.

"Wait," said Frank, talking into Buck's mouth.

"What is it?" Buck asked, his eyes still closed in bliss.

"The nuns."

He checked the tree branches with concern. Their faint observation focused on the other children playing tag football on the lawn, eager to point out an infraction and inflict punishment.

"What about them?"

"I don't want us to get caught. Why don't we go in there?"

He pointed to the nearest willow tree right behind them. The hollowed opening was dark. The two edges of the base fashioned a triangular shape like the aperture of a tent.

"The tree?" Buck asked.

"Yeah," Frank said, holding Buck's hand, jerking him enthusiastically toward the entry. "This can be our little hiding spot. Those nuns won't be able to find us here."

"Okay."

The duo chuckled, slinking their way inside the hollowed out base of the enlarged tree. The rooted foundation of the interior cascaded upwards, greeting the swirls of years of the earthy woodgrain, streaks drifting and twirling free like delicate brush strokes on a traditional romantic painting. Frank leaned back to pick up something on the ground, smiling eagerly to reveal a sharp, chalky white rock. The adonis belt of his slender abdomen came to light when he stretched over the top of the opening. He jabbed the stone into the wall of the miraculous work of nature as though he were drawing a toddler's picture. His pride emanated through his staggering breath, ignoring the exertion of his loving, whittling craft as lines became letters before turning into words.

Buck + Frank.

Buck's heart fluttered with joy, and his grin grew like a plant basking in a scorching summer sun. He advanced his steps closer to Frank as he tossed the rock back outside the tree, depositing in the grass.

"None of those nuns are small enough to fit inside here to find us," Frank said, his hands wrapped tight around Buck's waist. "This is our spot. Nobody will take that away from us."

Buck couldn't contain his self-control any longer, like a volcano about to erupt. He grabbed the back of Frank's head by his reddish-brown hair and forced him in for a long, wet, romantic kiss. Their cold hands glided over all parts of their bodies, warming up as their lips kissed little by little. Toasty, moist breaths heated their exposed necks, escalating their desires further. Their love grew stronger with each gentle touch of their warm, trembling bodies; the affectionate heartbeat of their young, beloved hearts beating as one unified force.

THE CLOCK TOWER BELL clanged an hour later, echoing in the ears of the children to signify them to enter congregate at the chapel before supper. The kids jaunted up the staircase like a herd of sheep being chased by a dog. They passed the monitoring nuns, who were pleased by their innate compliance. Buck and Frank leisurely strolled through the branches, clasping hands for a concluding moment before being exposed in the public courtyard. Their gigantic smiles of adolescent love radiated off their sweaty, pale skins while they readjusted their sweatshirts over their bodies. They distanced themselves as they drew close to the final cluster of foliage. They ran through the open patch of grass to catch up to the rest of their classmates, gliding up the mountainous cement. A displeased nun clutched onto her chipped, wooden yardstick, rolling her eyes at their two biggest offenders while she trailed after them with disgust.

Buck and Frank made their way across the well-lit entrance hall toward the chapel, the force of the main door shutting behind them, encasing their taste of freedom. The first couple of pews seated the rest of the kids. Their stillness intensified as Sister Magdalena stood at the altar with her hands on her waist, exhibiting their rapacious, squinting eyes and tightened lips.

"You two are late yet again," Sister Magdalena said, hissing with disdain.

"We're sorry, Sister Magdalena," Frank said as he and Buck removed their hoods and bowed their heads in shame.

"This has been becoming a pattern between the two of you, hasn't it?"

"It's only happened a few times," Buck said, his tone cowered with defeat.

"Tardiness is next to ungodliness! This will no longer happen! Got it?"

"Yes, Sister Magdalena," the two responded, their gazes lowered, shrinking between their shoulders.

"Now, I need you to pray for forgiveness," she commanded, waving her arms to usher them to the altar. "Come up, now."

Their muddy shoes shuffled across the carpet until they got in front. Their knees met the ground quick, heads bowed over their palms sandwiched together over their chest, prayers muttered from their mouths to convince the sisters that they were taking their rules seriously. A lukewarm spritz of water caused their tresses to become wet. The ladies swarmed around them like savages preparing to devour a filling meal.

"CLEANSE! CLEANSE! CLEANSE!" the nuns chanted together, their bottles of holy water emptied onto their drenching clothes.

Their locks became saturated, letting droplets trickle down their foreheads and cheeks. The fibers of their clothing clung to their bodies as they prayed louder to tune out the nuns' chanting. Their commands barked, making it harder to ignore the chill growing with every splash of liquid. Their teeth gritted in annoyance, once again allowing the theatrics of their practices to mold them into something they believe would be a better version of themselves. Counting down the minutes yearningly, they only needed to play along with the guidelines set forth for a couple more months until it released them back into society. Then they could move from their homes and on with their lives together, happy with no restrictions, judgments, or nuns.

Chapter 24

June 2006

SONYA TRUDGED INSIDE the entrance hall, water squirting from her toes with every bend of her feet. The sisters stopped their chores to scan her drenched defeat; sorrow read on their faces as they dusted the cobwebs out of the nooks and crannies of the building. Sheldon was frantically speaking on the phone, his dialogue's speed at the pace of a medicine commercial reading the neverending slew of side effects. He waved his hands in frustration as he endured the intensity of his call, teetering a stack of papers. After entering the common room, Cora stood there waiting for her like a bully preparing to gain lunch money. Her arms crossed over her chest, her foot tapping like an agitated typist's fingers upon a keyboard.

"What the hell happened to you?" she asked, smirking with pleasure as she studied Sonya's misery.

"Nothing," Sonya said, not stopping. The squishing of her shoes sounded like a soaked sponge being squeezed repeatedly.

"You think you're so tough, don't you?" Cora said, her arms thrust to her side.

"No."

"I've been getting pretty fed up with your shit."

Her knuckles crackled like dry wood over a harmonious campfire, each one annoying Sonya more.

Sonya sighed, frustrated, having to witness another provoking gesture from her within inches of the knob.

"What did I do this time?" she asked, exasperating a generous amount of air from her lungs, impatient to endure Cora's instigating. "I haven't done shit to you. Ever since I got here, it seems like you have a problem with me."

Cora walked toward Sonya to caress her hand across her dripping shoulders. Sonya's spine tingled from her personal boundaries being intruded. Cora craned her neck to give a passive-aggressive kiss upon Sonya's ear lobe. Her chapped lips were soaked with minuscule drops of rainwater.

"I just don't like you," Cora whispered. "I don't like people like you. The way you walk. The way you talk. The things you represent."

Sonya flinched with disgust, holding herself back from the conflict. Her head perched closer to her shoulders with disdain before shutting herself into her room. A maniacal laugh left Cora's mouth as she exited the lounge with excitement. The lamp vibrated from the force of Sonya's slammed door. She exhaled another deep breath to calm herself down, throwing her shoes and socks to the wall to release her ever-growing anger. She peeled her t-shirt from her chest before throwing it to the floor. The wet fibers scratched against her pale legs as she battled her pants that clung to skin before pelting them at the window.

She stood there in her black underwear, vulnerable and alone while enduring the consuming loneliness of Griffwood Manor, the patronizing of Cora, and the prowling of an assailing and relentless nun. She didn't know if she wanted to scream or cry. The idea of escaping came to mind, but where could she go after abandoning a distant spot, ignorant of what was in the vicinity? Her outpour of emotions halted when she saw a folded-up piece of paper on her windowsill. She walked with hesitation over to it, breathing heavily, fearful with anticipation. The crispiness was strange on her water-logged fingertips, her eyes blinded with angry tears as she tried to decipher the barely legible chicken scratches.

WE NEED TO TALK IN private. Let's meet up after lunch!

-Tom

SHE CRINKLED UP THE piece of paper and threw it across the room before collapsing onto her bed. Her dry, warm bed sheets gave her body a relieving welcome while she caught up on some much-needed rest to clear her mind and refocus her wilting spirit.

AFTER EATING A MEAGER lunch consisting of soggy sandwiches and a handful of stale potato chips, the three children parted ways. Cora was separated from the group to head up to an empty room. Sonya caught up to Tom, who paced in front of Sheldon's office.

"So, what is it you wanted to talk about?" Sonya muttered under her breath, curious to know what was on his mind.

"Shhh!"

Tom hushed her as Sheldon exited his cubicle, intrigued to know what was on their mind.

"Ophelia gives her regards and plans on having some hard-hitting work tomorrow. I will leave more sandwiches for later this evening, and will be meeting with the others now. She requests you take this afternoon for some reflection. Can't do too much here anyway, with all that rain still pouring!"

Sheldon cradled his wobbly pile of documents and folders before departing for the nearby staircase. The door slammed behind him, a lone sister fleeing nervously, abandoning the two teenagers.

"Okay. What is it you wanted to tell me?"

"So, after breakfast, I had some time to think about what brought us all here," said Tom, reaching his arm around Sonya to escort her into the chapel.

"We got into trouble with the law."

"True. But if we were in *big* trouble, why weren't we taken to some juvenile detention center? Why here?"

"I'm not sure."

Her interest slowly piqued. The two sat at the front of the chapel on the step facing the rows of pews, the ghostly congregation of empty seats illuminated by faint candlelight.

"What's the one thing we all have in common that would've brought us together? Why us?"

Sonya thought long and hard, resting her chin on her fist to reflect on all her short encounters with everybody.

"It's going to be difficult to put the pieces together without hearing a single thing about Cora," said Sonya, rolling her eyes with irritation. "Has she said anything to you?"

"No. Not a thing."

"Well, then, we have little to go off of," Sonya said, throwing her arms up in desperation. "Plus, we have nothing on Isis since we only knew her for minutes!"

Sonya reflected on her happy moment with Isis, envisioning a fantasy of her frolicking in a bright meadow. Her poppy-printed sundress brushed along the petals of friendly flowers. She bit her lip, hoping that one day the two of them might meet again to create actual memories to replace her fantasies.

"It must be possible to look up something about this place."

"Aren't they all gone for a meeting?" Tom said, his head turning to Sonya, his orangish-blonde eyebrow raising toward his hairline.

"Yes, and?"

"There is a computer in the office. And I *did* end up here for hacking...."

Sonya's head perked up like a stimulated dog hearing a concerning noise. She reached inside the pocket of her jeans to pull out the manipulated paperclip, poking her finger on the sharp tip before caressing the long, thin shaft. She smiled with confidence as she got up from her seat, reaching her hand to assist Tom onto his feet.

"Let's go! We won't have much time."

They left the chapel, tiptoeing across the empty entrance hall toward Sheldon's office door. The room was free of Cora, free from authority, free of nuns. She guided her paperclip into the ridged keyhole, gently placing her head upon the wooden grain to listen for diminutive clicking, hoping for success. Her breathing staggered; her fingers cramped as they fumbled with the tool, clasping like tweezers on a children's game of "Operation," silently praying for her plan to work.

Click!

An enthusiastic grin glared back at Tom, who chuckled. Static tingled from the brief snooze on her feet. A slight, creaking echo roared from the door, overtaking the space.

Manilla folders and stacks of papers greeted the two. The shelves were hung on the wall, stabilizing an excessive amount of fake plants, bobbleheads, and homemade knick-knacks overpowering the area. She grasped a chrome filing cabinet underneath his desk, jerking her shoulder with tension from the handlebar.

It didn't budge.

She tried to use her paperclip to unlock its drawers inside the neighboring keyhole, but the tool was too large to fit.

"Shit!" Sonya yelled, her yanking increased. "Now what?"

"Well, there's still the computer," said Tom, falling back into Sheldon's rusty-orange office chair. "I know how to hack into this one easily. I looked up porn yesterday while he was in the bathroom."

Tom began typing energetically, quicker than Sonya had ever viewed someone typing. His fingers traveled over the keyboard like the legs of a scurrying arachnid, dancing lightly over every key as he started unlocking the system with ease in his natural environment.

"Bingo!"

"Now, let's see if there are any files on us," said Sonya, leaning over the desk, becoming hypnotized by the rapid clicking of his fingertips onto the buttons.

Tom's face remained focused on the screen, not even blinking for one moment as programs opened and closed while he surfed the entire system. A gray pop-up overtook the monitor, giving him a hard stop.

UNABLE TO OPEN FILE. PLEASE INSERT DISK.

"DAMMIT," TOM HISSED with anger. "He has our information saved on a disk! I'm not able to pull anything up."

"I bet it's inside the cabinet, and we can't get in."

"Well, if we can't figure out why we all ended up here, maybe we can find out about this god-forsaken place."

He opened the internet browser, pulling up a search engine. He typed "Griffwood Manor" into the bar before hitting enter. The limited bandwidth, only a few results had pulled up on the results page. He clicked the first result, an archived newspaper article.

WELCOME TO GRIFFWOOD Manor

June 26, 1971

Is your child misbehaving? Have you tried different options, only to end up with minimal change? Well, then there may be a solution for you to explore!

Griffwood Manor is a safe haven for children to learn and grow. In the quiet countryside and away from distraction is an establishment built for structure. Our program balances a structured environment to champion discipline and develop responsibility. Complete with a full staff of nuns to shadow the growth of children, our curriculum will result in breaking negative habits while remembering that kids can still be kids. Contact our office to learn more and set up a consultation! Our friendly team is looking forward to working with you and the next chapter of your child's life!

THEY BACKED OUT OF the page, and the browser slowly loaded the list of results. They spotted each other's disbelief that there was history; the functionality of their program was once successful. Tom clicked onto the following link and loaded the next article:

UNETHICAL PRACTICES Cause Manor's Demise

December 15, 1996

Operations at the establishment previously run by Mother Superior and taken over by Sister Magdalena had been shut down due to lack of funding. As Griffwood Manor took in smaller amounts of children, there were fewer options for them to assist with the healing and development of juvenile delinquents. Former student Craig McBride stated the nuns used constant prayer, fasting, and electroshock practices. Once the government discovered the excessive use of electroshock therapy, they pulled the plug and ended the program. This information was discovered over ten years after the disappearance of Sister Magdalena, while being taken over by Sister Tate in its final years. These practices cured violence, theft, vandalism, and homosexuality.

"HOMOSEXUALITY?" SONYA asked, turning her head toward Tom with concern. "You mean like conversion therapy?"

"I guess so," he said, backing out of the screen and typing something else into the search engine.

"Craig McBride"

He pulled up the images; a familiar face of a slenderly muscular teenage boy popped up. His reddish-orange hair and freckles speckled from the tip of his nose and spread out to the apples of his glowing-white cheeks.

"Does that look like somebody we know?" Tom asked, full of shock, when he glimpsed back toward Sonya.

"Is that *our* Craig?" she said, placing a hand over her mouth.

SLAM!

The sound of a door blared from outside the office, startling the two. Her hand knocked a stack of papers onto the congested floor. Tom jumped out of Sheldon's chair and closed the programs with haste, logging out of the system and turning off the monitor. Sonya collected as many scattered papers she could before slamming them back on the desk.

"We need to get out of here," Sonya whispered with fear, throwing the last bit of documents in their place next to a framed portrait of Sheldon and his child. "We'll be in deep shit if we get caught."

They shut the door quickly behind them. She removed her tool and toyed with the lock, attempting to ignore the frustration pouring out of Tom that persisted tapping her shoulder. Her heart raced as the instrument moved in every direction, as though it was going through a garbage disposal.

Click!

The two of them composed a deep breath. The heat from their faces ceased as their sweaty palms dried up. They looked at each other and chuckled, relieved that it didn't catch them breaking the rules.

"That was close!" Tom praised, tapping his hand on her shoulder one last time before resting.

"I know. Now, let's get out of here before anybody finds us."

Their smug grins instantly changed into nothing as though their lips shifted into plain, straight lines. Sonya gasped in fear as she squeezed Tom's forearm, almost cutting off his circulation. They stared at the doors to the dining hall that welcomed the addition of another guest. The stoic, cold stance of a black-gowned figure with a white headdress and a blood-orange ghostly mask joined their encounter. She wheezed heavily, trying to hold back her panic.

The hidden nun unquestionably found them.

Chapter 25

June 2006

"IT'S THE NUN," SONYA said, her body frozen with fear; joints locking like a fresh cadaver.

"Relax, Sonya. It's just Amber or Joseph trying to scare us with another one of their stupid jokes!" Tom said, unimpressed with the costume as he walked closer to it.

"No. It attacked me last night."

"What? You're saying this clown attacked you?"

"Yes."

"You've got to be kidding me! Now you're in on the joke, too?" Tom said, laughing in disbelief.

Tom turned toward Sonya, unconvinced, placing his hands on his hips, matching Leslie's sass with his knee cocked. The nun pulled its hands from behind its back, and a wooden cross was grasped tight, clenching the end like a baseball bat.

"TOM, WATCH OUT!" Sonya screamed. The nun looped the weapon around its body, preparing to swing.

Tom's cheek met the immediate slam of intersecting pieces. Splinters dug into his face as it knocked him straight to the floor. Sonya flinched, empathizing with his pain, not knowing what to do. The nun lunged forward toward the boy, who remained petrified in pain. Tom's jawbone pulsated as though it had its own heartbeat. The assailant stood over the shaken child. Tom's hands glided over his face in defense.

The forceful shove of a wooden chair thrust into the front of the villain, knocking it back and loosening its sword-like grasp. The nun fell to the floor as dozens of chipped, wooden pieces flaked over its stunned body.

"Come on! Let's get the hell out of here!"

The two ran inside the empty dining hall, passing the lone table before heading to the other side. Stacks of sandwiches toppled over the closer they got to the kitchen door. Not a single sister was in sight for her to find refuge.

"We can take the back exit and make a run for it," Sonya said, her breath staggering with panic. "How does that sound?"

"Fine by me," Tom said, panting between each syllable, ignoring the pain radiating from his face.

The two advanced toward the door; their legs tightened with a strain on their calves. Tom moved first, his face nudging the door's hard surface when it swung back at him. He thrashed against the wall before collapsing onto the floor, his limbs heavy. Sonya screamed as the nun rushed toward her, grabbing Sonya by the hair. The painful memory of the locker room emitted from every pore of her scalp. Her palms slapped the nun's arms while pained tears exited her eyes. Her footing was constantly being driven backward before sensing the abrupt feeling of plummeting back, floating away from the nun as it pushed her down the basement stairs. Tumble after tumble, the space around her spun with her stomach turning after each bounce off the wooden surface until her body planted onto the cement floor. Immersed in the darkness, Sonya became unconscious and defenseless as the nun closed the door behind her.

The nun shifted back toward Tom, who remained protectively stiff with fear. The taste of blood seeped into his lips, gifted from his nose. Prayers were mumbled while his chin quivered. The tingling in his fingers overwhelmed him. He wished he could be home with his family, not caring about how much he disliked them. Tom's hair was yanked. The nun ignored Tom's desperate defensive swings lessening in power, soon succumbing to his peril. His scream pitched higher than Sonya's, screeching through the walls. His chest palpitated fiercely with his tightening throat rejecting the urge to vomit. They fought their way through the kitchen door; the nun struggled with Tom's squirmy compliance. Its other hand reached over Tom's cheek that was quickly changing its flushes of hot and cold. His pain pulsated horribly out of his head before meeting with the forceful push onto the counter, stunning him with the room going pitch black.

Tom halted his defensive struggle, diminishing to nothing. His eyelids began to fall, his sense of consciousness out of his control. The nun hoisted him over its shoulder, his lifeless figure hauled closer to the door. His limbs dangled like wet noodles while his helpless body and mind drifted to a quieter place in the raging storm's chaos.

THE BELL RANG INSIDE the empty hallways of the high school, barely resonating before becoming interrupted by the swinging doors of impatient children. Jocks tossed around a withered football to practice for their next game. Cheerleaders primped up their hair and makeup while admiring the oozing testosterone of the athletic boys competing for their attention. Academia-loving students balanced endless stacks of books filled with requested extra credit to fulfill their souls and impress their teachers. Tom carried his backpack over his shoulders, gripping the straps over his bony shoulder. The isolation of the cliques thriving in their natural habitat surrounded him.

He walked toward his locker for a quick break to get his required possessions to take home. The locker door swung open, the rusty latches screeching desperately for a shower of WD-40 while an avalanche of textbooks and notebooks plummeted to the floor. Tom sighed, aggravated, as he bent down to pick them up, rolling his eyes as he shut the exposed books before pushing them back into his locker. The force of a spiraling football tackled his hand and knocked the final textbook out of his hands. His wrist stung like a rabid animal bite, flinching toward his chest as he witnessed the book spin away from him. Through the pool of chattering classmates resonated a loud cluster of chuckles from the team. He turned to them, their black and navy letterman's jacket sleeves, high-fiving each other with cocky praise.

Raging heat fumed from his ears as he walked home, being reminded of the constant ridicule, day in and out of every type of person. They ensnared him in an unavoidable jail, aware that his peers teased him for being gay, which was bearable to a degree. But being picked on for being gay *and* weird was another. Even the other bullied kids rejected him. People who looked for like-minded individuals who wouldn't judge them still alienated Tom. He never felt appreciated as a part of anything and his identity wasn't embraced. The educators wouldn't take any action about it since they don't want any grievances from the parents of the kids who have set up a reputation for their town. It was better for the teachers to pick their battles, allowing the torture to commence, avoiding the revenge of the gossiping parents jeopardizing their image.

His teeth gritted tight, and a slight crackling crush clicked in his mouth. He'd had enough of the bullying. He'd had enough of the exclusion. He'd had enough of the ridicule.

Tom walked inside his house, removing his black tennis shoes before crossing the textured carpet to walk toward his bedroom. His mother and father watched their favorite daytime talk show at the security's climax, breaking up a fistfight between two women over a cheating boyfriend.

"Hey, honey!" his mother said with disinterest, her eyes fixated on the television.

"Hi," Tom said, the monotonous depression making him solemn.

"How was school?" his father asked, his fist scavenging for a handful of salt and vinegar chips.

"It was stupid! I hate it here!"

His knuckles stung in pain as he clenched it. His angst increased as his nail dug deep into his palms.

"Why?" his mother asked. Her eyes rolled with knowing the same complaint and no interest in acting upon it.

"I'm so sick of this fucking school."

"Another bully?"

His father sighed, groaning with minimal care. His vexation heightened, realizing that he had to endure his son's plea for aid for another day.

"You already know! Why don't you two do something about it?!"

"Why don't you?" his mom asked, turning the television volume up to tune him out.

"How many more times do we have to tell you? If you tone it down, then maybe people will leave you alone," his father said, his carefree rationale sharp with cold passion.

"What the hell does that even mean? You either are gay, or you're not. And besides, if what you mean by 'toning it down' by not being feminine, have you looked at me? I'm just like everybody else! And why does it matter?"

"I don't know what to say to you anymore," said his father, his voice raising. "We have given you all the guidance you need to get these kids off your back. We have nothing more to say."

"All you tell me is to tone it down," said Tom, stomping toward his bedroom door. "Maybe if you were more involved, you'd look like parents."

"If we weren't great parents, then why are we making the time to attend parents' night with you tonight?" his mother said.

"I'm not going!" he yelled back, slamming his bedroom door behind him.

"Yes, you are! You better be ready to go by six! And you better cut that shitty attitude when we leave!" his dad said as he picked up the remote to turn the volume louder to spook the whiny groans out of his head.

Tom leaned against the entrance, heartbroken with misunderstanding as tears fell down his cheek the closer he collapsed to the ground. His parents don't understand him. Even worse, they didn't have his back to comfort him, even in the toughest of times. Every time they found out about their son getting into another fight at school results in their recommendation to "tone it down." Tom knew their advice wasn't to protect him, but rather to spare themselves. They cared more about the well-being of their image as parents than about their child's safety and happiness. The frustration of being alone and out of place in this world brought more rage than he had ever felt before, roaring like a ferocious lion. He reflected upon the years of being ignored since he came out to them. The one set of people he assumed would have loved and nurtured him through thick and thin, through hate and adversity. Through heartbreak and triumph. This anger propelled him to get back, not only to his classmates, but to his parents, too. He walked over to his desk and logged onto his computer. He began to work as his fingers pelted the surface of his keyboard.

HOURS PASSED BY, AND the family arrived at the gymnasium. Groups of children accompanied their proud parents while the seats filled up. Tom felt like he was in a teen movie. Even the parents of the cliques were part of groups of their own. The football parents bragged nonstop about their boys and their star-worthy performances. The cheerleaders' mothers adjusted their overly primped hair while focusing on their compact mirrors to ensure that they polished their makeup to perfection. Parents of the academics conversed about neuroscience and engineering, comparing the molecular structure of atoms and chatting about the evidence of rapid global warming.

The microphone felt the tap of the principal's finger wobbling on the brown podium. From the clearing of the speaker's throat, the adult chattering began to dull down.

"I want to welcome you all to our annual Parents' Night!" the principal said, an enthusiastic greeting to the sea of people. "Before we begin our slideshow, I would like to take a moment to acknowledge a few folks that made this year possible. I hope you all have helped yourself to the assortment of snacks provided by our local churches."

Her hand waved at the kind members of the congregation. The group of five acknowledged her gratitude, finishing the plating of cinnamon rolls and cake doughnuts.

Tom looked at his parents, disinterested, while they stared at the principal with glazed regret that they missed out on their evening reality television schedule.

"Can I go to the bathroom?" Tom whispered, irritated.

"Yeah, sure," his father said, flicking his hand to shoo away his son like a gnat. "Be quick. You don't want to miss out on the slideshow."

"I sure won't," he muttered to himself.

He crept out of his chair, mouthing apologies to the neighboring parents and classmates he blockaded before getting to the clearing in the aisle.

He walked fast out the gymnasium doors. The hallways were emptied with nobody in sight, permitting him to sprint to the stage entrance. The clapping of his sneakers stormed the abandoned corridor. He ignored the cramping of his unathletic legs. He quickly rushed up the backstage stairs and found the projector. A disc containing the program's slideshow composed by the parents of the quarterback was ejected from his touch. Thoughts of the meticulously organized pictures of the same ten or so students with the possibility of a picture or two of everybody else motivated his cause. After throwing the disc across the room, he dug into his pants to grab his own. He kissed it for good luck, his lips contacting the spackles of lint before placing it on the tray.

"Time to expose you all as the pieces of shit you are," Tom said to himself, chuckling menacingly. "We'll see how proud your parents are after seeing all the secret pictures from your computers! Your days of tormenting people are over!"

He giggled as he raced around the hallway to get back inside the gymnasium. He hastily walked back to his parents as if he were an elderly lady at a mall. The adults remained sleepy by the drawn-out speech of his principal, pretending their support as parents with an occasional acknowledgement. Parents who took the time to show up and appear caring to their son in the eyes of their ever-so-judging neighbors. Tom's forehead dripped profusely with sweat as he paused to breathe, sitting back in his chair.

"What the hell happened to you?" his father asked, feeling his son's moist breath on his arm.

"What?" Tom asked, huffing.

"You're all sweaty."

"Oh, I had to go number two. It was taco day at school."

"Gross."

His father shook his head with disgust, turning his attention back to the principal as she concluded her speech. The audience roared with gratifying applause, cheering at the principal's over-the-top passion. She walked to the edge of the stage, pressing play on the projector while the Goo Goo Dolls soundtrack started to play. The first few images were cliques standing together with their pretend smiles. Macho football players stood in a line, flexing their biceps, growling fiercely at their opponents like gladiators. Cheerleaders clustered, laughing like a group of sorority sisters piled together on the lawn in an unstable pyramid. The slideshow then proceeded onto an image of a couple of those girls, gruesome in their chunky, avocado-green facemasks, plucking their nose hairs. One girl had shaving cream above her upper lip and pinched a Venus Embrace over it.

A burst of dull laughter erupted as the two girls in the photo collapsed lower into their chairs. Their bronze skin darkened with blush while they covered their faces.

The following image was the entire football squad going from the manliest and macho with victorious screams after their games. Awkward, feminine poses unflattering the fit of their matching bras and panties contrasted their egos. Their burly stomachs peeked over their hiked-up lacy underwear, their peach-fuzzy chest hair highlighting cleavage. Their pectorals were big enough to fit inside the cups of training bras. One was crouched down in a thong, exposing more than anyone should have seen with their black leg and lower back hair covering the fragile elastic band.

The crowd roared with laughter as more images continued to appear on the screen, exposing the side of the classmates documented for memory. Parents stormed out of the room, embarrassed that their perfect child was not as pure as they let others believe. The kids followed, chasing their parents as they fought their humiliation.

They begged for forgiveness from their distraught parental rejection. Football players broke down in tears as cheerleaders heaved up their doughnuts in panic.

"This is not the slideshow I approved!" the principal screamed, appalled as she ran over to the other side of the stage, trying to stop it.

Another image popped up with Tom. His middle finger was flung high in the center of the screen. Neon-yellow rubber bands highlighted atop the heavy metal of his braces shedding a flippant grin. Below his face was some text, bold as can be, to relay the message he had yearned to tell:

"Not so perfect kids you have, after all! Don't be so quick to judge what you see on the outside. We all have the same feelings on the inside!"

Tom exploded in chuckles, swaying to the brink of toppling out of his chair. One of the teachers marched up to him and clutched him by the ear, yanking Tom from his seat as they dragged him out of the gymnasium. He ignored the growing pain as he flipped his middle fingers to the entire audience, mimicking his image. His laughter grew over the embarrassed group of aggravated classmates and parents. His parents followed right behind him, apologizing to every person they walked past, humiliated by the unforgiving actions of their child.

HE SAT IN THE PRINCIPAL'S lounge, fulfilled. His pride was magnificent for standing up to the group of classmates for teasing him for all these years. He had no regret for embarrassing his parents after choosing the qualities they wanted to love about their son, but only considering their image and dismissing their child's safety and happiness. His stomach aches in pain, still laughing, still reminiscing.

The door opened; the principal exited, followed by his parents. Their severe glares of disappointment drew no intimidation out of him.

"Mr. Sackett, what you have done is inexcusable," the principal said, scolding the smug grin on the child.

"Compared to what everybody has been doing to me for years?" he asked, hissing in defense.

"I haven't heard of these troubles you've had with the other students."

"Yes, you have! All you do is ignore it so that you don't punish them and not piss off their parents! Did they bribe you to make their children have clean records and perfect grades? Because some of these kids are so fucking stupid."

"That's enough, Tom!" his father said, stomping his foot onto the floor to halt his child's argument.

Silence overtook the room, pausing as elegant stilettos clomped, growing with each step.

"We had a long discussion, and we feel you would benefit from some help," his mother said, barely making eye contact with her son as she focused on the secretary's desk behind him. "I would like for you to meet Ophelia. She is here to take you away for a while to help you."

"Who?" Tom asked, confused.

The woman glided into the room, her black feathered poodle skirt was stiff. She looked like she came straight from an Alexander McQueen fashion show. Her black mesh veil covered most of her face and part of her mustard-yellow plaid jacket, revealing the ruby red lipstick that showed a slight grin.

"Hello there, Thomas. I'm Lady Ophelia."

THE BACK KITCHEN DOOR thrust open, being assisted by the heavy wind. Rain pounded relentlessly down upon the stupefied teenager while being pulled by the nun across the back yard toward the mucky garden. His heels trudged into the thick, claylike ground, like a tiller in a field preparing to plant a fresh crop. The tree branches appeared to be multiplying in numbers, dizzy, while his consciousness drifted to his mind. The muscles of his arms and legs became paralyzed, unable to move as the fibers of his clothing got heavier. He mumbled in pain, which was not capable of being heard through the god-like storm overpowering any outdoor noise. The nun hoisted the injured boy back onto his feet, his skull tilted toward the side of the crimson metal gardening shed. He spotted the raindrops pelting into the wooden trough filled with never-ending drops of water vibrating its fragile surface. The back of Tom's head felt the grasp; his ear slicked the plastic surface of the nun's mask. Its warm breath tuned out the whistling winds before belting out a word:

"CLEANSE!"

The nun shoved Tom's head with full force into the trough. His arms locked. His elbows crackled with tension, his forearms and biceps burning with pain as he tried to push himself out. His feet slid in the mud while he attempted to shuffle his footing to save himself. Bubbles of air rapidly surrounded his submerged face, surfacing past his ears as he screamed for help. Gulping bunches of liquid, the oxygen in his lungs became replaced with mother nature's nourishing liquid that weighed down like water balloons. His throat stung the prick of a thousand needles. The whites in his eyes turned into a dark red while he stared at the bottom of the barrel that deepened like an endless pit.

His hands slipped from the edge, losing strength, falling to his side as his consciousness drifted from his body once again, drowning in his regrets, his sorrows, and the feeling of being unloved.

Chapter 26

June 2006

THE LIGHT SWAYED OVER Sonya's face, flickering in and out of sight. The lone lightbulb swung like a pendulum, tormenting her memory of her prior encounter in the prison-like room. Every muscle in her body strained as she hunched herself up, groaning from the extension of every pull. Her legs were unsteady; her weight bore heavy on the nearby railing to assist her back onto her feet. Clenching the bar, wooden slivers penetrated the surface of her sweaty palms, pulling herself up the stairs with every ounce of her strength.

Sonya thrust the door open to interrupt Ophelia and Amber's casual conversation over a simple meal. Contents of their sandwiches became an anemic salad after they collapsed onto the table, jumping from their seats and running over to her. The sole of Ophelia's shoes clapped audibly on the hardwood floors. Amber crouched under Sonya's loosened arm to assist with cradling her, guiding her toward the exit.

"What the hell happened to you?" Amber asked, concerned as Sonya's footing hobbled from her dragging feet.

"And what on earth were you doing in the basement?" Ophelia asked.

"The nun," Sonya answered, slurring her speech with exhaustion. "It was the nun."

"A nun? That's ridiculous. The sisters have better things to do. They wouldn't hurt a fly!"

"Let's take her to her room to get some rest," Amber said as they approached the spiral staircase, the collapsing weight of Sonya's body becoming heavier.

"There was a nun with an orange mask and green eyes who attacked me," said Sonya, reliving her trauma, her breath short.

"I'm sure she fell down the stairs and bumped her head," Ophelia replied, brushing her off. "She must be seeing things. It's the portraits, darling. You were seeing the faces from the portraits."

"It wasn't a hallucination! Why the hell would I do this to myself?"

"Oh, sweetie, I'm going to forgive you for the inappropriate use of profanity since you're hurt. But with all due respect, you are a criminal. How are we supposed to believe *you*?"

"Isn't the basement supposed to be locked?"

Ophelia had no response to defend against Sonya's logic. She continued to assist Sonya up the staircase, digging her fingernails deeper into the teenager's armpit. Amber's disgust grew with the lack of empathy and disregard for the child's well-being. She glared deeply at her with every opportunity she could glance at her oblivion. They rushed her down the hallway toward her bedroom and placed her on her bed.

"I don't see any signs of a concussion," Amber said, observing Sonya's normal-sized pupils, the intense fear in her frazzled mind showing. "She just needs some rest."

"Very good. And rest is what she will get."

"Why are you gone all day without checking in on us?" Sonya asked. The intensity of her pain in her gut escalated higher.

"Joseph was feeling under the weather, darling. We just took this moment for him to get some rest while the rest of us were planning."

"Wait," Sonya said, the sound of a skipping record echoing inside her racing mind. "Joseph wasn't with you?"

"No, he was resting," Amber said.

"Not for the afternoon meeting?"

"No."

Thousands of thoughts raced through her mind.

Where was Joseph when all of this happened?

Then she started to assume the worst, her paranoia rationalizing.

Could he have something to do with all these unexplained disappearances?

Sonya began wriggling with panic flooding her body. She squirmed frantically like a fish suffocating on land, her arms and legs flailing as though she was drowning in a deep blue sea. Amber and Ophelia, startled by Sonya's panicked disposition, stepped toward the door to blockade her.

"I NEED TO GET OUT OF HERE!"

"What do you think we should do?" Amber asked as they watched Sonya try to hoist herself up from the bed, groaning in pain like a mummy. "Would you like for me to stay with her?"

"Oh no, sweetie, that won't be necessary."

She reached inside the pocket of her suit jacket and pulled out a syringe, removing the cap and tossing it to the floor. Tapping the plunger, she produced a tiny amount of clear liquid from the tip of the needle.

"What are you doing?" Amber asked Ophelia.

"Just a mild sedative," said Ophelia, stomping toward the panic-stricken child.

The needle penetrated her arm, pricking her like a small bee sting. A slight, cooling sensation flowed into her bicep as the medicine took its course.

"This will help you relax."

"We don't have the licensure to administer that type of medication!"

"What she needs is a little rest. I just need her to calm down," Ophelia defended, placing the syringe onto the dresser.

"This is unethical!"

Amber stormed out of the room, appalled by her actions. Sonya's muscles started to relax as though wet sandbags had been attached to her limbs. Her head collapsed onto her pillow, the fluff cradling her pain. Defenseless, her eyelids became weighed down, drifting into a deep sleep.

"Where's Isis?" Sonya said, her voice slurred as she dozed away from reality, trapped by the shackling of the medication. "I want to see Isis."

THE NIGHT SKY DISSIPATED the rampaging storm clouds as the thrashing rain calmed into a slight drizzle. Crickets chirped throughout the grounds, echoing inside the hollowed-out base of the tree next to the abandoned clock tower. A final gust of wind blew the branches like blow-drying hair, slapping the door and swinging it open. The ground was covered in rubble and wood shavings, puddling the base of a circular wooden stairwell that ascended up the walls of the decaying interior. Hundreds of cobwebs ensnared every corner and crevice of the ruined edifice. The stench of wet, rotting wood and mildew competed fiercely with the aroma of dormant death. The wooden planks groaned a cacophony of uncertainty where the structure could fail at any time.

At the pinnacle of the long staircase was a ceiling containing a hatch to the highest point. Along the plethora of open holes from the absence of floorboards sat a person, imprisoned, her body bound tight to a chair behind the clock's face.

Isis.

She peered through a broken chunk of glass onto the overlook of the property. Her happy place was unobtainable from the bird's-eye view of the trees looking like a braided ponytail exploding with punches of dreadlocked hair drifting in the calmed breeze. Her mouth muttered prayers for somebody to save her, hoping ever since the nun knocked her unconscious two days ago that someone would come and rescue her.

Sonya.

Isis wriggled in her chair, bound and gagged. Her once vibrant yellow jumpsuit was now tattered and muddy, torn at the knees. She was isolated and powerless as the days went by at Griffwood Manor, with the occupants unaware of her captivity. Nobody knew where she went. Would they even care? Hope was starting to dwindle, and she didn't know how much time she had left.

TWO WEEKS AGO WAS THE three-month anniversary with her girlfriend. Isis and Creed were inseparable. Creed displayed many masculine qualities that made Isis feel safe to be around. If anybody had any extreme differences in opinions about two women being together, Creed would be there to set them straight. Her muscled physique and intimidation tactics were her form of conflict resolution. Creed always would make her physical dominance known as her bulging muscles popped through her white beater tank top and the arsenal of knives buried in the deep pockets of her baggy jeans poking out. She would also bring fun wherever they went, being twenty-one years of age compared to Isis's seventeen.

Isis's parents never understood her preferences, nor did they have any particular interest in investing themselves in her happiness. They were too busy with their corporate jobs, too consumed with the "white-collared" family ideology. Once they learned about Isis's preferences, they neither embraced nor rejected it. All they would do was tell her that "they didn't want any of it in their house." The rejection stung worse than any child with parents who flat-out told their kid that they disapproved of their life. Because of her parents' lack of acknowledgement, Isis would sneak off late at night to go visit Creed. After all, it's what her parents didn't know would spare her from becoming disappointed with every insensitive comment that distanced her from her family. Sometimes, she would lie to them and say she was staying with one of her classmates for an after-school study session.

Isis left her home on a Saturday afternoon, strutting her upright confidence in her brand-new sparkly cocktail dress. The red and blue beaded fringe swirled around her like a tornado of crimson and periwinkle. She savored the emancipation of being who she was meant to be while she ambled the streets toward Creed's apartment, conveniently eight blocks away from her house.

I can't wait to see Creed. She makes me feel more normal than my parent's fantasy.

Isis arrived at the front steps of a worn-down brick building. Antique lamp posts paralleled the door like a small town's post office. She ventured merrily down the ivory marble hallway. Her black rhinestone high heels echoed inside the dark corridor as she approached Creed's apartment at the end. She entered the industrial-looking residence where most kitchen counter space and appliances were chrome, mimicking the interior of a five-star restaurant. The brown leather sofas were well organized atop the Chester hardwood flooring congregating around Creed's wall of expensive flat-screen television and rolling minibar. She searched for her girlfriend in the heavily scented sage and cedar cloud. The underpart of her feet vibrated; she tried to remain focused as the loud hip-hop music boomed through the stereo system.

"H-Hello?" Isis said, immediately being tuned out by the base's thumping. Her joints vibrated.

There was no response.

"Creed? Are you here?"

Answer the door already!

She stepped inside the dark, candlelit bedroom, straightaway noticing the hot, radiating warmth of two people romantically expressing their love to each other. Movements pulsated with arms and legs bulging under the thin surface of delicate ivory bed sheets. Waves of giggles and moans entered her eardrum, unwelcomed.

Isis felt steam leaving her body, not from romance, but from betrayal. Her white teeth ground upon each other like a knife sharpening onto a wet stone. Her fist clenched tightly. Her knuckles crackled like a crushed candy wrapper.

"What the hell is going on here?!"

A startled gasp halted the two fornicating individuals. Creed snuck her head to the surface, miffed that her moment of inflicting pleasure had ceased.

"Isis," Creed said, panting for air. "What are you doing here?"

"The real question is, what is *she* doing here?"

"This is my place. I can have whoever I want here!"

"But having sex with them? I thought you were committed to me?" Isis said, placing her hands on her hips, her fingers disappearing underneath the red and blue strands.

"Oh, please! We've only seen each other for like three months."

"You said that they have been the best you've had!"

"Get real," Creed said, brushing off Isis's case. "I say that to everybody."

Disappointment weighed Isis down, suffocating the remaining ounce of joy out of her mood.

"And besides, people like you will do the same to us, going back and forth between men and women. I don't have time for your indecisive shit."

"Indecisive?" Isis asked, appalled. "You don't know me like that!"

Creed sighed a frustrated breath, shaking her head.

"Can't you see I'm busy?"

"Busy?"

"Yes, busy," said Creed, her tone rising impatiently. "Now, can you please leave my key on the counter and get the fuck out of here so I can finish?"

Creed sank underneath the covers, resuming her intimacy. The sound of skin rubbing against each other was intensifying with the proceeding of giggles.

"Go to hell!" Isis yelled, storming out of the bedroom and slamming the door behind her.

Isis cradled her hands upon her face. The agonizing defeat of being betrayed was too much. She slammed the key onto the metal countertop and ran out the apartment. She felt alone with giving her trust, only to have been taken advantage of.

THREE HOURS PASS AFTER a long session of breaking ferociously into tears inside her car. Soft rock music roared over her wailing heartbreak in a nearby mall parking lot. Her grief outstripped her fury, perceiving the moment she was going to declare her love to Creed vanish. Instead, her heart had been torn out of her chest and shredded into a million pieces. Along with sensing ambivalence, she cringed at the justification of Creed's rationale.

Why can't people like me be taken seriously in relationships like other couples?

Concealing her bloodshot eyes, she placed her sunglasses on. She exited her vehicle, grabbing a plastic shopping bag from the passenger seat.

She paced through the sea of cars and shoppers of all ages, walking around a slow-moving elderly couple, zipping her hoodie up toward her chin while they stared at her with nervous energy. She followed a pale-skinned adult male; his dress shirt and brown pants oozed professionalism as they both entered the store.

They passed by clusters of unorganized sales racks as one lone associate frantically attempted to fold a knocked-over stack of shirts. The mother beside him disassembled the pile of meticulously organized clothing he had just finished, disrespecting the merchandise.

Another associate cradled a pile of clothes, exiting a fitting room with fear, avoiding the haunting glares of the store manager who stood there micromanaging her productivity. Her fear of getting her hours cut exuded from her as the endless amount of clothing piled. The department supervisor was sweating from juggling the impossible task of set design and maintaining customer service and teamwork with his staff. Isis waited patiently in line, overhearing the male attempt to make a transaction. The red-headed woman, in her mid-twenties, assisted him as she warmly greeted the gentleman.

"Hi, there! How can I help you today?" said the associate.

"Hi, I would like to make a return, please," replied the gentleman.

"Okay, do you have your receipt?"

"No, ma'am. I don't."

"Okay," she said with her pitch heightened. "I'll gladly place that on a gift card for in-store credit."

"Sounds good," he said, gracious. "Thank you."

The cashier grinned with ease as she reached over to the other side of the register to grab a navy-blue plastic card. She swiped it through the slot and handed it to him.

"Twenty dollars is all yours to use at your convenience!" she concluded with kindness. "I hope you have a wonderful day."

"Thank you. You too."

The gentleman passed by Isis, eager to unload the money from the card. Isis placed the bag on the counter, her nerves at ease.

The sales associate's demeanor changed, her grin straightening as though she were conversing with her in-laws. Her orangish eyebrows lowered her freckled forehead closer to the sockets of her eyes. She placed her hands upon her hips, and her hip bones felt the pinch of her unwelcoming change.

"Hi."

"Can I help you?" the associate asked. Her tone deepened, atypical of the kindness she gave to the gentleman.

"I would like to make a return, please?"

She took the blue and red dress she had worn earlier in the day out of the plastic bag and laid it on the counter. Her fingers brushed the strands of fringe, feeling the sadness of its original intent being foiled with each comb.

"Do you have a receipt?" the associate asked, grunting like a teacher reprimanding a misbehaved student.

"No, ma'am."

"Well, how do I know you didn't steal it?"

"Excuse me?" Isis asked, appalled.

"How do I know you didn't just take this off the rack just now and come up to ask for money?"

"I paid for it. I bought it for my anniversary with my girlfriend," Isis defended with conviction, offended by her accusation. "And besides, it's store credit that I would get since I don't have a receipt."

"Please don't patronize me, ma'am!" the associate hissed.

"I'm not patronizing you," Isis said, her tone shaky. "You gave store credit to the man in front of me."

"That's because he was following policy."

"I'm doing the same thing as he was. We both walked in at the same time and went straight to you. We both didn't have receipts. Why are you treating me differently than him?"

"I don't believe you. I know customers like you. Coming in and stealing just to make money from workers like us."

"People like me?" Isis asked, baffled by her anger across the counter.

"Yes, people like you! And you have the nerve to come to me with your aggressive tone and demand money out of me!"

"Aggressive? I bought this dress last week with my savings. I would've kept the receipt if I'd known I was planning to return it."

The sales associate's eyebrow raised, her lips pursed with cockiness.

"I guess I'll just keep it. Thank you for your time."

Isis grabbed the dress off the counter and stormed away. Overwhelmed, her hands trembled in embarrassment, troubled by the stress of her mistreatment. Her heart fluttered like a terrified bird rattling in its cage.

"Call the police! That girl is stealing from us!"

"I didn't steal!"

Isis's steps went faster as she walked closer to the exit. Before her arms reached the glass door, her hair tugged from behind her head, pulling her away from her stressor. Her scalp screamed in pain as it yanked from the hateful clenches of the worker. The associate grabbed the dress, looping her hand with the straps. Fringe shook crazily like a handmade puppet's hair, and the seams began to separate from their stitching.

"I can't let you steal our merchandise!"

"I bought this!" Isis said, yelling as her fingers digging into the unraveling hem.

"People like you have stolen from this store for too long!"

"I didn't steal!"

Why won't you believe me?

The dress freed from the employee's grasp, thrashing like a mop head. The associate lunged at Isis, tackling her to the floor. Painful scratches pelted at her neck and forearms like a rabid feline being tormented by a child.

What the hell is this bitch doing?

Isis's palms became lacerated from her digging nails; her fist clenched before landing on the cheek of the employee, shoving her back. The associate wiped the oozing blood trickling from her lip. Her front teeth squeezed onto the wound, forcing it out quicker, gassing her up to pounce on Isis.

Why are people so cruel?

Isis and the assailant tumbled over the dirty floors, and clothing sprinkled over the tiling as racks were nudged with force. Her fury grew from the reminiscence of Creed's infidelity and the employee's accusation, fending the fighter off with forceful punches. Isis lunged her knee into the associate's stomach, causing a low-pitched howling roar that blared over the elevator music. The glass door quickly swung open. Two police officers sprinted inside the building, guns out of their holsters and aimed at her.

"Freeze!" one officer commanded.

Isis and the employee halted their brawl. Their hands hovered above their heads in compliance. Their hearts stopped in fear, stopping instantly with threat.

"She attacked me!" the associate said, breaking down in hysteria while she shuffled from Isis.

"No, I didn't!" Isis defended, her hands vibrating with trembles.

"She stole from us. And then got aggressive at me when I wouldn't refund her, and then she attacked me!"

"That's not true!"

The other officer ran toward Isis and tackled her to the floor. He grappled with her writhing body as she reacted to the intense pain while wrapping his handcuffs around her wrist.

Why won't you believe me? Someone please step up and tell them I'm not lying!

The sharp metal detainments cut deep into her tiny wrists as the officer perched her back on her feet. Unsteady, her ankles were weak as she teetered around, glimpsing every customer that was now eyeing her with intimidation.

"Officer, you've made a mistake," Isis said, pleading with every remaining ounce of energy she had.

"That's enough from you! We've heard enough."

As they escorted Isis out of the store, she looked behind to the cluster of customers staring at her with profound judgment, appalled at witnessing the brawl. The employee drank in every bit of encouragement from her manager, who tenderly placed his hand on her shoulder. She wailed with victimization, fanning her hands over her face to conceal the sudden eruption of tears as customers proceeded with their shopping. The employee glared back at Isis, and a huge, smug-like grin grew on her face, as though she was a toddler who won a tattling fight as the parents punished the innocent child.

Bitch.

ISIS SQUIRMED UNDER her constraints, vigorously trying to break away to freedom. The tiny fibers of the rope abraded against her aching wrists. Threads of dried twine flew from the constant friction of her frenetic movements. She used every ounce of her remaining withering strength to get to Sonya and escape. She ignored the angry roar of her stomach screaming to be filled with sustenance and erase the two days of emptiness. Her mouth barely produced saliva as her tongue rubbed against her parched lips underneath her burlap gag. She spread her arms wide, her arms crying out for ease.

The ropes began to separate from her arms, falling to the floor as they gave into the tension. She expelled a tremendous sigh of ease, digging her chipped nails into the ropes around. Her newfound energy rose, ignoring the pain, motivated to release herself as her ankles felt loosened.

The rickety floorboards creaked as she tiptoed with apprehension while she approached the heavy hatch. Her shoulders shuddered in agony as she lifted the door, using the weight of her falling body to pull it open. Clutching onto the railing, she descended the long-winding stairs to get out of the clock tower, her balance uneven as she battled falling over the edge.

She ran out through the cluster of sleeping willow trees, splashing her sandals into the deep puddles of water, drenching her tattered jumpsuit. Droplets from the leaves brought a slight reprieve on her dry tongue.

She approached the nearest spiral staircase through the kitchen and entrance hall. Her body became heavier and sluggish while she crutched herself up the stairs, clutching onto the metal railing tighter with each step.

I'm coming, Sonya!

The motivation of reuniting with Sonya was all she needed to push through the cramping pain of her biceps and thighs, combating the strain that felt like she was moving underwater.

She walked across the hallway, glancing at the lineup of paintings, recognizing the eerie expressions on each of the nun's faces, disregarding their presence. Catching herself on the bookshelf, the stare of Mother Superior halted her. Her green eyes pierced into her soul, leaving her frozen in fear. Her breath stifled, silenced by the grip of a black-gloved hand. She wriggled in panic as the other wrapped around her waist, digging deep into her tender gut, disabling her, pulling her back. Isis tried to scream through the muffled fibers of the glove. Her throat scratched horribly, her vocal cords rattling in pain.

Nothing came out.

Helpless, she didn't know what to do. Her imprisonment would slowly kill her, drying her out like a withering plant.

She needed help.

Using her last bit of hope, she removed the black rubber bracelet before a pinch stung her right bicep. A syringed sedative jolted into her body. Her eyelids drooped down, drifting out of consciousness. Her hands fell to her side like a dead body. The bracelet tumbled out of her palms, falling to the floor right in front of Mother Superior.

SONYA'S EYELIDS OPENED slowly, the faint soreness of her muscles discharged achy alerts to her brain. Her strained abdomen tensed as she hunched forward, shaking off the grogginess from the sedative that had knocked her out the night before. She swung her bruised legs over the edge of her bed, blood rushing toward her cold toes. Her foggy vision blurred over like a muggy summer morning in the Midwest countryside. She winced in pain as she struggled to adorn herself in her usual black clothing. She placed her pants and shirt on slowly, catering to the extreme sensitivities of her tender body.

She exited her room, not even hearing a peep of a roaring snore she expected to thunder out from Cora's door. Her patience was worn out thin that she had no interest in trying to endure anything related to her. In the hallway, she stopped at the portrait of Mother Superior, glaring into her green eyes winking at her.

"I hate you," Sonya hissed at the painting before proceeding to breakfast, scuffling her feet.

She walked toward the door, the sole of her sneaker cracking as it ground upon something. Removing her foot, a black elastic bit bounced away from her. She stopped to observe the object to pick it up. She regarded the similarities to the other bracelets wrapped upon her wrist, remembering the person she had gifted the accessory to. Her fist hugged the bracelet, frustrated.

Frustrated with the number of lies that she had received from the people.

Frustrated with Cora.

Frustrated with being assaulted by a masked nun and nobody believing her.

She stormed out of the hallway and stomped down the spiral staircase to search for answers. She needed to know where Isis went. Now.

"Ophelia!"

Chapter 27

June 2006

A THUNDEROUS ECHO FROM the door overtook the empty dining hall as it slammed into place, interrupting the deep conversations between the entire group. For once, Cora appeared to be invested since arriving, smiling in Ophelia's direction before snapping into her serious demeanor with annoyance toward Sonya.

Sonya's stomping footsteps shook up the table of breakfast cereals like a slight earthquake trembling the assortment of nourishments.

Captain Crunch cringed.

The Trix rabbit felt trapped.

Charms weren't feeling so lucky.

Noticing the young lady's frustration, Sheldon braced the shaking glass of orange juice trickling a tiny droplet down the side. Ophelia shed a startled expression, her jaw dropping with nerves interrupted by the teenager's wrath. Amber showed cringing concern toward the tantrum, moving closer to their table. Joseph's milk fell from his cup from the force of Sonya's palm, slapping the surface; the white stream seeped around her clenched fist before she let go of the bracelet.

"Sonya!" Joseph scolded, reaching for a towel to wipe the substance, minimizing the drops soaking his penny loafers.

Ophelia sat there, not bothered by Sonya's behavior. Her stony expression remained solid like marble.

"Is that one of those *atrocious* bracelets that you wear?" Ophelia asked, taking a sip of her tea.

"Yes, it is."

"I never understood the point of those *ghastly* accessories, if that's what you kids call them. It doesn't even have any pearls or diamonds. People shouldn't consider those bracelets. So cheap!"

"Well, some of us can't afford gaudy jewelry like you."

"You should focus on bettering yourself so that you can succeed in society. With my help, you could one day obtain the nicest of things."

She took another sip, allowing the heat to clear her throat.

"Such as profiting from troubled children and then making them vanish?"

Ophelia choked on her beverage, startled by her accusation. She patted her lips with her napkin, the fibers barely touching the red of her lips.

"Yes, and?"

"I gave this bracelet to Isis on the first night we were here. I found it this morning!"

The adults studied the simple black rubber band, solemn, staring as it swam in a small puddle of milk. Tiny bubbles clung around the piece, looking like the top of a latte.

"Perhaps she left this for you to have when she departed?" Joseph asked, unimpressed by Sonya's behavior, clustering wads of soaked paper towels away from him.

"Maybe. However, this was in front of the portrait of Mother Superior. I have been by those paintings many times since I got here, and this was never there any other time."

Believing Sonya, Amber looked with concern at Ophelia. Eager to dig into his meal, Sheldon's hand shook as he scooped up his cereal. His Raisin Bran flaked away from his mouth in his trembling grasp. The program master stared deep into Sonya, squinting her eyes with fury like a predator.

"What are you trying to say, child?" Ophelia asked, placing her tea cup onto the table and adjusting her chandelier earrings from her clavicle.

"I'm saying that Isis wasn't removed from the program. I think she's still here," said Sonya with assurance, her focus not distracted from the mixed reactions.

"Really?"

"Yes, really. And I think you have something to do with this!"

"Me?" Ophelia asked, fluttering the tips of her fingers on her chest, barely meeting the top of her breasts.

"Yes. And did you tell anybody that Griffwood Manor was used for conversion therapy?"

Amber's eyes widened in disbelief, blindsided by Sonya's accusations. Unaware of what she signed up for, her appetite diminished with the drop of her spoon.

"Ophelia, is this true?" Amber asked, shoving her plate away from her.

Ophelia said nothing. Her nostrils huffed a gigantic breath, her arms crossed, challenging Sonya's hypothesis.

"Nothing?" Sonya said, leaning over the table. "A wise woman full of *so* many words, and you say nothing?"

"Ophelia?" Amber asked again, her pitch heightened with clear heartbreak. "Why didn't you tell us about this place?"

"None of that matters," Ophelia said, responding without care. "That is irrelevant."

"Oh really? Then why are only gay and bi teens here for your program? Tom, Leslie, and I are. I'm going to safely assume that Cora and Isis are as well. Did you know?"

"I didn't know!" she hissed coldly, her eyebrow twitching.

"Did you?"

Amber bowed her head at the table, full of guilt. She was ashamed for signing up to be a part of Ophelia's staff, blindly unaware of her intentions. Cora rolled her eyes, obliviating conversation, digging back into her lukewarm porridge.

"Coincidence?" Ophelia said.

"Coincidence? Coincidence that you tricked our parents into enrolling us in a program used for conversion, but telling them it's because we were in trouble with the law."

"Well, all of you needed help."

"Help? I guess attacking your subjects dressed up as nuns is part of your therapy plan, is it?"

"Pardon?" Ophelia questioned. Her charcoal penciled eyebrow perched toward her well-groomed hairline.

"One of you has been dressing up as Mother Superior and hurting us."

"Mother Superior?"

Ophelia placed her hand back on the table, no longer playing along with the child's antics. Her confusion perked from the sudden update.

"The nun in the painting!" Sonya said, barking with fury. "Joseph and Amber told Tom and me about Mother Superior. She creeps around the grounds late at night and takes all the misbehaved children or some stupid shit like that."

Joseph hissed, laughing with disbelief, milk flying out of his mouth.

"Come on, Sonya. It was just a dumb story. None of it is true!"

"Then who the hell keeps attacking me and the rest of us?!"

"Maybe you're all doing it for attention," Cora said, her antagonistic tone sharpening.

"Excuse me?" Sonya said, turning quickly toward the last person she wanted to deal with, whose arms were perched across her chest like an unbothered mafia don.

"Ms. Martin, let us handle this," Ophelia said, irritated.

"I'm getting fed up with your 'pity me' shit," Cora continued. "All of you are whiny, weak, and don't deserve to live."

"What did you say?" Sonya's gut jolted.

"You heard me. You're weak. You're trash. You're nothing!"

The word "weak" echoed repetitively throughout her mind, reliving the trauma from the girls in her class, Darris, Blade, Pastor Ryan, and even her parents. Perspiration beaded on her face as her fist clenched tight. Her blonde hair felt like warm acupuncture needles on her forehead, appearing whiter from the deep pink hues flushing her cheeks. Her stomach knotted a dozen times. Her past ridicule overwhelmed her as the room closed in on her, blacking out.

She sprang over to Cora, hitting her hard in the nose and sending her back to the floor. The chair shattered to dozens of pieces, breaking upon the impact. Sonya straddled over her, continuously punching Cora's cheeks. Ignoring her sore muscles, she didn't stop her fury.

Startled by Sonya's rage, Cora didn't fight back. Her hands flinched away from her face, retreating to cowardice. Screeching like a bat, she screamed at the highest pitch she could to negate her attacks. Blood accumulated on the floor, puddling around her body and soaking her jeans. Teeth rained like vicious drops of hail as Ophelia and Amber rushed over to stop Sonya's brawl.

"Joseph, the sedative!" Ophelia panted, her lungs tightening with nerves as she sprinted over to them.

"I don't have any," Joseph said, intimidated as his footing slowed the closer he got to her. "My supply is missing!"

"What?! Are you kidding me!"

"We don't need that crap!" Amber said.

Amber grabbed the back of Sonya's shirt, the fibers ripping as the child's relentless punching continued. Her bloody knuckles pounded into the victim's face, grunting ferociously, her mouth spitting blood like a sprinkler.

The taste of iron invigorated her tongue; tiny fibers of hair brushed against Sonya's teeth. Cora's odor was foul, with Sonya's nose buried in her scalp. Her eardrums screeched in pain from the bully's scream as Sonya's teeth dug deeper into her ear.

"Sonya! Sonya! Enough!"

She grabbed Sonya's arms, using all her strength to push them down to separate her. She covered her saucer-like pupils with trickles of tears, clearing a path through the blood over her cheeks; the sweat wiped away at the fluids dripping down her mouth and chin. Sonya's nostrils flared, huffing like a charging hippopotamus. Her teeth gritted so hard they started to form small cracks.

Sonya glanced at Amber's sorrowful expression, the tears of fear shining atop her empathy. The warmth of her body left her as she looked down at Cora who was flinching jolts of shock. Her bruised face swelled up and poured out a rapid rush of blood. Her consciousness diminished as the twitching movements of her arms became sluggish.

Sonya sobbed, collapsing onto Amber's shoulder with her usual innocent persona taking over. Her regret only internalized a bit. Her pride silenced the bullying voices with gusto.

"I'm not weak," Sonya whispered to Amber.

"I know."

The women left, crutching Sonya as the weight of her pain took over her again. Her shoes increased in mass as if someone poured cement.

"You two go get the first aid kit!" Ophelia commanded Joseph and Sheldon, already leaving the room, scuffing around with fear.

As the door slammed behind the women, another one opened from the other side. A shadow marched toward Cora while she coughed a wad of blood to add to her puddle on the floor. Her head fell to the side as her legs became elevated, her body dragging toward the other end of the dining hall. Her once tough exterior had now been exposed as the cocky, overcompensating character as she collapsed defenseless and alone. Blood drifted alongside her, leaving a trail of her truest self as she went closer to the open basement door.

THE WOMEN ENTERED THE office doors with haste. Sonya's weeping intensified into panic, echoing in the silent entrance hall. The sisters cleared the path, terrified of the bloody gore. They noticed the faded cross imprint on the wood grain before planting Sonya into the mustard yellow chair, now turning to blood-orange. Amber coddled Sonya as Ophelia walked to the other side of her desk to grab a box of tissues.

"Now, my child," said Ophelia, intimidated as her once frantic tone leveled back to a more approachable one; timid from her inmates' unpredictability. "Violence is not the answer."

"I'm sorry, Ophelia." Sonya said as she wiped her tears, clearing her face like windshield wipers. "I don't know what came over me. I-I just blacked out."

"I'm glad you're okay," said Amber, swiping Sonya's sweaty hair away from her forehead, her heartbreak taking over her sorrow.

Sonya's heartbeat refused to settle as she clenched the arms of the chair, angered that they had left her questions unanswered. Her temples pulsated quickly. Motivated, she hunched her head at Ophelia, squinting her eyes fiercely back at her.

"Now, are you going to tell me about the nun?"

"I don't know what you're talking about."

"Cut the shit, Ophelia! How can a ghost story of Mother Superior get made, and then some nun miraculously shows up to attack us?"

Ophelia remained frozen; the glares from Sonya and Amber intimidating. The delinquent's eyebrow raised, her predatory focus desperate for answers. She was trapped, paralyzed from her delusions.

"There's a nun here! I know it. It's Mother Superior! Isn't it?"

"Just tell her the truth, Ophelia," Amber said, insisting from fear of Sonya's escalating intrigue.

"There is no nun! It wasn't Mother Superior! Mother Superior died of cancer! That story is made up!"

"Made up? How do you know that?" Amber asked as her spine tingled, cradling Sonya's head upon her shoulder for comfort.

"Because I made the story up!" Ophelia admitted, sighing as she helplessly collapsed into Amber's chair. "I used to be a resident at Griffwood Manor."

"As one of the children?" Sonya asked, startled.

"As one of the nuns! I'm Sister Ophelia Tate."

Chapter 28

October 1986

BRANCHES SWAYED TO the upbeat symphony of chilled wind; their arms danced like a patron at a rock concert. Leaves whipped the faces of the wandering children during their recess. Birds took roll calls before venturing south for the winter and flying to their temporary destinations. Two girls in matching tangerine sweatshirts playfully skipped in and out of Mother Nature's subtle and hypnotic movements. They giggled with glee, chasing each other in the frigid playground. The boys in the open grass continued their tackle football match, knocking each other to the muddy turf and sliding along the wet terrain.

A muffled groan came from the foot of the furthest tree next to the clock tower. Pleasure moaned as Buck and Frank enjoyed their escape. As the climax of their session wrapped up, the squishing footsteps of a wandering nun approached the base. The underpart of her oversized yellow rain boots sank into the deep piles of accumulating mud.

"That was great!" Buck said to Frank as he sidestepped outside. The zipper of his jeans let a tiny growl as the chain closed up.

"Thanks!"

Frank followed behind him while he adjusted his sweatshirt over his waist, fastening the brown leather belt through his pant loops.

"We should hang out after supper."

Buck reached his hand to guide him out of the rest of the crevasse.

"Maybe we should wait to do this again on another day," said Frank with apprehension, gathering his balance on an unsteady pile of mud. "I don't want us to give off any suspicions."

Buck remained silent, staring at the clock tower with disappointment; his face remained vacant as though he had spotted a ghost.

"I don't want us to get caught and have to deal with another one of their ridiculous punishments."

"I think we're too late for that," Buck said quietly.

Frank followed Buck's pointed finger toward the tower door where Sister June and Sister Tate stood. Their authority struck disappointment in their exposure. Their hands crossed over one another, perched close to their robed chests. The two women shook their heads as they walked closer to them, ignoring the unsteady terrain.

"Shit," Frank whispered as he bit his lower lip.

"Come with us, please," Sister June said firmly to the two boys.

Their hands dug deep into their biceps to guide them out of the wet, mucky paradise.

Buck and Frank bowed their heads near their shoulders. They marched with shame back to the establishment like dead men walking to the guillotine. Their unsteady footsteps from their soaked tennis shoes slid on the ground's slick surface, and fingernails embedded deeper into their skin, crutching them. Football players paused, ignoring an upcoming touchdown as they all stood up to acknowledge their shameful march. The two tagging girls giggled, concealing their smiles behind their drenched sleeves.

Chunks of fertilizer-like mud trickled behind them as they trudged up the stairs, leaving a track of the clumpy earth toward the entrance doors. The group turned to the open office door. They met up with Sister Magdalena, sitting at her desk enjoying her afternoon reading, eyes focused deep inside her pages.

"Sisters," she said sharply, shutting the book with a sigh. "What is going on here?"

"Sister Tate found these two fornicating by the clock tower," Sister June said, her tone matching one of a tattling child.

"Is this true, Sister Tate?"

Sister Tate stood there frozen in fear, afraid to tell the truth. Her moral guidance of being honest was being blinded by her connection with Frank, reminiscing about the sad innocence from his first date. She said nothing, only nodding her head to acknowledge the accusation. Turning her head from Frank's saddening glare, she ignored the betrayal by the once welcoming and trusting persona that she once shed to him.

"Very well," Sister Magdalena said, pursing her lips. "Sisters, I think we need to resort to advanced practices."

"No, no, no!" Sister Tate said, interjecting with apprehension as Sister June cut in front of her, marching toward Buck to grab his arm. "It was just a simple mistake. These boys mean well!"

"Sister Tate, are you having second thoughts about what has been taught to us to follow for the sake of eliminating sin?" Sister Magdalena asked her, pacing closer to Sister Tate to where they were inches apart. Her lip quivered as she stared into Sister Magdalena's jewel-green eyes. Her intimidation drew away from her like a polarized magnet. Sister Tate began pinching the fibers of her wet, black sleeves as she shook her head.

"Great," Sister Magdalena said, grinning with falsified glee, grabbing Frank as she escorted the two boys out of the office. "Off to the basement for treatment!"

"The basement?" Frank asked, concerned. "What's down there?"

The door swung open to the entrance hall. The forceful yanking of Frank's arm was so taut that he felt his arm was being ripped out of his socket, his bones grinding away from his joints. Buck wept in shame and had nothing to say while he complied with Sister June's guidance, followed by Sister Tate's quiet sobs, who followed the group toward the dining hall and swung the basement door open.

"Sister Magdalena, are you sure you want to do this?"

Sister Magdalena shoved Sister Tate's arm back to her side before caressing her chin to encourage her obedience.

"Solitary confinement is just what these children need in order to be cleansed."

Sister Magdalena trudged down the stairs, tugging on the solo light bulb's string, causing it to leap away in terror from her focus. The ghostly whaling of children greeted them, crying to be freed from the clutches of the occupied rooms in the dark, deserted hallway. Panic flooded Buck and Frank, combating the closing of their throats rejecting their nervous gulps of saliva. The impending sense of dread of being abandoned in pure darkness grew with nobody to hear their cries.

Nobody to care for them.

Sister Magdalena opened the nearby door, a white, padded room with a grubby mattress on the floor. Frayed fibers flaked along the seams of the stitching. The stench of rotting death reeked as flies danced around the fecal remnants along the wall next to the metal bucket in the corner. The space personified the fusion of a mental hospital and a prison cell fit for any neglecting adult that would punish a non-compliant inmate.

"Buck, you'll be staying here for a few days," Sister Magdalena said as Sister June ushered him inside.

"A few days?" Sister Tate asked, startled with shock. "Those poor boys will starve!"

"It's all part of the process. These two need their slate cleaned so their true healing can begin in reflection."

"Please, don't do this!"

Buck's throat choked on his tears as Sister Magdalena slammed the door in his face before locking it with her oversized key ring.

"And for you," Sister Magdalena added as they trekked down to the end of the corridor, turning to the left to go into the open exam room, which was more lit than the dark hallway. "You've been troubled since you stepped foot on these grounds. I think you need a little something extra."

"Extra?" Frank asked with confusion as he studied the metal table with a bright dangling headlight above it like a spotlight on a vital prop of a stage performance.

"A little electroshock therapy will jolt out those perverse thoughts in your head."

Frank's arm throbbed from Sister June's grasp, sweeping him off his feet. She carried his squirming body toward the table, ignoring his thrashing limbs.

"NO!" Frank screamed, full of fear, his throat scratching with desperation. "PLEASE!"

Sister Magdalena and Sister June strapped his squirming arms and legs down with the tan leather belt straps, followed by his chest and forehead. Rapid tears flew as he broke down, the dangling light blurring over his head.

“Please don’t do this. I’ll be good. Tell me what I need to do and I’ll do it. I promise!”

The wooden piece sliced his tongue; he gagged on his spit as they forced it into the back of his jaw.

Sister Tate placed her hands over her mouth in disbelief that the sisters were facilitating this treatment to children. Her breath shortened, saddened by their torment.

How could she do this? He's just a kid.

The machine powered on, giving a gradual charging roar over the silence. The two nuns bowed their heads, prayers mumbling as they ask for cleanliness and purity. Frank looked up to the subtle grin that was shed on Sister Magdalena's face as the fabricated forked prong was placed over his temples.

"May peace be with you," she said as her finger flipped the switch.

Without a second to breathe, jolts of shock rapidly took over his body from head to toe. Sparks rained onto the floor. His spine arched back as though he were being exercised from a demon. His teeth cracked as they embedded hard onto the wooden piece, crunching into the gag. He groaned while the overhead light danced in and out of his sight like a relentless strobe. After a minute, his figure straightened to normal, allowing the last bit of electricity to course through his system. The never-ending convulsive twitching of his muscles settled.

"He can handle another round. Don't you agree, Sister Tate?" Sister Magdalena asked as her fingers caressed the nearby dial, turning up the voltage. "Maybe a stronger dose could get all those thoughts out of his system for good."

"Please, stop!" Sister Tate said, her tears of shame spewing from the underparts of her eyes. "This is immoral! I'm begging you!"

Sister Magdalena placed the fabricated fork back onto Frank's temples. His body jolted even worse than before, his bones cracking in hyperextension. Glass from the medicine cabinet broke behind them, unable to tolerate his high-pitched scream. His screech silenced the mourning cries of the nearby children. The overhead light flickered from the excessive power.

I'm so sorry, my dear Frank.

Sister Tate couldn't handle seeing any more of Frank's punishment. She ran out of the room, her hands cupped over her ears, hoping to tune out the electrifying pain inflicted as she sobbed horribly. She collapsed by a nearby padded room door, the shame and guilt pierced into every fiber of her being as though she were being shocked herself. The bellow of Frank's anguish resonated deep within her brain as the children howled, begging to be freed from the inescapable containments of Sister Magdalena and her punishments.

Chapter 29

June 2006

"YOU USED TO BE A NUN here?" Amber asked, her hand hovering over her dropped jaw.

"Yes," Ophelia responded, bowing her head in shame.

"So, you took part in conversion therapy?"

Sonya rose from her chair to lean over the mortified leader, interrogating her like an aggressive detective desperate to solve their case.

"It wasn't like I was in full support of the practice."

"You administered unethical treatments to innocent children! What's the problem with letting kids just be who they want to be?"

"Well, the book says—"

Sonya's fists pelted onto the chair's wooden arms. The wood creaked a painful woe as her knuckles pained.

"Forget what the book says! It seems like all you thumpers do is use a passage or two as a crutch to alienate and mistreat people while you disregard everything else!"

"That's not true," Ophelia said with her arms crossed, her eyes avoiding to look at Sonya.

"Bullshit! You all judge and ridicule, then pray for forgiveness so you can all repeat your hatred all over again!"

"Sonya, that's not how *every* religious person is," Amber said. "Many people are loving and accepting no matter what the teachings are."

"Well, they don't stand up in the face of sin and call them out on their crap!"

"That may be true, but we shouldn't categorize all of them into a certain box. I know your experience with the church wasn't the greatest ever since they outed you. But you shouldn't think of all of them as corrupt."

"Right," Sonya said, glaring at Amber. "We just remain silent as their leaders shove their personal beliefs mixed with loosely written passages and *hope* that the congregation can filter out the bullshit!"

"That's not it at all!" Amber said, reclusing toward her desk.

"And besides, this isn't a session," Sonya said, stomping her foot, shaking the leaves of Amber's sunflower decoration. "Therapy is over!"

Ophelia and Amber froze in silence as Sonya's frustration dominated the room. She paced around the office with her anger being ready to go off at any minute like a loose cannon. The adults leaned onto each other in protection, hoping neither one would fall victim to the young girl's wrath.

"So, you stood by the church running this conversion therapy camp, and you went around telling these kids a little ghost story about Mother Superior that ended up being a stupid lie?"

"First of all, Griffwood Manor didn't solely do conversion therapy," Ophelia said, placing her hands gracefully back onto her lap. "We took in many troubled kids."

"All of which happened to be gay or bisexual?"

"Some of them have had attraction toward members of the same sex, yes," Ophelia confirmed. "And the story about Mother Superior was to add a little fun. They're kids, after all."

Sonya's foot tapped like a ticking old-fashioned stopwatch. She tried to contain her indignation against Ophelia's contradiction; her fingernails dug into her hand.

"Mother Superior passed from complications with her health. These kids needed some excitement in their lives here. I saw the sorrow and loneliness of being away from their loved ones. I felt like if I did some under-the-table humor with them to help ease the seriousness, it would make their time here somewhat enjoyable."

"Then who keeps dressing up in the orange mask with green eyes?"

"Green eyes?" Ophelia asked, confused. "Mother Superior's eyes were blue!"

"Who is the lady in the portrait?"

"That's Sister Magdalena. After Mother Superior died, she took over. She was far more traditional and despised certain people, and she would add more intense treatments to the program to combat their feelings. None of us were fond of her."

"Intense treatments?" Amber asked, her interest steeped in disbelief as she rose from her chair.

"All we did was prayer and scripture reading. When she took over, the time for prayer became much more common, along with the use of holy water, fasting, solitary confinement, and electroshock. Things of that sort."

"Electroshock?" Amber asked, gasping with disgust.

"Yes, electroshock. I was stunned to find out we were giving this treatment to the children. I couldn't bear to witness another child go through such torment as a cover-up to convert them. I was about to turn her in for her excessive practices, but she disappeared shortly after. She used it on poor little Frank."

"Who's Frank?" Amber asked.

"Frank was a sweet little boy that meant no harm. He was full of potential. He was the last person to have electroshock administered.

The sadness in his eyes stung deep into my soul and I wanted to make things right."

"Which is why you started this program?"

"Nobody could get through to Sister Magdalena. It was too late to change things when they shut us down after she disappeared."

"Disappeared?" Sonya asked, concerned.

"Yes, nobody knows where she ran off to. It was like she vanished into thin air and never returned."

Amber and Sonya looked at each other with equal shock at her confession. The tables turned as Sonya had to secure Amber's heartbreak, caressing her shoulder when noticing her quivering chin.

"Soon after her disappearance, they pulled the plug on the program. I brought this program back to help any struggling child. I've seen so much harm done to these children. It killed me. I wanted to ensure that I could do everything in my power to better them with no use of harm or torment. No conversion techniques, just therapy and trust exercises. I swear."

"Then why were all of us chosen?" Sonya asked. "It wasn't a coincidence that we ended up here."

"It has to be a coincidence," said Ophelia. "I knew nothing about you all. I get the call that a fitting candidate is qualified to participate in this program. And then I rush over and do my part to convince the officers to allow this chance for you all instead of being locked away in a juvenile detention center and possibly repeating your mistakes."

"Calls from who?"

The office lights flickered horribly, startling the three and pausing their conversation. Amber walked closer to the door, desperate to settle her nerves.

"I thought you said that the power was all updated?" she asked Ophelia.

"I had it all updated, darling," Ophelia said, her face frozen as she got up from her chair. "It must be some excessive use of power that is causing the lights to weaken."

"Well, then we should check it out," Amber said, opening the door to usher the other two into the empty entrance hall.

"Sonya, wait!" Ophelia said, grabbing Sonya by her arm to stop her. "I never wanted to do anything to hurt you or anybody else here, I promise."

Unconvinced, she ignored her plea and swallowed her pride. Now was not the time for argument. Somebody was up to no good once again; somebody who had inflicted trouble before.

"Let's just get everybody else and get out of here."

The three raced across the entrance hall. The flickering of the lights danced in and out like the offspring of a techno nightclub and a haunted house. They entered the emptied-out dining hall, where a streaking trail of blood led to the open door of the basement. A cloud of white smoke emerged from the dimly lit doorway as the stench of cooked meat engulfed the once-stale room. Chills crept up the spines of the clustered women. They clenched each other's arms, the sharp dig of their fingernails embedding into tender skin. Their bodies tensed as the warmth of their rising body heat became stuffy.

"Come on, we need to find the other three," Sonya said, shaking off her fear and jogging toward the basement with brave gusto. "Let's go!"

"Sweetie, shouldn't we split up and look in the other areas?" Ophelia asked, her body quivering in faint apprehension.

"No more splitting up! Come on."

Ophelia trailed behind Sonya and Amber with cowardice, descending the staircase toward the basement corridor with trepidation. The memories of wailing children echoed in her mind while she relived the pain and torment inflicted by Sister Magdalena. The whining pleads for mercy blinded her. Her eyelids fluttered;

temples pulsated. Her sorrow took over her when she recognized she had cosigned the confinement of innocent children locked in the padded rooms created for torment and reflection as punishment for trying to live their lives as their truest selves. The crevasses of her defined crow's feet streamed tears of heartbreak before falling down her wrinkled cheeks.

The smoke became heavier the closer the three were to the end of the hall. Sonya and Amber joined Ophelia in the episode of tears as the burnt aroma blinded their vision. Their lungs became heavy from inhaling the charred stench of burning meat.

Sparks rained along the lone opening, spackling in and out of the thick, gray veil. A machine hummed loud, drowning out their eardrums. Limbs danced through the sheet of smoke; arms jiggling, legs wiggling, flailing mercilessly, waving the clouds away from the chrome table. Blood puddled on the floor, creating a moat around the table. The frayed-denim edges combusted, cinching the fibers of her clothes. The body groaned horribly from the remaining bits of air.

It was Cora.

The remaining flesh from her burning skin began to peel away from the ruthless jolt of the electroshock machine, wiping out the last ounce of life pulsating through her veins. The ladies' shoes crunched on the shards of shattered teeth that continued to sprinkle out of her mouth to the cement floor.

"We need to get out of here!" Sonya said, yelling as the machine's power roared down. Her voice was barely noticeable over the pitchy scream penetrating their ears.

Sonya and Amber waited for Ophelia to lead the way. Their hands were doused in hot sweat between their fingers. The smoke drifted away while they scoped the room, looking for the third part of their trio to exit first.

But nobody else was there.

Sonya and Amber squatted closer to the floor, checking under the block of grayish-black air for the remaining pair of legs.

Nothing was there.

They grabbed arms and squeezed tight as they found their way out to head back into the dining hall, facing the realization that Ophelia was nowhere to be seen.

Chapter 30

June 2006

"WHERE THE HELL DID she go?" Sonya asked, confused, the two waving their free hand to disperse the fumes out of their path.

The waltz of smoke died down as they reached the hallway. The tempo of their footsteps increased while they sprinted closer to the stairs, desperate to escape. Light bulbs extinguished as the duo rushed into the dining hall, only disclosing a small ray of light from the half-closed curtain. It showcased an overcast beam of light shining through the untouched part of the gigantic window. They panted for a reprieve; their chests lightened as they hacked out their bodies' toxic remnants of burned flesh.

"We need to find the others!"

A hefty wad of chester-brown mucus expelled onto the hardwood floors from Sonya's mouth. The impact of her spit echoed loud in the darkened, deserted room. Not a single sister to be found to come to their aid.

"I think we should call for help," Amber said, her arms placed above her head to open her chest to its fullest capacity. "Where are the nuns?"

"It won't do us any good. We're in the middle of nowhere. It will take them *forever* to come!"

Amber grasped Sonya's arm as she walked to the nearby kitchen door, halting her from venturing further away from her.

"Sonya, I know you're trying to be brave," said Amber, trying to calm the wound-up patient, her hand clenched to her bicep. "You're not alone in this like you've been before, and you don't need to feel like you have to show strength. It's okay to be scared and trust other people for help."

"I know."

"You and I are in this together. I have your back. We need to call the police and let *them* handle this. Okay?"

A tear glistened from Sonya's eyes. Nobody had ever gifted their full support to her. She always felt like she was a lone wolf having to navigate through this world with acquaintances who either broke her trust or individuals that were temporary social fulfillments. The comforting ease from Amber's thumb as it swiped the tear of pain kept her focused.

"Okay, but one more thing."

Sonya ran into the kitchen. The door swung back and forth while the chiming sounds of silver clashed feverishly. The jingle of utensils ricocheted off the tiled floor like the legs of a wind chime flailing zealously on a gusty morning. Within seconds, the door's swinging replenished from Sonya's exit as she carried out a handful of large knives, reaching out to Amber to hand her a few.

"Take these," Sonya said, her face reflecting off the blade. "We need to protect ourselves."

"From what?" Amber asked, taking two thin steak knives and clutching them into her palms.

"The nun," she said coldly.

Sonya led Amber out of the dark dining room into the even darker entrance hall. Amber's heart thudded against her shoulder; the atypical irregularities tapped her back.

"Where can we find a phone?"

"My office has one," said Amber, pointing the tip of one of her knives toward her door.

They meandered into the waiting area next to Amber's office. They entered the well-lit room where they were once a trio. Their eyes flinched from initial blindness, white blurring their sight before the outlines of furniture became clearer. The open window illuminated the room better than any other. Amber thrusted the phone quickly and pounded the three digits to call the police.

Nothing.

"The power is out, duh!"

A boom of thunder shook the grounds. The two women flinched from the shrieking of mother nature's harmony accompanying the horrific events as the ground trembled. The overcast sky darkened, diminishing the sole ray of light that once assisted the two, concealing its brightness to one of a lone tea candle. They couldn't find each other as the darkness engulfed them.

"My cell phone," Sonya said, chiming in. "Sheldon locked all of them in his office!"

"Okay, let's go."

They walked out into the entrance hall, the relentless pelting of raindrops beating against the door like a bully on its victim in a ravenous pursuit of lunch money. Their pacing increased with the rapidity of their pounding heartbeats. Their muscles twitched in fear, jolting fiercely with each strike of thunder. Sonya reached inside her pocket to grab her paperclip tool as they approached Sheldon's office to prepare herself for another break-in. Her fingertips tapped around the cold frame, trying to find the knob to begin her work. Her fingernail sunk into a sharpened and indented hole along the edge.

"What the hell?"

Her two fingers inserted themselves through the hole as she realized the doorknob had been broken off, chipped from its foundation.

She pulled the door open. The office was engulfed in complete darkness that made the room stuffy with mystery. Amber ushered herself with haste around Sonya's minuscule movements to navigate the premises to find any phones.

"He locked them in a steel box," Sonya said, gliding her hands upon the desk, the smooth papers grazed underneath her fingertips.

"Okay."

They resumed fumbling through the piles of documents and knick-knacks, knocking trinkets to the floor. The impact resonated throughout the emptied room next to them. Frustration settled, the two could find no use in recovering any trace of steel lock boxes while navigating through the darkness.

"This is pointless. I can't find a damn thing."

"Don't lose hope," said Sonya. Her elbow knocked another stack of papers to the floor, and there was a faint fluttering as the sheets plummeting downward.

An uproar of power revved up from all directions; lights from above flickered, awakening them from their brief snooze. The electricity had returned to the establishment. Relief was unsuccessful at returning to Sonya and Amber as they comprehended the entire room as being covered with splotches of red liquid. Blood had engulfed the palms of their hands from blindly guiding themselves around the clutter of possessions. Amber quivered with terror, disgusted by the gore. The overwhelming doom of being surrounded by what looked like a crime scene in a slaughterhouse was too much. Every bobblehead had at least one drop over it; some were utterly doused.

Sonya bit her lip to conceal her crippling anxiety as she acknowledged the single portrait of Sheldon. His child had dripping blood splats overshadowing their picture's joy. It covered most of Sheldon's face and hovered over the top half of his young, barely revealing the joyful smile and prominent mole on its cheek.

Her toes felt the retracting cushion of a heavy block as she tried to move it. Her heart dropped, turning the blockade with her heel. The paleness glowed through the spackles of dried blood. The blue-green checkered shirt was drenched in crimson. A fleshy nipple peeked out of the tear from the disheveled pocket next to his heart.

"Sheldon," she said over Amber's shocked gasp.

"We need to get out of here," Amber said, combating the tickling gag in her throat while her hand yanked Sonya's arm to escort her out of the office.

"Where should we go?" asked Sonya, wiping the blood off her thigh.

"We'll make a run for it," Amber said, insisting, ushering her toward the front entrance. "Come on! I'll be right behind you!"

Amber used all her weight to barge open the door, allowing Sonya to exit into the thrashing rain. Her spine tingled from the chill of the wind, her eyes blinded from the relentless drizzle as she crutched herself along the railing.

The lights went out again. Amber froze in fear, holding the door handle tight for comfort. She muttered silent phrases to herself, trying to remain calm.

The power came back on once again. Amber took in a deep breath before following behind her. A frosty pain slapped her forehead like microscopic ice cubes asserting themselves onto her skin. Her blouse weighed her down as the hem continued to accumulate water. She tried to combat her aching chest that took the beating of her racing heart.

A tug coming from the back of her scalp, causing Amber to screech in pain as it prevented her to continue like a stimulated dog on a leash. Another pull thrust her back as though a divine force shoved her into the imprisoning abyss of the building. Her breath shortened as she disappeared back inside the Manor. Sonya ran back up the stairs; catching Amber tumbling back to the center of the entrance hall, plummeting onto the rugs.

"Amber!" Sonya said, crying out in desperation, racing to beat the door as it closed in on Amber, separating her from the one partner still on her side.

Amber rubbed the back of her head as she gathered her bearings, wincing in pain while her fingernails scratched her scalp for relief. Pulsating aches began to die down with each press of her fingers. The pounding on the door became muffled by Sonya's frantic knocks. The metal screeched as she tried to yank the sturdy handle. Her jaw fell closer to the floor as the cloaked figure stood between her and the door. The shiny orange mask reflected in the light. The jewel-green eyes glistened with a wink as its hand latched the door shut to lock Sonya out in the freezing chilly rain and Amber inside.

Chapter 31

June 2006

AMBER HYPERVENTILATED while the panic paralyzed her body. Persistent knocking echoed inside the entrance hall, growing with the frantic pounding of Sonya's fist thrusting upon the door. Lights flickered repeatedly, highlighting the orange plastic of their face. The nun revealed the sharpened wooden cross behind them, clenching its black glove around the intersection between the two stakes. Drops of opaque red trickled down the tip from the rainwater mixing with blood.

Amber's eyes widened in disbelief; Sonya had been telling the truth the entire time. She wasn't making up these visions of an assailant, and now she was trapped inside the building with nobody to help her.

Nobody to save her.

"Amber!"

Sonya screamed at the top of her lungs, hoping it carried over the aggressive gusts of loud, whistling wind.

"Open this door! Please, don't leave me out here alone!"

Amber scuffled back, trying not to shed any sign of her fear to give the killer satisfaction. The nun lunged toward her, allowing the weapon to guide its upcoming strike. Amber rolled over as the cross missed her by less than six inches; its sharp point ground against the floor and permitted her to hook her arm into her assailant to shove them aside. She thrusted herself back upon her feet to run into the chapel behind her, closing the door without hesitation to lock them out.

Her breath trembled while her arms slid down the door, secure from being away from her attacker. Her pulse tapped like an insistent door-to-door salesman.

BANG!

The door moved from a forceful thrust with the latch fastening the two pieces of wood together. She gasped with terror, pacing away as the nun attempted to shove open like a bull ramming toward its confining gate.

BANG!

PELTING DROPS OF WATER drenched Sonya's clothes, her back stinging like tiny needles. Her breath floated around her like a thought bubble, engulfing every part of her shivering body. Her hair drooped over her eyes, the wet tips poking her eyebrows. She climbed down the stairway, squinting to make sense of the countryside with rain continuing to haze.

She ran around the building, her sneakers slipping with each step on the mud as though she were gliding on black ice. Patches of ground gripped her ankles like quicksand, impeding her attempt to sprint toward the back door. She had no choice but to take the longer route through the thick jungle of willow tree branches. The heavy raindrops trickled down the vines, forming deep puddles of water.

She grasped the foliage to guide around the pools. Her footing became easier to navigate with the relieving assistance of her upper body, bracing her balance to pull herself out of the wet cement-like mud. The soles of her sneakers drifted away from the heels of her feet. Branch after branch, she guided herself through the thickened terrain like a caveman swinging on jungle vines.

Sonya's biceps screamed with throbbing pain while she used all her upper body to maneuver through the ever-so-thickening path of muddy terrain. They engulfed the lower part of her shins. Her balance became unsteady as the weakness of her trudging caught up to her. Her calves stung in agony, drawing closer to the end of the patch of willow trees. A door flailed open to the blistering winds sweeping it. Her knees buckled like a geriatric person trying to walk without their cane. Her ankle crackled, giving into its sprain and losing her balance. Her palms burned as leaves broke off, sliding into the mud.

AMBER STEPPED BACK in fear; the blitzing charges against the chapel doors grew in strength, cracking the fibers of the aged wood. The candles shook like a hypothermic victim, desperate for warmth. Cobweb-encrusted banners neighboring the religious accessories flailed off the altar. Books thumped from the underside shelving of the multiple rows of pews, hindering Amber's vision, splatting gracious wads of dust upon impact like a cloud of chalkboard clouds caused by banging erasures.

Her tailbone caressed the sharp edge of the wooden altar, shaking the rest of the items toward the floor. The backside of a cold, hairy knuckle brushed against her disheveled brown hair, startling her. Her palm was shoved over her dropped jaw; gagging disgust reached its pique at the grotesque entanglement of Craig strung up, cradled alongside the wall. Hundreds of black and red beads glistened from the liquidity of the drops of blood sprinkling down to the carpet. His pale face was whiter than a crisp piece of paper. Every ounce of life drained out of his gasping expression. His bluish-pink lips pursed out, desperate for air. His arm reached out for a reprieve in the snare, like a fly spun upon a spider's web before being feasted.

The doors cracked further, the base of the entryway breaking more and more. Amber gasped as they were closer to coming in. Her eyes scanned every inch of the space, looking for a place to hide. Blood rushed through her veins quicker when she discovered the only place to hide was the grand piano in the corner, which was too obvious. Her kneecaps crackled when she squatted to the floor. The floor was cold under her forearms and legs as she crawled under one of the front pews. The door succumbing to the thrust of force made her heart stop.

The nun's footsteps reverberated through the emptied chapel like thunder as Amber attempted to calm her panicked breathing. Her hand grasped over her lips; the kitchen knife tucked securely into her pant pocket. Her chest rubbed against the carpet as she slowly crawled, her elbows trembling as they tried to stabilize her.

The nun scoped out the room, observing the emptiness, celebrating the reminiscent of their kill. Candles collapsed to the floor. Banners piled under their once peaceful home.

Amber moved past the nun who marched closer to admire Craig's corpse: its prized kill. The nun opened the top of a flask, showering the dead body for another passionate cleanse. Drop after drop, the water moistened the dried-out blood, replenishing the vibrant blackish-red hues before trickling to the carpet, joining a congregation of gore.

Amber got to her feet and ran out the door with haste. She pulled open the dining hall door with the remaining bit of strength, cringing at the rusty squeal of the hinges. Her footsteps clapped against the hardwood floors, creating a loud thunderous noise as she sprinted toward the kitchen. She drew closer to the swinging door, panting for a reprieve of fresh breath and freedom from her assailant.

Her fingertips grazed the door, safety becoming closer to her reach before retracting and pushing her back. Helpless, she flung herself to the floor and moved as fast as she could away from the killer entering the room. Her heels slid out of place, stuck in puddles of water, while she attempted to use them to push herself back away from the nun's predatory steps.

The nun rose its cross over Amber to attempt another strike. Her foot swiped at the nun's boot, giving her enough time to run back out as it toppled to the floor. She unsheathed her knife from her pocket and held it up like a tiny dagger, preparing to fight.

"All right, asshole!" Amber panted, hissing at the nun. "If you want to fight, let's fight!"

The nun cocked its head to the side, admiring the gusto coming from her as she slowly paced back. Silence engulfed the tension between the two as she strode to the center, drawing closer to the window, cornering her; her heart sprinted, and her extremities tingled numb. The room began to spin, barely making sense of them as it drew closer to her. The nun once again rose its cross to prepare for a strike. Doom crept over Amber, under-equipped with a dull utensil compared to a sharpened wooden weapon. The cross swiped down toward her, and she flinched her arms in front to defend herself. A pelting jab knocked her body back, thrashing into the window.

Glass shattered, slicing her back before she collapsed onto the muddy ground. Shards sprinkled onto her chest. The sharpening pain cut into her face upon impact. The hazy sky turned dark; her eyelids weighed down. Her body ignored the freeze as she drifted further away from consciousness.

GRAVITY PULLED SONYA down to the ground. Her face was planted into the moistened earth, spitting a heaping wad of mud before squirming toward the other end. She couldn't move fast enough from the earth's entanglements. A knotting pull came from her fingers like strands of rope were buried around her. She pulled the branches out of the ground, allowing the rain to wash away the mud caked over it.

She used the branch to guide her out of the trees to the end. Pull after pull, as though she were climbing a rope. Her shoulder blades screamed in pain as she utilized everything she could to aid her weakened self toward safety.

She crawled out of the pit, using her loosened knees to get herself on more reasonable terrain. She threw the branch back into the ground, gracious that mother nature was on her side while kicking off heavy chunks that weighed her down. Globs were shaken from her shoulders and shook her hands to sprinkle what she could so the rain could finish the rest. Between the rapid movements of the willow branches behind her, she could see Amber, who was lying in a pool of reflective, shattered glass. Coming around the corner was the nun circling past the gargoyle statues. She ran to hide for cover at the nearby tree, concealing herself into the hollowed-out base.

A temporary reprieve came from dodging the rain. Her hands touched a blockage coming from the inside, impeding her trek to safety. Wet, cotton-like fibers grazed her fingers. Two heads tilted as she pulled them back. One was a bluish-pale boy with orange hair caked in mud, and the other was a brunette with a wooden cross impaled through its skull. It was Leslie and Tom, lifeless, as the whites of their eyes barely peeked through the earthy remnants on their stiffened corpses, gasping for a second chance at life. Sonya screamed, falling back to the grounds. She hyperventilated, noticing the nun's eyes focused on her, its black cloak becoming bigger the closer it got. She looked back at the open door of the clock tower and sprinted inside, slamming the door behind her.

Sweat and rainwater trickled down her terrified body, shivering as Sonya observed the hay puddling the floor of the tower. The ever-winding stairs gradually built up to the ceiling of the unsteady structure. She started stepping one after another as fast as she could, wobbly creaks reacting with the step of her toes. Her calves burned as she reached closer to the top. One board breaks in half, causing Sonya to almost fall through. She grabbed onto a wooden pillar that braced the shingled walls, trying to ignore the embedded nail cutting deep into the raw palm of her hand. Pulling herself back up, she wiped the blood off her newly inflicted gash before continuing.

She reached the end of the stairs, being met with a heavy hatch, still with no nun in sight. Her hope was minimal, not knowing what is on the other side, if it can indeed open. Nervous, her mind scrambled to think of a different plan if it didn't work, being trapped on the stairs and the nun appearing at some point. She can't give up. She needs to live through this for everyone.

Her bloodied hands were joined by the slivers of wood poking into her. The muscles in her lower back pulled, the strain cried for relief as she dead lifted the door. It swung to the other side, swooping a cloud of dust into the dirty, dried-out attic. Broken, yellow glass surrounded her; the wind whistled pitchy through the cracks of the weathered-out tower.

In the corner sat a young woman, her marigold jumpsuit full of filth, tattered up, revealing the rope burns and cuts on her shins and thighs. Weakened with lethargy, she struggled to perch up her head to observe the new guest. Her baggy eyes drooped with heavy dark circles as she squinted to observe Sonya. Her melancholy expression showed through her gag as she huffed a sigh of relief.

"Isis!"

SHARDS OF GLASS CLATTERED as Amber regained consciousness. The stinging rain entered the gashing cuts on her face, rinsing out drops of blood from her cheeks and forehead. The velvet curtain joined the party of stormy weather while it danced outside the broken window. It flailed with the winds as she crawled out of the fragments that kept cutting deeper into her hands and knees. A door slammed in the distance, the panes of the clock tower lit, standing above the heads of the trees.

The gray sky cried tears of sadness upon her face. Her regret for not believing Sonya strained her heart. The aches of her muscles validated the damage she did for allowing danger to become inflicted on the children. Her neglect for safety paralyzed her.

Voices accumulated inside her head; mumbles gathered her attention. Above her in the demolished opening in the window, a slew of black and white grew as her focus gained the visibility of heads multiplying.

It was the sisters.

"Please protect our guests," said one of them.

"Please help him find salvation," said another.

"Get help," groaned Amber, her shoulder blades stung.

They ignored her, and the growth of chanting overwhelmed her. The lack of urgency irritated her.

"Please, help us!" she panted, ignoring the pain throbbing out of every part of her body.

She got back to her feet and trudged quickly through the mud. Rain whipped at her face like a slew of hands slapping her, whipping her senseless. The closer she made it to the trees, she noticed that the farthest tree neighboring the toolshed was an entangled body. Strung up with bunches of branches wrapped around his neck like a hangman's noose, his hands dangled and moved with the gusting of the relentless blows of the wind.

It was Joseph.

It motivated her to use every ounce of her strength to rescue Sonya. Someone needs to protect the child.

SONYA TIP-TOED ACROSS the unsteady planks of the floor, getting closer to Isis as she smiled with relief. She took the knife out of her pocket and started to cut off the rope that bound her feet to the chair. The dull blade sawed through the thick layers of twine, making minutes feel longer. Her eyes kept peering at the open passage, hoping that nobody else would join them.

"I'm so glad to see you," Sonya said, her arms jolting, full of control to loosen her quicker. "I missed you!"

Sonya took her other hand and removed the cloth gag tied around her mouth, wriggling it past her chin and neck.

"Sonya," Isis groaned, her raspy tone exiting through her peeling lips.

"We need to get out of here," Sonya said, the knife now venturing halfway through the rope.

"You have no idea how happy I am to see you," Isis said, her body squirming slowly, trying to free herself.

"Me too. A nun is out to get us. We're going to die if we don't get out of here soon."

Isis's eyes widened with shock as thundering footsteps distracted her, her state of ease dissipating slowly.

"Sonya!"

The nun stood at the hatch. Its hands grasped the wooden weapon as flashes of lightning illuminated its glossy orange mask. The green jeweled pieces in the eyes reflected from the dim light, jumping in and out of the enclosed space. Sonya stopped her rescue to face the killer, grasping at her blade while guarding Isis. She ignored the fear that once took over her when she was in the face of adversity. She would not let it paralyze her.

"I'm not afraid of you, you little shit! You can take off your mask now and fight me, Sheldon."

The nun cocked its head, intrigued by Sonya's bravery. A faint echo of wood slapped against the rotted planks as they dropped its weapon. The gloved hands wrapped around the white and black headdress to push it back and onto the floor, unlatching the straps that firmly fastened the mask. The mask lifted to reveal a yellowish grin, maniacal as it extended closer to his ears. His unibrow darkened from the room's shadows, blending with the deep wrinkles on his forehead. The lightning flashed on the exposed scalp of his faded comb-over as he picked the cross back up.

"Say your prayers, kids!"

Chapter 32

October 1986

FRANK ROCKED BACK AND forth, his hands grasped tight into his hair, padding the temples of his head to fortify the happy memories that began to fade away. His hunger pains roared like a ravenous lion communicating with its pack. He could barely see the pan filled with feces and urine that forced the musty aroma down his throat.

Solitary confinement had taken its toll on him, starving the urges out of him. He'd lost his desire to be with Buck; his yearning to be loved no longer existed. Muscles twitched from the memory of high-voltage shockwaves flooding his body. The voices of his happiness being diminished away, becoming overpowered by chants of cleanliness from the extreme forces of conversion therapy taking its course.

A click of a lock creaked the doorknob, and the padded door swung open. A younger nun walked in with a sandwich teetering like The Leaning Tower of Pisa. Her innocent demeanor oozed guilt with an open hand lent to assist Frank back onto his feet. It was Sister Tate; her long face showed guilt to have been a cosigner to his punishment.

"Sister Magdalena sent me to release you from your treatment," said Sister Tate, somber, her eyes focused on the grime on the surrounding walls.

Frank said nothing. He continued to rock back and forth, trying to unblur his shaky vision. He mumbled sweet-nothings, buzzing like a bumblebee.

"I'm sorry that all of this happened to you."

She stepped closer to him, reaching her hand onto his trembling leg.

"I'm not in support of Sister Magdalena and her methods. If I had it my way, we would kill off any negative forces with positivity and encouragement. If I had it my way, Sister Magdalena wouldn't be running the show the way she does."

Frank made little sense of what she was proclaiming to him. Only one word left her mouth that kept echoing in the back of his mind.

Kill!

Sister Tate sighed with disappointment, ashamed of herself. She crouched down to Frank. His eyes wandered, his pupils bouncing in every direction.

"Look, I promise you that this will be the last time she'll administer this type of treatment. One of these days, I'm going to take over this establishment. I swear to you I'll do everything in my power to mend the awful ties that have weighed down the troubled souls of this earth."

Kill!

Sister Tate reached her arms over Frank and guided him back onto his feet; his buckling knees unsteadied her. He mumbled louder to himself while he tried to regain his balance, feeling the blood go back into his feet as the tingling white noise in his toes lessened. The door swung shut, creaking loud to tune out the chorus of crying moans—wailing children begging to be released from their punishment. She handed him the sandwich and aided his hands with compressing it against his chest. His palms touched the porous fluff of the bread, and the wet slime of the bologna seeped through his shirt.

"Let me take you outside for some fresh air while you eat."

The two trudged up the rickety stairs; the percussion of the wood harmonized with the inmates' cries.

"You could use some after being locked away in that room for a week!"

They exited into the crowded dining hall. Long tables were squeezed into clusters of four, with dozens of children socializing over their lunch. The audible sound of laughter and yelling muffled the crescendo of commands growing in his mind.

Kill!

They walked through the kitchen, where two of the sisters were handwashing an excessive pile of dirty dishes. Foamy suds clung onto the sleeves of their black ensembles. They glanced at the frail, lethargic boy, acknowledging his weak haunch. The bags of darkened circles under his eyes stood above his sunken cheeks.

Sunlight blinded him as though he was in a heavenly kingdom when the white flash overwhelmed his sight. Fresh air began to wisp inside his nostrils, detoxifying the molded stench of death that brewed his senses for days.

The two walked by another trio of sisters, hunched over the sprouting garden to admire the blooms. They plucked every unwelcomed weed that antagonized the health of the vegetables, hoping to save their rations for upcoming meals. One of them placed a shovel next to the shed, crutching it against the watering trough. Dried dirt sprinkled onto the wet surface of the filled barrel, slowly drifting down to the bottom.

Kill!

Sister Tate seated the weakened Frank on the cement bench. The bones on his butt felt the cold slab, and his clavicle clicked from her hand as she placed her arm over his shoulder to comfort him.

"I'll give you a moment to enjoy your lunch. I'll be back to help you inside shortly. You'll be okay, I promise."

Sister Tate bowed her head before leaving; a silent prayer of forgiveness mumbled to herself as her shadow disappeared into the trees. His lower eyelid twitched with every breath of fresh air to reset his mind. The nausea of deprivation flinched, tasting the salty abundance of his lunch meat. His abdomen combated the nourishment, his throat ready to reject it. He stared at the open country landscape; the diminishing cornfields were quaint. The slight humming of tractors buzzed from miles away as they plowed their crops.

"Surprise!" yelled a familiar voice. His hand tugged Frank's shoulder, foiling his balance.

Frank groaned like Frankenstein, turning to Buck who smiled with glee at him. Buck's elation grew, the relief of Frank's presence brought ease.

"I'm glad you're okay!" Buck said, his warm arms caressing Frank's malnourished biceps. "I was worried sick about you."

Frank said nothing. He resumed staring beyond his head where crows cruised the sky. Buck's smile wilted, shedding concern. The uncharacteristic zombie-like presence that his partner was emanating became troublesome. Their disconnection was unsettling.

"Are you okay?" Buck asked, observing the vacancy in his eyes.

Frank still said nothing.

"I know you need some time for yourself. Hell, I would if I was in there as long as you. They only made me stay there for two days, so it wasn't as bad as yours," Buck said, trying to relate to him. "I think we should be careful for a bit. I don't want the others to catch wind of this."

Nothing.

Buck hesitated to leave. His body locked every time it wanted to give him space. Apprehensive, he couldn't hold himself back. He leaned over to Frank, soaking his wet lips into his, like he was smooching sandpaper. The scaly pieces of skin poked his peach fuzz. The grotesque rot of his rancid breath coated his taste buds.

Frank's eyes widened; his awareness retracted from his ambush of affection, overwhelmed by their embrace. He held Buck tight with his arms over his chest. His fingertips brushed over his delicate Adam's apple, touching the firm crevasses that his skin cushioned. The rapid beat of Buck's carotid artery sent waves back into him. The perspiration of his neck guided his grasp closer together. His fingernails began to penetrate Buck's skin.

Kill!

Frank's knuckles trembled, too weak to squeeze any tighter. His body lacked nourishment, desperate for strength. His breath was staggering, tired from exertion. The jubilant memories of love and laughter had faded into mush, seasoned with the overpowering garnish of lust for bloodshed. His anger had reached its peak, tolerating all he could. Punishments have taken their toll. His fury craved satisfaction, yearning for a kill. Why not Buck? Why not the one who got him into this mess?

Their lips parted as Buck lifted himself off the bench and walked away, his face showing hope as a gentle smile appeared through the curtain of tree branches.

"I love you, and hope you recover soon," Buck said, blushing with care as his body disappeared. "We'll be out of here before you know it. Together."

Frank smiled back at him before letting the corners of his lips straighten out to anger. The desire for pain became a yearned craving. His teeth gritted as his tongue pressed aggressively against the roof of his mouth. Feeling Motivated, he picked up his sandwich, not neglecting a fallen crumb flaking onto his chest. The voices made sense. He knew what he had to do. He needed to find the right time to do it.

Kill!

TWO WEEKS PASSED AS the sun set over the chilled horizon. Two nuns adjourned the congregation of boys to prepare themselves for their nightly slumber. The boys argued about a tall tale they heard from one sister.

"I heard *her* ghost comes out at midnight and walk the grounds," one said from outside his room.

"I hear she terrorizes naughty children!" said another.

With sudden curiosity, Buck joined the others to inquire further about their claims. His innocent intrigue wanted him to know more about their conversation.

"Who are you all talking about?" he questioned, his fingers fiddling with the roots of his shaggy hair.

"Didn't you hear?"

"No," said Frank.

"About who?" Buck asked.

"The ghost of the late Mother Superior. Haven't you heard?"

"No."

"She died a long time ago. They say that her spirit still haunts the old grounds, punishing any children who disobey the rules of the land."

They wanted to know more; their monotony needed something more. Their conversations craved uniqueness to spice up the blandness of their day.

"Do you know how she died?" Frank asked.

"No. I heard she died from too much evil in her heart!"

"No way," responded Buck, unconvinced. "You can't die from an evil heart,"

"Yes, you can!"

"Who could've told you such crap? She's a *nun*, for goodness' sake!"

"Sister Tate," one boy said with confidence. "She told me in the infirmary couple of weeks ago."

"Sister Tate is a *joke*!" Buck spoke coldly.

"She also told me that when the clock strikes midnight, her ghost comes out of the clock tower to check on the children. She makes sure that all of them are well behaved."

"And what will this *so-called* Mother Superior do if there are people that don't follow the rules?" Frank asked as he huffed out a gust of air from his nose.

"She punishes them!"

"You are so full of shit!" Buck hissed, not believing a single word coming out of the other children's mouths; their passionate defense meant nothing to him.

"Well then, don't believe me! You'll see!"

"I'm sorry to break up a close and touching moment," one peer jumped in. "But we should get ready for bed before Sister Magdalena returns. She can be quite the grouch if we piss her off."

"You're right!" said the other child, grabbing his toothbrush and rushing into the bathroom with the rest of the kids.

They ran closer to the entrance where the rest of the group patiently waited to empty their bladders and perform their evening hygienic tasks. One by one, they ventured around the hallway into their rooms to prepare themselves for bed, their frantic movements exhausting them. Frank and Buck glared at each other, feeling mutual interest welcomed by the slow glide of a raised, bushy eyebrow.

"Mother Superior, huh?" asked Frank, intrigued.

Kill!

"You don't believe this crap, do you?" asked Buck.

Kill!

"Are you thinking what I'm thinking?"

Kill!

"Oh, you know it."

"Tonight?"

"Tonight."

AS MIDNIGHT DREW CLOSER to Frank's plan to take out Buck came closer, the two exited the building, where they were immediately greeted by a brisk chill tingling up their spines, causing them to both shiver.

"Are you sure you want to do this?" Buck asked Frank, his jaw chattering.

Kill!

"Yes, I do."

They proceeded past the tool shed complete with a stump and an ax located next to the vegetable garden. Their faces got slapped by the ever-drifting branches swinging frantically with the increasing speed of the wind. They ran across the back of the building toward the clock tower and rushed inside, slamming the door behind them.

"Oh, thank goodness!" Frank said with gratitude. "Away from this horrendous wind!"

"No kidding! It's colder than a witch's tit out there!"

Kill!

The two huddled closer to warm each other up, being surrounded by a never-ending wooden staircase ascending to the top where the big bell awaits. They anxiously waited for the make-believe ghost. They couldn't wait to prove themselves right in discovering that the story was made up.

"Do you think we'll see anything?" Frank asked.

He rubbed his hands onto Buck's forearm to warm him up, squeezing him tight to suffocate Buck with his regained strength.

Kill!

"I highly doubt it!" he answered.

A thud roared near the door. The two boys became startled and jumped in closer for protection.

"What was that?" asked Frank.

"Probably just the wind."

The thudding continued again.

"Enough of this," Buck says as he walked to the door. "Let's go back!"

He opened the door; a dark figure blended with the night sky, causing them to cradle together in fear. The stories were indeed true. Mother Superior has returned to take the naughty children away.

But it was not Mother Superior.

Sister Magdalena was fuming, her cheeks flushed with deep red hues, huffing like an instigated bull. Her stance was stoic, leaving no room for them to run past her to escape her fury.

"What on earth are you two doing in here?!" she yelled.

They said nothing.

"I have about had it with your behaviors! Ever since you two arrived, you have been nothing but trouble! You are both a disgrace, and I will see to it you both shall be punished!"

"But Sister Magdalena, we—" Frank attempted to defend their behavior.

"BUT NOTHING! NOW COME WITH ME THIS INSTANT!"

The two exited out the clock tower full of shame, with Buck leading the group. He walked toward the nearby tree, and the wind overtook his body once again. Frank was irate that his plan to kill Buck had been foiled. His desire for revenge made the blood rush to his head. His lust for bloodshed couldn't be contained anymore. He had to kill somebody right this instant.

The clock struck midnight, with a gust of wind whispering into their ears. Frank grasped a bundle of branches and knocked another over, pushing Buck deep into the heart of the tree where layers of thick branches entangled him. He screamed for Frank to save him, but the gusts were too loud and too strong as they muted the sounds of distress from Frank's maniacal stare into Sister Magdalena.

"What on earth are you doing?" she asked, startled, barely audible over the wind as Buck continued to scream for help.

The clock tower kept ringing as he ran away, with Sister Magdalena chasing after him. Branches slapped her face as his shadow disappeared further away from her.

Why is he acting like this? He was never this bad!

A sudden thud of a metal shovel whapped her on the back of her head, the clank of the metal bursting inside her eardrums. The stinging pelt made her black out into nothing.

Frank threw the tool to the ground and began hog tying her with the wads of broken tree branches. He dragged her into the clock tower and shut the door, looping another cluster around the doorknob to prevent her from escaping in case she awakened from her assault and ruin his plan once again.

Buck was desperate for help as the clock continued to chime its twelve deep, loud, and strong bells. He panicked, screaming again as Frank ran back to him to cover up his trail and not to lead any suspicion. He reached inside to rescue his partner from the entanglements that he created as a distraction. The two made their way inside to conclude their adventure and pass out together to forget the night ever happened...at least that's what Frank wanted Buck to think.

AN HOUR PASSED WHEN Buck finally slumbered away from the terrifying night's events. Frank did what he promised: remain by Buck's side while he fell asleep in his arms to ease his anxieties. But instead of returning to his room where Frank said he would go, he went back outside. He stomped out the back kitchen door, ignoring the chill winds as his body temperature boiled from the pent-up rage taking over. His patience whittled away, not interested in deferring further.

Kill!

He walked past the stump to take out the planted ax at the center, growling at the handle while he pulled it out like Excalibur being released from its stone. He ventured through the sea of trees, angrily slapping away the leaves as they got in his way, swatting at them like hungry mosquitoes.

Kill!

He reached the clock tower; the wind accessorized his dramatic entrance as it blew the door open, slamming against the wall when he strutted inside. Startled, Sister Magdalena crept back to the opposite end in fear; her hands grasping the strands of hay.

"You just don't know when to keep your fucking head out of people's lives, do you?" Frank snarled, creeping closer to her terror.

"Please, don't hurt me!" she pleaded, wincing, the dried gashes of blood along her hairline cracking. "I'm sorry for all the pain I've inflicted upon you!"

Frank paused and stared deep into her tearful eyes as she bawled for forgiveness. Her jaw was trembling, her jowl rippling. The wind's growing howl eclipsed her screams, silencing her.

"Magdalena, you didn't cause pain. You cured me."

"Cured you?"

"Yes. Believe it or not, your practices did what you wanted to do. You've cleansed me of my indiscretions. And now, it's time to pray."

"Pray?"

Her body remained frozen in fear, her focus on the blade of the ax shining her petrified reflection.

"ON YOUR KNEES!" Frank commanded like a drill sergeant to a fresh cadet.

Sister Magdalena's body jolted, whining like a spooked horse. She squirmed to her knees, bowing her trembling head to remain obedient to his demand. Her clasped hands shook in front of her. Tears rushed down her wrinkled cheeks and onto the dry straw.

"Go on!" he said, hunching over her, the point of the ax grazing her cheek. "You know the prayer!"

She groaned, asking for mercy. Her body trembled before starting her prayer as though she was being administered her own dose of electroshock. Her high-pitched mumbling began reciting the words. Thoughts of hope raced in her mind that the person she believed ever so firmly in would save her. The person used as a shield to disguise her hatred toward people who weren't like her. The person whose message of love and acceptance only applied to a small demographic and singling out most.

She finished her prayer, and her heart rate increased as though it was about to explode, cramping tight inside her chest. Her head trembled upward as she couldn't face the ground any longer. Frank was no longer there; only the mound of straw and the tree branches blowing in the backdrop beyond the open door. She sighed a deep breath of relief, assuming the punch-line of a prank coming up. The ease of a joke set comfort; her gratitude for her prayer satisfied her.

The sharp blade of the ax leveraged behind her neck, cleanly detaching the head. The surface of her eyeballs pricked the strands of hay. Blood splattered out of her wound like a fountain at a shopping mall while her body collapsed. Her torso piled on top of her feet while the whites of her collar darkened into hues of black and red.

Frank raised the ax back to his face, breathing heavily upon the gore of Sister Magdalena's blood as it trickled down the sharp edge.

His chuckle grew into a laugh, relishing his desires. He brushed it against his cheek, taking pleasure in the fresh death of an innocent soul. He tasted the satisfying drops of her ended life, his spirit fueled.

"Amen!"

Chapter 33

June 2006

ANOTHER STROKE OF LIGHTNING shook the hollow foundation. A flash illuminated Sheldon's murderous grimace with his unibrow arched angularly, his teeth glistening, and the veins on his temple bulging. Isis remained frozen from the revelation of her kidnapper, her arms burning from the rope, unable to break herself free as she repeatedly flinched from underneath the half-cut coils. Sonya stared at him as he circled the outside perimeter of the space, her sweaty palms grasping her kitchen knife, lubricating the handle.

"It was you?" Isis asked with shock, her breath exacerbating with each thrust of her body.

He chuckled at his own success. Sonya blinked, unimpressed by his demeanor.

"I knew it was you," Sonya said, focused on his direction as he paced to a neighboring corner to lean cockily upon a wooden stud.

"Oh really. What could've given me away?"

He began twirling the wooden weapon in circles like a cheerleader and a baton, playfully challenging her.

"Your child."

"What about them?"

"I remember that kid."

"From where?" he asked with entertained anticipation. "*Do* tell!"

"You were there the day I got kicked out of the church," she answered, her blade shaking in her hands as the memory of her trauma sent chills down her spine. "As soon as I saw that birthmark on their cheek in your picture, it came back to me. That poor child looked so happy when everything around me was full of shit before you made them give me that wretched piece of paper."

"*You are going to die a slow, painful, sinful death. You will burn in hell!*" Sheldon recited the paper's contents with enthusiasm, cackling at his work. "Pretty good stuff, don't you think?"

"Pretty cowardly to allow your child to do the dirty work for you!" she said, hissing with hatred, stabbing the air with her blade. "Great parenting."

"Are you judging me on my parenting skills?"

"She wouldn't do that," Isis said. "Everyone else will do that for us when they discover how spineless you are."

"You better watch yourself! I have my plans to keep you alive. Don't make me have some fun with you before I turn you to the police."

"You won't get away with this," Sonya said, voice calm.

"Yeah, nobody will believe you if you tell them I did all this."

"Well, nobody is going to believe you if you tell them you didn't," Sheldon said with confidence. "Like when you got into the fight with the store associate?"

"Wait," said Isis, confused, "how do you know about my fight?"

"I was there! I was there for all of your crimes! How else did Ophelia get the call of her future inmates?!"

"PLEASE DON'T PATRONIZE me, ma'am!" the associate roared, her defensiveness sharp.

"I'm not patronizing you," Isis said, her tone shaky in defense. "I saw you give store credit to the man in front of me."

"That's because he was following store policy."

"I'm doing the same thing as he was. We both walked in at the same time and went straight to you. We both didn't have receipts. Why are you treating me differently than him?"

"I don't believe you. I know customers like you. Coming in and stealing to make money from workers like us."

"People like me?"

"Yes, people like you! And you have the nerve to come to me with your aggressive tone and demand money out of me!"

"Aggressive? I bought this dress last week with all my savings. I would've kept the receipt if I'd known I was planning on returning it."

The sales associate's eyebrow raised, and her lips pursed with cockiness.

"I guess I'll just keep it. Thank you for your time."

As Isis stormed away from the customer service desk, she walked past three individuals lingering behind her. A middle-aged woman with a metal box of meticulously sorted coupons and her binder with every store policy in the tri-state area; an elderly man rocking back and forth to retain his uneasy balance upon his walker. Then, there was Sheldon, intrigued by Isis's intentions to buy the dress for a date with her now ex-girlfriend. He smiled as he picked the phone out of his pocket. His fingers danced upon the keypad, spotting the beginning of their altercation. He waited for the dial tone to end as he took in every thrashing punch coming from the girls.

"Ophelia, I got another one for you," Sheldon said, grunting quietly as the customers congregated around the fight. "I'll send you the address."

He walked over to join the group of customers, who were displaying a mixture of amusement and fear as they regarded the two women brawling. His smile grew like a vine, wrapping closer to his ears. He draped the legs of a pair of pants over his arm, halting his shopping trip to bask in the intense altercation.

"I WANT TO WELCOME YOU all to our annual Parents' Night!" the principal greeted with enthusiasm toward the sea of guardians. "Before we begin our slideshow, I would like to take a moment to acknowledge a few people that made this year possible. I hope you all have helped yourself to the assortment of snacks provided by our local churches."

Her hand waved at the kind members of the congregation. The group of five acknowledged her gratitude, finishing the plating of cinnamon rolls and cake doughnuts.

"Can I go to the bathroom?" Tom whispered, irritated.

"Yeah, sure," his father said, annoyed, flicking his hand to shoo away his son like a gnat. "Be quick. You don't want to miss out on the slideshow."

"I sure won't," he muttered to himself.

He walked fast down the aisle and out the doors to the gymnasium. The hallways were emptied with nobody in sight, sprinting to the stage entrance. Out came Sheldon, hiding inside the dark entryway of a nearby classroom; Tom's rushing footsteps clapping on the floor enticed him. The child rushed to the stage and found the projector, pressing the eject button to take out the disc containing the slideshow. Sheldon became amazed from behind the curtain, eager to find out the plan this genius young man would entail.

"Time to expose you all as the pieces of shit you really are," Tom said to himself, chuckling at his master plan. "We'll see how proud your parents are after seeing all the secret pictures I hacked from all your computers! Your days of tormenting people are over."

Sheldon smiled as he took the phone out of his pocket to make the call. He crept behind Tom as he sprinted back to the gymnasium and took his seat to enjoy the show.

"Ophelia, I got another one for you," Sheldon said with confidence as he approached the gym doors.

The adults gasped as they started storming out into the hall. Their scolding remarks toward their children sent excitement through Sheldon's veins.

"I'll send you the address."

He proceeded to join the disappointed parents and aggravated teenagers, stopping at the table of treats he had stocked. Feeling entertained, he took a bite of a moist chocolate chip cookie. He sat in one of the vacated chairs next to a crying mother as she discovered a photo of her child passionately making out with a hotdog. Sheldon enjoyed the slideshow, wishing for popcorn as Tom got escorted out of the room by his ear toward the principal's office.

LESLIE ROLLED HIS EYES in disgust, walking to the neighboring aisle to scope the shelves. His finger caressed the assortment of liquor bottles; the texture and girth of each bottle distracted him from the corporate disarray.

"What're we even doing here in the first place? We're not even old enough to buy this."

Something caught Sheldon's attention as he stopped reading the nutritional labels on the back of a can of clam chowder. His gaze became focused on Leslie's conversation as the teenager rationalized their purchase.

"Shhh!" Leslie hushed his friend, his confidence oozing. "I got it under control. Do you want to have fun tonight at Anderson's party or not?"

"I do, but this is wrong."

"Don't worry," Leslie said, grabbing a small bottle of vodka. "I have somebody that will pay for all the goods we need."

He pointed to the end of the aisle. A college-aged male winked at them, his beefy fists tucked deep inside his letterman's jacket.

"He owes me a favor for some fun we had last week," said Leslie, giggling. "Maybe I'll call him later tonight after I'm a little sauced, and we can have our own after-party!"

"Are you going to drive?"

Their cart caused a traffic jam that frustrated an elderly woman who double-fisted bottles of gin and tonic water.

"I'll be fine. I know my limits," Leslie said confidently.

As Sheldon followed the kids leaving the store after Leslie handed off the liquor he requested, he picked up his phone and called Ophelia.

"Ophelia, I got another one for you," Sheldon said, boasting as he went into the checkout to place his groceries onto the slow-moving conveyor belt. "I'll send you the address. Take your time on this one. It needs to cook a little bit with some juice before you take it out of the oven. Be ready."

"Wait, what?" asked Ophelia.

"Just give it a couple of hours!"

He let the slow, hypnotic beeps of the scanner drown away in his mind. He envisioned the torment he would enlist upon the underage delinquent he found.

"That will be twenty-seven dollars and fifty-eight cents, sir," the young cashier said kindly as she bagged up the contents of his groceries.

He turned to the cashier. His creepy grin made her uncomfortable as she reached out her palm to take his money.

"Can you take a check?"

Chapter 34

June 2006

"I WAS THERE TO WITNESS all your crimes and confessions to who you were," Sheldon boasted, his weapon raised like a sword toward them as though she were a fire-breathing dragon. "It was as easy as shooting fish in a barrel."

Sonya and Isis were stunned by Sheldon's plan as he marched over to a lone wardrobe; its planks were three-dimensional, like part of the wall.

"I think we should invite our little guest of honor to join us in our get-together, shall we?" Sheldon said with a cocky half-smirk as he turned the knob.

Ophelia collapsed to the floor, her arms bound by the same black, thick rope as Isis. Her head cracked one board, muffling her moaning pain upon impact. Her gown was tattered to shreds, and the hem of her skirt was coated in mud. Her pristine ensemble was now grimy, blackened, like she survived a fire caused by an unaccompanied lit cigarette during a heavy snooze.

"Get up, hag!"

Sheldon grabbed her by the back of her shirt, bracing her onto her feet. The tension of her button-down placket broke. Blood dried up along the side of her head, streaming around the strip of duct tape concealing any sounds from her lips. Sheldon's hand slapped her across her face to interrupt the scream roaring from her lungs from the sudden rip of her gag.

"Sheldon!" Ophelia screeched with fear, gasping for air. "What on earth do you think you're doing?"

"I'm carrying out Sister Magdalena's legacy. I thought it was obvious?"

"How do you know about Sister Magdalena?" she asked, bewildered, her smudged eyebrow perched toward the center of her forehead.

"What's the matter, Sister Tate? Are you *shocked* that I knew about Sister Magdalena?"

Ophelia's panicked breathing slowed down as the realization hit her. Her recollections overwhelmed her as she gazed into his green eyes. Her ambitions clouded what was always in front of her; the blameless spirit abandoning his body the day they set the electroshock machine to complete limit. The pain behind his vengeful face plucked her heartstrings. Memories of cries and pleading coming from the boy broke into her oblivion.

"How could you forget about me?"

"Frank?" she asked, her tone becoming raspy as tears fell from her eyes. "What had gotten into you?"

"Sister Magdalena had cured me from all the demons that had consumed me...before I chopped her head off. "

"Just to be clear," Isis said, annoyed as she huffed with irritation. "We're not demonic."

"SHUT UP!" Sheldon barked at the two girls, turning to raise his weapon toward them. They flinched, and Sonya shielded herself over Isis.

"Ophelia, how did you not realize that Sheldon was Frank? You had to have known that it was him."

Sheldon dragged the helpless lady with him as he braced the cross against her neck to stabilize her against his chest.

"Frank was my nickname. My full name is Sheldon Franklin. And as for her not recognizing me, well, that was thanks to Father Time for thinning out my hair and allowing the good ole' aging process to take its course. And besides, Ophelia had been so consumed with revitalizing this ridiculous program that she barely noticed I was there. She did her thing. And, of course, I did mine."

"Killing people?" Sonya asked with sarcasm.

"Luring people like you to see if Ophelia's idea of encouragement would work. And if it didn't, then I took care of it like I did with my pal Buck."

Sonya then realized the sequence in which the three teenagers were killed. Leslie continued to hook up with Craig behind closed doors while Tom hacked into the offices to print off pornography. She questioned why Cora wasn't killed off the minute she set foot in Griffwood Manor, since she had demonstrated nothing but chaos and disobedience the entire time.

"And now," he added, turning back to face Ophelia. "Your job is done. You should be proud that you tried *so* hard to change evil with kindness and encouragement. Perhaps it won't be such a failure in your next life."

Without a second after punctuation, he forced the cross into her abdomen before it broke out on the other side. She flinched from the excruciating pain radiating from her stomach as blood coughed out of her lips and splashed onto the layers of tulle. Her knees buckled, using the slippery grip of her hands to grasp the stick. Feeling the weight of her loosening limbs, she collapsed onto Sheldon.

Smiling with ease, he took in the satisfaction of ending the life of the one person who believed in his growth twenty years ago; and the leader that failed to keep her program in compliance. He removed the weapon from her lifeless corpse. He thrashed her body away, many floorboards cracked surrounding her impact.

"Ready for your final treatment?" he asked as he perched his head back toward Sonya and Isis.

Sonya trembled with disbelief, facing the reality of nobody there to assist her. It was her and Sheldon in the final faceoff. Isis's strength faded as she continued to wriggle out of her confinements, grunting with every thrust of her body to loosen her imprisoned state.

"You know, Sonya, I had a lot of faith in you. I was going to allow you to be the lone survivor. I saw so much potential in you."

Sonya's breath quivered as he ventured closer to her, stepping over Ophelia's bleeding corpse as blood seeped through the cracks of the floorboards, raining down onto the bed of straw below.

"You could've had a perfect life. You could've gotten married and even had a kid or two. Find a fulfilling job and be a contributing citizen while Isis takes the hit for all of us."

"You can still do that as who you are, you idiot!" Isis said, barking back.

"Not how *it was* written."

"Who's going to believe that Isis did all of this?" Sonya asked.

"Well, who will believe someone like her?" he responded confidently. "If only you didn't have to step in and be a hero to discover my plan."

"Too bad I have morals," Sonya said, voice cold. "Isis is a kind and loving person. People just need to give her a chance and not make assumptions."

Sheldon shrugged, flicking the remaining drops of Ophelia's blood off the end of his tool.

"Well, I guess I'll have to kill off the final character witness, now, will I?"

Sheldon leaped toward Sonya. She raised her hands to block his attack, the knife shielding his impact, causing her to fall onto the floor. The blade tumbled toward Isis, and Sonya became helpless with him on top of her squirming body. She panted as her palms continued to slap his chest before the godly punch of his fist knocked into her jaw. With Sonya stunned, he tucked her sluggish arms under his knees to prepare his last strike. She stared hopelessly into his arched unibrow that framed his eyes. The tortured soul of a teenage boy trying to break free became masked by his hatred.

"Time to cure you of all your sicknesses!" he said, hissing with full gusto.

He padded his hand behind him to search for his cross. His smile began to fade away as confusion settled in. The weapon he once placed at his side had now disappeared, nowhere within reach. The cross he needed to cosign his final blow was nowhere to be found.

"Looking for something?" said a shaky voice.

Amber held the cross like she was about to swing a baseball bat. His jaw dropped as the intersecting stakes whapped him across the face, coming at him with the speed of a firing bullet. His body launched off Sonya and collapsed on top of Ophelia. The floorboards gave into the unsteadiness, breaking apart, causing Ophelia to sink down the steep opening to the long drop toward the ground. Neighboring planks rained down on Ophelia's splattered body as Sheldon and Sonya started to sink into the ever-growing pit of doom. Amber stepped back to the edge of the space, stricken with fear she would fall to her death. Isis wriggled out of her restraining ropes; her muscles stretched, awakened from confinement. She reached her arm to Amber, trying to help her move to the more stable side of the attic with more floor to walk upon.

Sonya dangled over the open pit, one drop away from her death. It cramped her biceps, her last remaining ounce of strength used to brace herself to loop around the plank that had become her final saving grace. Her sweaty and bloody palms moistened, loosening her grip and causing the impending doom to creep closer. Amber and Isis cautiously moved toward her, attempting to support their balance as Sonya kept begging for help; furniture sliding to the aperture.

"We're coming, Sonya!" Amber said, desperately trying to reassure her.

"Hang on!" Isis called.

Sonya's legs dangled like wet spaghetti noodles. Her feet felt the heavy pull of gravity as she tried to swing her arms to the plank to brace her safety. Amber and Isis crept to Sonya, their fingertips barely touching. From the corner of Isis's eyes, somebody else had been in the same predicament. Sheldon had also been dangling over the edge on the other side, but his strength had proven to be more successful than Sonya's as he swung his leg to climb toward security. In front of his grasping fingers sat the wooden cross.

Isis gritted her teeth. The anger of her imprisonment filled her with rage, empowering her for justice. She would not allow him to survive while they took away all these innocent lives from them. She eased closer to him, stepping over Amber's reach. With every step, he climbed. The leg to her jumpsuit shortened, ripping quickly from the exposed nail on the wall as she shimmied along the edge.

His fingers were within centimeters of his weapon, his fingernail tapping the grain. It slid away from his touch, with Isis holding it as though it were a sword. He stared at her with fear, his forehead wrinkles deepening as she caught her breath. She fought the tears of anguish that imprisoned her; the loneliness weighed her down like a veil. Her vengeance was hungry for satisfaction.

"Go to hell!"

The blade penetrated his shoulder, jabbing into his bones. He shrieked as he fell back, losing his grip on safety. Yet, he smiled with satisfaction as his menacing grin crept closer to his ears. His pride went with his fall, reminiscing his kills before the jolt of the ground's impact crushed his body when he plummeted onto the ground. His happiness exploded out of him.

Chapter 35

June 2006

BOARDS SPRINKLED ABOVE Isis as she ventured back to the group. Sonya's grip was dancing with death by the grasp of four cramping fingers. Isis guided the intersecting stakes to Sonya's extremities as they tapped her knuckles.

"Grab on! Amber, grab hold of the cross!"

Sonya swung her free hand to grab onto the pieces of wood. Amber grabbed the apparatus like a firehose with one hand in front of the other, securing her footing as though it was about to emit a rapid stream of water. Sonya clenched the weapon to swing toward the wall. Splinters dug deep into their palms, the tool started to slip. The strength of Isis and Amber wasn't enough to pull her up, but it provided her momentum for her to swing to the nearest step below her. Their balance was questioned as it launched her to a nearby plank.

She grasped the wall with the grip of her fingers and toes like a cat climbing a tree from the embrace of a barking dog. She screamed as a rusty nail embedded deep into her wrist. The other two sighed with relief, hugging each other before walking to the hatch to meet up with her.

The duo descended the long, winding stairs to reunite Sonya on the main level. She glared at Sheldon's body as she ripped the sleeve of her shirt to put pressure onto the gash on her arm. She stared at him as he lay there, sprawled out in the cluster of broken floorboards and straw blanketed him. Her panting declined as the realization hit her that the torture and murders were over. Ignoring her aches and pains, Isis ran around to give Sonya a long, loving hug. They felt their heartbeats return to normal as she massaged Sonya's achy muscles. Their warmth and comfort magnified as Amber joined in, collapsing over their drenched bodies.

"Thank you for saving me!" Isis said, breathing hard into Sonya's neck.

Sonya squeezed her body, weakened from the wear and tear catching up to her.

"It was *you* that gave me the strength to continue."

Isis perched her head back; her tears blurred the definition of Sonya's scratched cheeks. Isis's hand caressed her chin, confirming the validity of her presence. They stared into each other's eyes, grinning as their teeth shined through the peeking sunlight creeping through the open door. The storm cleared away, and the dawn of a new day greeted a new chapter in their lives. They reached closer to express their affection with a long, wet kiss.

Their hands glided around their backs, admiration radiating out of their bodies. Their hearts pulsated as the comfort of their love warmed the pit of their once panicked, stricken souls like a thick blanket. Amber smiled as she witnessed the reprieve of their massacred experience.

The trees mellowed out their dancing with the sun peeking out the clouds. The congregation of sisters solemnly glared at the survivors. Their gratitude for their safety kept their smiles lightened. The hems of their gowns flying in the breeze as Sister Alice inched closer to Amber, who shielded herself in front of the others. Sister Alice bowed her head before her body drifted away into the air. The rest of the ladies disappeared into the branches; their spirits put to rest and their business finished. The evil that tethered them to the establishment had freed them into their happiness.

Amber ushered her arm over the two young ladies to assist them with leaving the clock tower. Sonya looked at Sheldon's collapsed body as he laid there. She took the cross out of Amber's possession and tossed it upon his chest before resuming their exit.

Sonya and Isis's hands clasped onto each other, squeezing tighter with each second. Isis's breathing shortened, her gut twitched as she stared at the beauty of her love, fighting back her thoughts. The continuation of a sole word bounced around in her mind, growing with each breath of fresh air.

Kill!

Acknowledgements

There are too many people to thank who made this book possible. I must thank my husband for being there for me during this process. Without his support, Nun Taken wouldn't have become what it is. I also have to thank my family for allowing me to express myself creatively through my work. In addition, I want to thank my dear friend Christine M. Germain, author of *The Brother's Curse Saga*, for encouraging me to keep going, even when I was doubting myself.

This book was conceptualized and drafted at the height of COVID-19. There were some recent losses before the pandemic that I needed to process that I wanted to dedicate to them. First, my teacher from high school was there for me and was a friend when I needed one. Without her mentorship and support, I wouldn't have had the confidence to survive high school.

Next are my grandparents. Willow trees were mentioned in this book to be the calm amongst the chaos. The willow tree on my grandparent's property always brought a sense of calm and security, watching the branches sway and even grabbing onto them for a good swing. It was their unconditional love and support that molded me into the creative person I am today. Words cannot describe how much I miss them.

Last, I want to thank my readers for allowing me to be in your lives as you read my work. I appreciate all of you horror lovers!

About the Author

Brady Phoenix

BRADY PHOENIX IS A self-published author. With a love for 1980s and 1990s slasher movies, his goal is to add diversity to the horror genre through his work. When he is not writing, he enjoys long nature walks, hanging out with his husband and two cats, along with reading and supporting the self-publishing and horror community.

Want more Brady Phoenix?

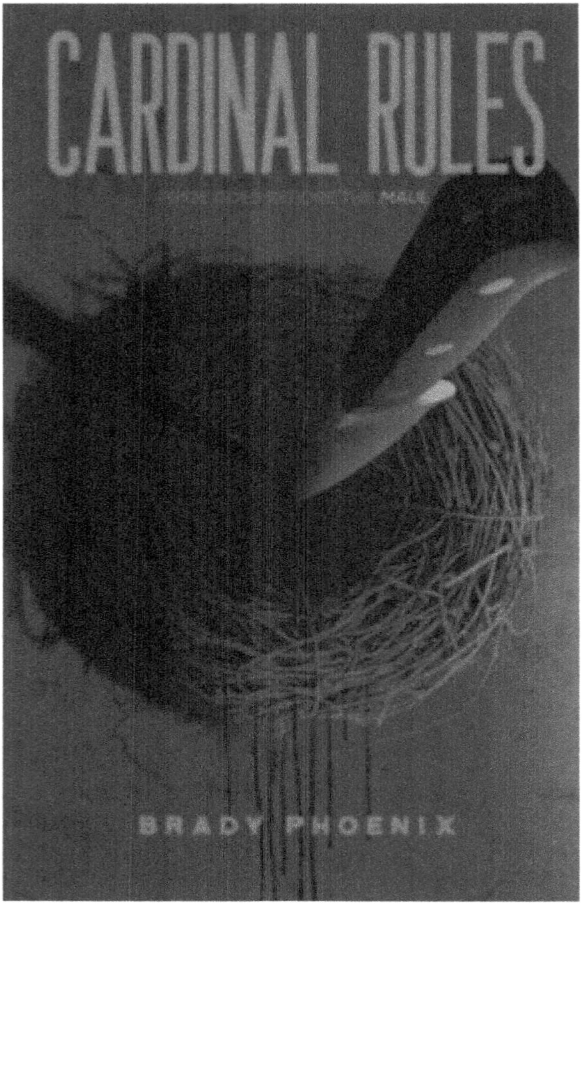

Printed in the USA
CPSIA information can be obtained
at www.ICGtesting.com
LVHW031132230224
772606LV00046B/861

9 781736 239421